The Hierarchy of Heaven

The methodology for attaining a grand unifying theory of the Universe may not lie so much in the mechanics of how it began and how will it end; but rather, to 'what end' did it begin, and to 'what end', will it end. Was there, is there, a purpose?

Our journey seems to be a search for the light of meaning and from which we may find our purpose. We and the fabric of the Universe appear to be irrevocably intertwined in shared experiences, perhaps with a common purpose, but as yet, undefined to us.

Alan Des Harnais

Contents

And to an End Comes a Beginning

A city bus is a microcosm of society, with the many faces, many destinations all measured by a collective patience as each passenger shares the others getting on and off points. When the weather gets interminably hot the passengers endure together, almost always silent. There are those with a newspaper, a book, or a forlorn gaze out the window arming themselves against boredom and to give the façade that they are able to handle the ever present urge that the ride will end soon.

Humid rainy days are much the same, passengers increasingly intolerant of those passengers who appear odd, smell bad or through stupidity or just a failure to know the particulars of the routine cause delays.

Yet, on other days, like very cold winter days when everyone feels just fortunate to be headed to the comfort, familiarity and safety of their homes, the hue of the collective consciousness on the bus ride is altogether different. A break for an old lady here, extra change tossed in for an odd ball without quite enough money there, adds some kindness to the exchange of human experience.

Today's bus ride was in the category of humid, damp with foggy windows and far too little room on the early morning route. Robert Delequa liked the mornings and despite the inconvenience inherent liked bus rides and the feel of animosity of the passengers all around him. Robert liked that he didn't feel that animosity, that he was apart from it, and that it reminded him of how far he had travelled in his fifty two years of life, from angry easily frustrated hothead to relaxed observant bus rider.

That little bit of contentment was enough to rush over Robert so that the many mistakes that takes a man to being content riding a bus at fifty two was pushed just aside his main thoughts. Robert had quite a few failures to put aside, failure to complete a degree at University when his friends and family had become lawyers and handsomely positioned businessmen. One in the Clergy, a brother in New York big into something that had to do with shipping, a sister happily married with four young mouths to spoil and minds to please.

There was another marker for failure, the six years he had spent with tender and pretty Janet, the son that had been born, and then the ending of family life. Robert had stood under the dark cloud of drug addiction for a life changing 15 years from 26 to 41 that had taken a lot from him. It had taken Janet, their son, their home, a reasonable job and income, prospects for retirement this side of 60 and replaced it with a bus token.

Yet for the Roberts of the world, just getting to the upside of 50, to the better side of a drug problem left enough self-respect and desire for contentment that just riding a bus early in the morning and not being upset over the drill could make a day worth living, even when it's your last.

Robert looked forward to his work as a security guard in a mall underneath the main terminus of two roads in a large city center. The mall allows access to shopping as well as the subways that run to the outer suburbs. The intersection of subway routes and a large subterranean parking cavern, with plentiful shopping above makes the mall a busy world, and that suites Robert well. He likes people and he likes helping them as he goes about the business of security in such a place.

Really security is just a job title because Robert and Al-o-mi, his African descended partner manage electrical circuits, help out staff taking deliveries, rescue elderly shoppers collapsing under the weight of being alive in a big city and any manner of trouble that can and often does present.

Each morning as Robert makes his way to this world beneath a world he makes the day's most favourite stop for cappuccino and to watch the comers and goers headed into the office towers above that hold the working lives of so many people. The many who toil through their careers for advancement, who can manage the steady pace, and whose considerable efforts maintenance and earn the fortunes of those who spend their days in the beautiful places of the world.

From the perch of the elevated tables at the coffee bar, and the point of view of Robert's observant mental watchtower, the office dwellers seem to be ever in pursuit of some distant treasure. Some right combination of financial security and power to make the dreary days but sign posts on the roadside in a journey to some better place.

Robert wasn't immune to that end goal. He had stopped drugging with its self-sabotage some eleven years before. And he had trashed smoking just 6 months before this bus ride when he recognized an ever-present sore throat and shortness of breath.

Even though that shortness of breath was still with his 210 pound 6 foot frame he had started to eat better and walk during the evening. And although Al-o-mi couldn't prompt Robert for an admission, Robert did secretly believe that if he worked some more on his health and fitness, that he might not live his life alone.

So he would sit at the coffee bar each morning when he arrived in the city and before heading down to work. He would shower the night before his 6 am muster, rush through breakfast and cut the odd corner on maintaining his small apartment for the sake of an extra 20 minutes to half hour on that stool. In part because of the familiarity of a routine and in part to see the familiar faces that showed themselves each morning; some tired and haggard, some full of purpose and energy, and some friendly enough to cast a smile his way.

Al-o-mi had a faithful wife and two sons in their life in the city to make complete a transition from a life in Europe. Immigrants weren't as able to make their way in a smaller country, where the space brings people very close together. So they had made their way here, to this country and city where there was space enough.

The family man that Robert worked with was truly a good friend and they shared a determination to do their jobs well. And Robert knew - that Al-o-mi knew - that he admired a life devoted to wife and to raising two sons.

Funny thing about that though, was that it wasn't ever enough to make Robert seek out his own son left behind when his life had tumbled carelessly down like a hurricane on its way to some unfortunate shore. Janet and their son had taken the form of that unfortunate shore.

Sometimes life is just a contradiction; the middle ground where lives are spent between the things that are wanted and the inexplicable actions or lack of that makes sure dreams are not attained. The artist at heart who can't ever make it to that first evening painting class, the driven employee just one plunge away from his or her own business but unable to find the resolve to take the first step, the singer who can't find the courage to step beyond lessons and put their belief of talent on the line.

Like Robert, a father of twenty years without a son to know, who spends his mornings smiling at well dressed women with a silly notion that one day one will step out towards him and a great romance will start. Somewhere inside himself Robert knew that those thoughts didn't ring true, but maybe it was a way of thinking so he did not have to face the definite possibility of being alone in life.

Robert had didn't think of such hefty matters though, or that his illusions were matters of reflection not to be - as he arrived at his revered coffee home - and took delivery of a frothy, strong brew. Treasure in hand, he glanced to his right in time to place his other hand on a morning newspaper, a rarity even at the early time of 7:16 a.m. He took his seat at a favourite stool at an elevated table just next to the right door into the coffee bar. Robert took laboured breaths as he pulled his weight to a rest on its perch.

At the table in front of him were two young women eager to replenish the caffeine the intervening 24 hours had robbed from them since their last meeting a day earlier. They were passionate in discussing some important matter that was hidden within their low voices. Robert recognised the women in the blue pants suit and the intensity of her eyes as she sipped her coffee and pressed her opinion on the morning topic.

Robert also recognised the two men busy at their papers and saying little, as if saving their power of expression for the debates, challenges and conflicts soon to be lived out in the offices high above street level. He did not recognise a woman sitting alone at the raised table to his left, by the other door. He gazed over and down at his paper in a rhythm that would allow him to make a careful survey of each person's essence – all that can be discerned from a few minutes of selfish intruding inspection.

Near the end of this favourite morning pursuit, Robert heard a sharp voice from one of the few irritants in his coffee house world. Danielle appeared through the door and did the one thing that Robert prayed to a God in any Heaven that cared to listen that she would not do - she sat at the free stool that was to his right at his table of solitude.

The pretty five foot two inch blond women of twenty eight shook her umbrella thoughtlessly, and then loosened her large, bright and unneeded scarf. The actions and garb of a person who wears strange things to gather the attention somehow withheld for far too many years. That was why Robert dreaded Danielle's visits, not because she talked about far out things, that she stayed on too long and talked to loud, but because she garnished attention that was draped in negativity.

Robert loved the blessed and treasured mental solitude of his mornings - observing all before him from that stool, reading a newspaper and drawing in the aroma, taste and effect of good coffee. But the game table was already set and Danielle joined him at the raised table with great leverage flexing of her elbows that left her feet dangling from the round stool platform.

"Know what I've been reading Robby?" the words reaching resentful eardrums. "Couldn't guess" was the uncommitted reply as mouth and eyes turned hopelessly towards the morning paper destined to be unread by the current handler.

"The Bible. Ya, the Bible. Really has been neat. I mean from a person who has always thought religion the greatest bullshit that was ever put to print for mind control. But you know I never really read it or listened to the message or any of that. But you know...HEY SHEILA...straight up black and a large please."

Chrrriist sake Robert mused. Why me, why this morning, why her. He heaved another deep laboured breath and turned his eyes kindly upward to acknowledge Danielle, his eyes inviting the explanation of what made reading the Bible neat. When self-absorbed Daniel bothered to return her focus to the table she had invaded without invitation, she offered her explanation.

"Well, I was reading about how Lucifer got thrown out of Heaven. The Bible says that there were *Heavenly Beings* and that Satan got the boot. Well how's that...like how does that work? I mean *Heavenly Beings* sounds like a species, like goldfish or racoons. If there was a big fight and poor old Lucifer gets his walking papers then maybe Heaven has a pecking order, sort of a boss and…Hey, are you OK?"

Danielle's words had drifted toward Robert's ears in the most peculiar way. They had in a space of a few seconds gone from being annoying harbingers of a meaningless conversation to being sounds that Robert could not hold on to. He first noticed that he felt wet under his arms and along the brow of his forehead. His mouth had gone dry and pasty, a foul odour noticed at the same time as he noticed that he felt nauseous. He felt certain that he was about to throw up.

Robert turned hard in his seat from left to right to make himself sit more upright the way people do when they are trying to shake off, tough out, something uncomfortable. He moved his left hand to his collar and pulled toward the new lady seen by the other door. He moved his right hand to his coffee and as he grasped it to move it to his mouth he felt dizzy and couldn't execute the manoeuvre. That is when Danielle had asked him if he was all right.

Robert felt confused and that the air in the coffee bar had grown thick and unmoving. He heaved his chest up and back to clear his head, his stomach, and the sweat that was now pouring from his forehead and leaving his palms clammy and cold. He tried to take to his feet when his growing sense of fear and panic met a deep pain on the left side of his neck, a feeling of pounding in his ears, and then crushing pain in his upper abdomen and chest that took all the strength from his left arm and left leg.

Robert stumbled forward and reached out for the raised table in a vain hope of preventing a catastrophic collapse to the floor, but it was partially missed. Robert could not prevent his plummet with the strength that he had relied upon without fail since he was a little boy. As his head bounced off of the carpet he curled his legs upwards toward his chest and then back down like a person trying to resolve the pain of a kick to the groin – or when the air is knocked out of the lungs by a blow to the stomach.

That had been the order of crisis that Robert now sensed was his final experience in life. A terrible fight for the feeling once again for air to be moving across the lungs and satisfying that thirst for tangible vitality.

The absence of air moving into his chest was the forewarning of impending death. Even more so than the feeling of an elephant standing on his chest, of the pain that was now endemic travelling down the left arm and upwards in the neck, Robert new that his struggle for air was to be the cause of his death. He had the terror of knowing that he was about to die. The onset of sweat and nausea to writhing pain and the sense of impending death was only a period three minutes.

Robert knew his face was contorted in pain as he looked up at Danielle, the two women and the new lady looking down at him with deep and real concern written on their faces. He could see the words being mouthed "...call for help, call 911, call 911" but he could not hear the spoken words.

Robert knew that a world of difference had now grown between he and the other occupants gathered above his deathbed on the floor of the coffee bar. On one side of the difference is the world of the living, who animated by the magic of life pursue the activities they strangely mostly refer to as the mundane. On the other side, the dark unknown of the cold place the living fear as death.

Robert's mind hastened towards some memories and reflections the way people do when they have experienced a very emotional event, some hurt that is all encompassing. He remembered being punched and humiliated by his older brother when he was four when he had tried to be accepted and play with the older group of children. How his mother had comforted him and cuddled him as he had cried. He thought of an accident at seven when he had had a serious fall on his bicycle that had caused a concussion and badly taken the skin off his leg.

Robert remembered being out all night at age13 when he and friends had risked all to jump a fence at a community pool to swim in their underwear. The lie that got a night without parental supervision for Robert and his brother and that turned into a night sleeping in the family car with wet underwear underneath pants that made for a terribly uncomfortable night. But, a night when risks were taken and a first kiss received from a girl he would remember throughout his life.

There was a memory of high school graduation and his first year in University when he felt freer than at any other time - and that his life would hold all the treasures that could be had. A time to feel the power that one's choices can lead to and that those choices can become creations. Then on to his marriage to Janet, the illusion that he was somehow in control of the process of damage that would end his family life once and for all and that would cause him to abandon his role as a father.

The final thoughts that came were not those that give reflection of some meaning for a life, of a recounting of the good and bad events, but instead were a collection of daily images. Some more important, a Christmas spent with his sister and her husband and four children, and others less important, a favourite restaurant and dinners there with Al-o-mi and his wife and children. Then a thought about a father who Robert had not bonded with or known well, of a brother who never seemed to value any kind of relationship, of friends lost and finally of the loneliness felt over the past many years.

A time comes when the body can manage no more of the environment of life, of the Universe that hosts living organisms. A time comes when the aspirations of the human condition, of the pains and joys, attention to tasks and obligations to others have lost all meaning. A time when human life no longer holds the wonder of what might be, of being able to shape history in ways large or small and joins history - of all that has been and is no more.

At 7:37 on a rainy humid morning 52 year old Robert Delequa left the realm of his life and entered that which is the eventual repository of all that lives. Death, and to that end, comes a beginning.

The Veil of Transition

Robert Delequa's end of life was searing pain and a fretful need to draw in just one more breath. Many-many thousands of breaths are taken in a lifetime with never knowing what a cool drink of life it gives. The sudden absence of drawing oxygen across the tissue of lung is the epitome of exasperation, and can cause a great fog of confusion to settle upon the soul when it ends in such a longing.

For Robert life faded away in panic and terror. It left his body through eyes that could not focus, blurred by the strain of dying and gradually unable to make out the figures above him. The last images of Earthly life, the last tie to a body and a world no longer able to act as a host for this soul.

And so in death was nothingness. There was not a looking down on a body once home to all sensations of the living by a soul now discarnate. There was only a darkness that fell like an anvil upon the soul - completing the process of living.

When life ends in such a trauma a soul may linger in nothingness for a very long time, unable to gain a footing in the realm that lies between the plains of existence. It drifts on the living side without light as no physical body is left to gather in the environment for the senses. Neither can it find the dark, as it has not yet sensed that it will now journey to another medium which will create a door to other realms.

The soul is the essence of the human form. It remains within the structure of living beings, radiating within the cells that themselves are independent living structure. It is the ungoverned animator of life, prompting it on through adversity whether primordial or highly evolved. When life is ended the vibration of the quantum structure of matter shifts and the soul responds by moving away.

All matter in the physical realm resonates with the energy of atomic structure in a harmony that is simple, beautiful, and fantastically rhythmic. From the tiny quark to the greatest red giant star, from an atom of hydrogen per square centimetre in the depths of interstellar space to galaxies of 400 billion stars and more, the rhythm of existence resonates at a harmonious frequency. The physical realm has a duality of structure, one governed by the laws of physics and the other not governed by it, the spiritual form.

Both are intrinsically connected, with the physical realm destined in each of its manifestations to termination and recreation. The atoms of a star gone supernova destined to be reborn as other stars and other solar systems. A tree that falls to the ground degrades and dissipates only to become a flower, or field grass, or to become the energy of a bird when eaten as a seed.

The energy of the soul is entirely different. It is evolutionary as matter forms into higher states of organism, developing and aspiring, growing and retaining learning from the lessons of living. It is pursued by karma, not of actions right or wrong, but as cause and effect; the long river of experiences that flows toward what seems in the physical creation as the end time.

Through countless incarnations the energy develops ever higher consciousness, and it remains as an evolving entity until that energy rejoins the larger river of consciousness – we know collectively as God – at least God as a place name holder for particular belief an observer may have. A spiritual energy, that is at once and forever central to everything in existence, unchained repeatedly from physical matter and able to transmigrate between many planes of existence.

The soul that animated Robert Delequa gradually sensed something. Motion and drifting in a slight direction within a vastness whose edges cannot be imagined let alone sensed. As the motion very gradually increased the soul became ever more aware of still being intact, of still being in some form of existence. With the impression of still being something, Robert's soul realized it was no longer a being in pain and even of having a freedom that had never been experienced in life. At that sensation, the motion sensed became greater.

Then a great curiosity came upon Robert's soul, not so much as to what had happened at the end of life but as to where he was, why he was in a complete darkness. Strangely, he did not immediately want to find a way to give light to where he was. He wondered if he was spinning in a circular fashion or that perhaps that he was tumbling head over heels, but he somehow knew that he no longer had any appendages, no hands, or feet or anything else that was Earthly flesh.

That sensation led to another, more familiar of the ending of his life, panic and terror. Robert's soul first realised that he had, in the moments before reaching this strange experience of existence, died. His centre of consciousness reckoned back to the last sensations of life, the pain and gasping for air, his falling and his dying. The panic that gripped Robert's soul was not because of those death throw reflections, but rather, because of the notion that in death he lived on, and may live on in a darkness and vastness, an emptiness and solitude that gripped everything that Robert thought he now was.

The sensation of motion became random, not in a general direction as before, but in directions wildly. For a long period the fear of everlasting nothingness, of a place between a heaven and a hell swept as waves across a consciousness that was sure it had been swept away from every other thing.

When so much of this panicked flight had gone by, Robert's soul came to realise that his gyrations were related in intensity and frequency to each wave of terror that swept through his consciousness. As he controlled the fear so he controlled the tendency toward random motion, so that when he could seek out periods of mental calm he could settle into what he sensed as being motionlessness.

Somewhere a spark crept in, at first it was just felt as momentary lapses in fear bluffed into being calm, and then as relief. Was this acceptance, surrender, apathy, or something else?

A realization then occurred that if emotion could cause an effect then what other emotion that was good could make things better. At once the most powerful need that Robert's soul could want came flooding through, a desire to find light. Slowly, the vastness seemed to contract, to gather in and narrow at a great distance. When it had narrowed to a point where the edges - what seemed to be curved walls were perceptible - the structure began to rotate slowly to the right.

A definite sense of relief took over Roberts's soul's consciousness. Not yet happiness, but that something other than the horrid emptiness could exist. And then there, in the distance, so very far and pin point in the distance, a speck of light, and as it grew, the walls of the structure became move visible. As the light spread generally, the walls looked like they were covered in clouds that began to glimmer about the edges with a brilliant hue.

The light was of an intensity that in its self - caused a wide range of emotions in Robert's soul; healing, forgiveness, peace, laughter, wonder, faith, amazement. The light, growing as Robert's soul was drawn closer to it was bright and a translucent white that emanated warmth even though there was no body to feel it. There was a sense that the brilliance of the light would not injure the eye, even if there was a physical one to see to it. A light that allowed the soul novel to death to instinctively know that there is a place of absolute refuge on the spirit side, a Heaven, a domain other than life, an afterlife.

Heading to that world was easy for Robert's soul. He was being drawn forward through a tunnel whose sides were slowly turning, and in bands of light that were of an aura he could only think of God's.

The only adverse feeling was of impatience to reach the tunnels end, and to become one with the loving light. Robert longed to reach out with arms that were physical and touch the light. When he did reach out with his mind, he saw what were clearly the arms of a body that had taken shape around him; a body of light, a spirit body.

With a desire to reach the blaze of nirvana Robert's soul accelerated culminating in union with the light, a communion of soul and its spirit world. And there drenched in the light stood Robert in the full form of spirit.

The tunnel's end and the light gate serve as the barrier between the etheric medium and the spirit domain, as does the tissue of life serve as the barrier between the physical world and the dark void of the inter-medium domain. As spirit Robert crossed through the gate he came to a flush, green pasture, with trees, crisp air that the spirit soul can breathe, a blue sky - all in colours that were vivid, sharp, and crystal clear like he had never seen before.

And there, standing before a soul as amazed as it was bewildered, was Mrs. Delorme, Robert's ever pleasant grade three teacher; and now, he was utterly confused.

A Subtle Domain

"Mrs., Mrs. Delorme? Mrs., Delorme." Robert tried to gather in some meaning, some context. "Mrs. Delorme?" Robert's spirit face was displaying the shock worthy of the experience he was undergoing.

"Hello little Robert, you're so grown up." The comment seemed incredulous. "When did you get so grown up?"

Robert looked down at his feet and noticed something different. More than just a body that now emanated light - where once was the bulk of more than fifty years of wrong diet - there was a slim waist and the sense of fitness.

"You have been through very much Robert, and you have now come to a world where over time, and through my help and others, you will find an understanding of the true being of you." The words were soft and radiated the warmth and reassurance that a child knows from their mother.

Robert walked forward and alongside who he remembered as a kindly grade three teacher but who was not a person who had stood out in his life as a child and who was long forgotten in adulthood. Robert's walk was robotic, although with an ease of movement that was more akin to floating than walking. The spirit host joined Robert's motion and moved alongside him as they passed through a meadow towards some trees.

"What do you know of what has happened to you Robert? Do you know what has changed for you Robert?" A few moments passed and Robert thought back to the last feelings that he had when he was in his body. Strangely, it seemed like such a long time ago, and then it struck him; it felt so distant that it was a lifetime ago, and in a way it was.

"I died didn't I?" The words seemed reassuring because they were the first words that placed a context over the strange experiences that had occurred. "I was in a coffee shop and I got really sick. And I think that I died."

"Yes Robert, that is right. You have died. But in a way, you have come to life, because where you are now is the real world that your soul, your being belongs to." Robert looked at the light being to his right and felt agreement with what he heard, only because the painful experience of his death seemed so far distant and because he felt in his soul a growing sense of unity with the world around him.

Robert worked at sensing more of his surroundings. The trees were pleasant in the aura they gave off, their leaves a lush green that swayed in a warm breeze under a clear sky.

Robert noticed there was no sun in the sky but warmth surrounded him everywhere. And then, for no reason or cause, he fell to his knees and began to swell with laughter, a laughter that cast out any lingering feeling of doubt or painful memory, or fear of the empty dark void of the inter-medium realm.

He laughed with an energy he had not felt since childhood. The laughter was that honest gut rolling type that children have when they pull a prank or fun is made of a playmate. Robert couldn't stop. And he laughed like a person whose worries in life are suddenly lifted. Like the few times in life that is felt when the magic of fate touches one with great luck.

Robert did not feel embarrassed by his outburst or out of place with it. His companion, all five feet of her, with glasses and a warm smile, her fine hair and middle aged complexion not seeming so strange after all. Robert oscillated with the rhythm of the wind, and he understood that the laughter and glee that had overcome him had come from the wonder of energy that was all about him, and that radiated in the very fabric of existence in this new world.

"Why?" Robert now thought his words rather than spoke them and the response came as thought to his mind in return. "Come Robert, come, you have entered a new world and there is much for you to learn and come home to. We will stay together for a time, and I will help you learn." The thoughts helped Robert to his feet and he sang in the fresh air and feelings that said a grand new experience was about to swell over his soul.

The two drifted through fields of flowers without any words or thoughts passing between them. Robert was consumed by the flickering light that came from the grass and flowers, the brilliant colours and the energy that flowed between his new body and all the things around him. He looked skyward at the blue sky that appeared at times brilliant in its blues but also at times a sort of grey and blue with great clouds that drifted by at a high height.

Robert noticed that his legs seemed to move slowly, rhythmically, in a manner appropriate to the pace of motion that they were moving at, but really not necessary for that motion. They were in fact floating along as easy as the particles of pollen that drifted across their path.

Nearing the top of a small rise in the landscape Robert noticed that other pairs of spirit bodies were off to each side at varying distances. At first one pair, then two, then four on either side - each pair drifting along together at calm tranquil paces. Robert noticed the others but did not feel ill at ease at what this new development meant, his mood still overcome by the environment.

At the top of the rise, Robert stopped and looked over the horizon to see a small town site of buildings all made of pastel coloured plaster material, and light. A feeling of tiredness came, and Robert sat down on the ground cross legged, and as his teacher sat next to him he surrendered to a fetal position, his head resting upon a welcoming lap. "Ready for a rest?" Even before the end of the words, a deep sleep had overcome him.

Robert's spirit body did not need sleep really, but his newly adjusted seat of consciousness had to position the relevance of three domains of existence in what the physical world would consider a short period of time; and it needed a quiet reflective time. Like the reflection or change in perspective that comes from the period from of just before sleep and just after waking.

In the physical world sleep not only recharges the body but also allows the soul to peer through to its real home, on the other side. It doesn't travel to that place but on a few rare occasions while vested on the physical side, but It does tap into a ground swell of energy that finds its way to the physical from the spiritual.

The mind still fresh with the physical orientates best to the world after life through a deep sleep from which it reawakens. That way there is a sense of departure from the events of transition, from a painful world of minor joys and terrible sufferings to that of a subtle domain; a domain for rest, reflection, learning and the making of next steps through choices. The soul does best when it feels that in rising from this spirit world sleep that it has come home to its true domain, and that was true for Robert.

In rising from his sleep, Robert pulled his arms back and his chest rose with what felt like morning air. So very strange Robert thought, was there a morning or afternoon, or night in this place? But Robert expected morning air and that is what filled his chest. He rolled his head from side to side, looked skyward and around for his teacher. There she sat, pulling her hand along a long blade of field grass, her hair pulled back by a breeze.

Robert's eyes stayed with her as they rose to their feet and in a way that signalled to both that it was time to move on. Time to begin the process of coming home, of relearning the true self and remembering the length of path both behind and ahead of the life recently shed for Robert. With the staying of his inquisitive eyes the teacher knew to begin the lesson.

"This place is the coming home for souls that have lived in the physical world and who have need of rest and reflection before they make other choices." Robert's eyes shifted away and back as if to prompt an explanation. "The dark world that you passed through is a medium that separates the energy of this world and the world that you came from, where you lived."

"What do I do here, where will I live? What does being here mean?" Robert knew the questions that rolled from his spirit body lips were the quintessential tip of the otherworldly iceberg.

"Come, let's go see, I have something I think you'll like." Mrs. Delorme took to her feet.

Robert and his teacher slipped down the slope leading toward some buildings. As they grew closer other pairs of souls were also slipping into the town area, apparently taking to their feet for motion as they gathered into the centre square area. Robert waited for his teacher to provide the cues, but there was no feeling of social ill at ease, not as there always had been in life.

After a few moments the teacher looked over behind Robert with a slight playful smile on her lips. Robert started to look back but then looked questioningly into his teacher's eyes. With her facial expression being that of 'oh go on', Robert turned his body around enough for his eyes to see a shop with chairs and spirit bodies sitting and standing. Then, it hit him, all at once and with pungent glory, coffee!

Coffee in Heaven? Heaven and coffee, but how! The answer didn't need to come, it didn't matter. The two entered the shop and took to stools with a cup of brew that was strong in taste and odour. Like everything else, the sensations given were both an unmatched sensational delight and as they were consumed in, enriched the energy swells that rose and set in Robert's being. Each drink was rich, and it provided a pleasurable context for the two to continue their discussion.

"Why are you here Mrs. Delorme? Why are you here to greet me? Is it because you were my teacher?" Robert said as he sipped his coffee from a cup glowing lightly and held in both hands.

"I am here because that is what you are wanting Robert." The answer was said flatly, without emotion.

"So from what I can think, is that that day I died and went into a dark empty place. Terrible aloneness, for I don't know just how long. Forever maybe and I don't know why, but then I came here through a bang of light, a beam of light."

"Go on." The teacher encouraged, rather than prodded. "Well, then I came here and found you. I am glad you are here Mrs. Delorme, but why you? I..." he stopped for a moment to avoid sounding insensitive, and the teacher added "I wasn't someone central in your life, was I Robert?"

"No" Robert added. "No, not really. And wouldn't my mother, or father, or someone like that be here to meet me?"

"Well Robert that might be hard to arrange given that your father is still alive." Both heads rolled back with laughter and Robert shook his in playful embarrassment when he spoke again. "Yes, yes he is. Of course, but my mother, or my grandparents?" Robert remembered that he was very close to his grandmother on his mother's side, and he missed her, and thought that he should meet those relatives on 'this side' sometime soon. He looked from side to side and at the door as if his thought of them should bring their appearance at any moment.

"Robert, I met you at the gateway because that is what you wanted." Her eyes met his as the second mentioning of this fact settled in on his mind. "Yes, sometimes your thoughts in this world will precede you Robert, yes, just like that they will. What you will learn most in this intervening period, is that what we desire makes things happen."

"In this world Mrs. Delorme?"

"In this world and in many others Robert." There was a moment or two of silence. "How many other worlds, are there?" Before the teacher could answer Robert asked, "...how is it that desire makes things happen Mrs. Delorme?"

"Remember the Earthly world Robert. Remember how you might like a fine dinner out, or ice cream? And remember how you would go to a restaurant and eat, or go to a store and have an ice cream? Remember how a company would plan to sell a product, and then they would? That was a series of people's desires made into reality. The same is with many other dreams that people have; a notion, to a dream or intention that becomes a desire for something to happen, then the reality of that desire coming true."

"So we build things here? We sell things here?" Robert was confounded.

"A little different Robert, on the earth plane, we use our hands and materials, forces of production to make things happen, to bring them real."

"Here thought in itself can form many things and cause many events to happen, shape the world around us and what is to be." That caught Robert's attention, and it prompted the teacher on. "Yes, what is to be. You choose that. You have chosen that, you have chosen this."

"OK, now you have me really confused." Robert wanted more coffee and with that a smiling young soul, a pretty female soul placed a cup of coffee in his hands. Robert looked over at the teacher to see if she would have coffee to but the young spirit turned and walked back toward other pairs. Robert wondered if his wanting coffee had produced the obliging young lady to provide it.

"No Robert that was because you probably looked like you could use some more, and you, and others, many others, are new here." Both settled back into the lesson.

"When you crossed from the other side, and think now, this will be a little more complex than you will grasp here, you knew in your soul, you knew from a previous decision that it might be me to meet you on this side, after this particular life." That wasn't registering well. "Because of the life that you lived, you were not close to people although that is a desire that you had for your Robert life, your life, Robert." That was registering less well.

"Like this. There will be a time here where you will sort out, come to grips with the life that you have lived, those that you shared with in that life and what will come next for you. The contiguous you, the you that has lived, does live, will live and will ascend knew that it would be best for you to be met by your teacher, someone in-descript who would not flood you with feelings of conflict that might, might, either keep you too long in the in-between realm. Or, leave you out of touch on this side of it."

"So you needed a person that would bring you a sense of trust, of familiarity, even though a familiarity that was long ago, who you would feel at calm with, even though a little confused."

Robert looked away and heaved a sigh. The teacher's lesson was taking some form in his mind, and he felt a moment of regret, another first feeling, as he sensed that the life past was one without much meaning, really.

Suddenly the teacher spun on to her feet, sensing Robert's melancholy, grabbed his hand and pulled him to his feet. "Come on, let's go explore this place."

The two walked the square for a long time, and what had seemed like a small area yielded many different streets and shops each time a corner was turned. Robert was eager to see each shop but through the windows, as he had begun the practise of saying hello to those passing by, each in pairs. Robert failed to notice that only those on the left of each pair were saying polite hellos to each other, and as they did, looking in shops.

The teacher did not grow weary of the tedious exercise that was playing out. She and Robert walking along, he looking in shops of all types, shoes, breads, wines, golf clubs, flowers that still waved gently in windows, the soup shop, barbers cutting hair that as it fell to the floors still cast a spiritual light. After each peer through a window Robert would turn to say hello another passing pair; the reply always the same with the pair member on the left nodding their head and smiling broadly and saying hello.

Only after a great period of time had passed did Robert break the cycle through an insight, he was not hungry, nor thirsty, nor did he have to use the bathroom or sit down. He turned to the teacher. "Do we stop to eat, do I buy anything?" The answer was given in a low monotone that neither endorsed nor discouraged, "If you like."

Robert became conscious of his clothes, he hadn't yet thought of his body. He noticed that his body and clothes were really of one, not attached but enmeshed in the presence of bright white light, pleasing to the eye and present in everything and everyone.

Robert thought of money and then that having any would be odd. The teacher spoke in to his thoughts. "No money Robert, none is needed. You have here, whatever you desire to have; anything and everything." Robert stood silent for a moment.

"Okay, how about a tall beer and club house sandwich. No Italian capicola on rye bread. " He was sure that that would stump his obliging teacher. With a slight grin the two turned the corner to the left and the teacher stopped, turned slightly to the left to move back a little, and with her left arm extended motioned to offer Robert to walk up three stone steps into a pub-deli. Robert's spirit mouth dropped open and he made his way with an impatient step towards the bar.

Robert glanced to his left and right and saw others socialising comfortably at their tables, mingling casually in a way that was quite opposite of how he felt. What sort of strange reality was this that he would find himself confronted with the challenge of what type of beer to order in a place that to his mind, must be heaven. He looked back at his teacher who, as she pulled herself up onto a stool and to the bar edge gave an approving nod and gesture with her hand to order.

After a few moments Robert stiffened his upper torso and flexed his back and asked for "...whatever you have on tap." The reply came from a pleasant looking women dressed in flowing gown that seemed to gently sway as did her hair. With a side smile she said "we have everything on tap here." Robert thought better of making inquiries from all he had seen he thought it likely that every conceivable brew throughout history would be somehow available. To test that theory he said, "...an ancient Egyptian beer, please, like the Pharaoh's had."

"Old Kingdom, or new, hops or barley based?" Well, who would know, so the answer was a guess "ah, old, hops."

"It'll taste like crap, you won't like it." The comment sounded pretty certain.

Robert looked to the teacher to see if the comment was based in telepathy of the consciousness or what had been a predetermined act of fate. Before she could answer the bar keep spoke up "...everybody thinks it takes like crap, probably even the Pharaohs."

Robert grinned and safely asked for a frosty Budweiser. The bar keep reached down and pulled up two glasses, one a large frothy oversized mug with some of the fluid and foam spilling over its cold side, and the other a green glass of medium size, narrow at the base and looking like an artefact. Robert noticed that the women had not poured either of them. He didn't ask.

"What's this" Robert asked, looking at the smaller glass. "It's ancient Egyptian beer from the Old Kingdom." Robert reached down, brought it to his lips and took a small sip and then a larger one. The taste was something between a stale sewer and a prairie slew. It needed an immediate response to remove its almost overpowering offence to the palate, even a spirit palate, and Robert pulled hard and passionately at the lip of the second larger container. The beer was smooth, cold, radiant and pleased every part of the body that Robert thought he could feel.

Half way through the beer filled mug Robert could feel a sense of being light headed and his mood jovial, almost playful. His conversation with the teacher was out of context, Robert knew, even without having much of a clue as to what the context of this new world really was. "How many people come here? Who owns a bar like this? Do you have to pay for this? Do you have to get a job here and find a place to live?"

The questions began to have greater importance and semblance of reason around the end of the second mug. The explanations that came from the teacher began to give some context.

"Robert, the way to understand the world that you have come to is to know that what happens here, what happens for you, is based on desire. What you want to do, whether to sit and drink beer, or take the roll of serving others who want to sit and drink beer, is what you will do. Some, as with a friend of mine, enjoy helping others find the story of their previous lives in the main hall library. Another, who watches children who came to us to early as they play in the school and others who sit and gamble all day."

The lesson continued, "Our desires that drove us in life follow us in this world. We live them for a time, either a short time or for a very long time, and then we decide to move on. To move on to learn about the nature of our soul's journey, to seek out the other realities that are available to us, sometimes to find others that we have been close to, and at times to return to the Earth plane." Robert was drinking in the information along with the beer.

"Sometimes a soul here cannot find the answers that it needs and is confused, it fails to find the calm that it needs to learn and comprehend. For those souls, the whirlwind of their experiences drives them back to life to early, and they are worse off for it. They can find no rest, and karma is a torment for them, relentless and compulsive."

What does compulsive mean, Robert thought?

"Compulsive at the beckoning of the only real task master of the soul, the self. The consequences faced in life are those that we plant as the seeds of our own actions, or failure to act, cause and effect. So those souls in torment can only find resolution to their pain through understanding their responsibility to their own destiny. Not a destiny of physical being, but as beings of light – beings of pure energy."

Robert looked down at his beer and rummaged through the fuzzy intoxication that draped his mind. He didn't feel much like an evolving being of light at that moment. Maybe that was the point. Somewhere, in time, he would need to come to grips with the tasks of his own soul; he knew, in time.

"The impulses of desire can keep us here for a long time. That is not to be avoided but enjoyed, like all things in life and in this true life here beyond the lives that we live. You see, these two, at the end of the bar."

Robert swung to his right and looked. He saw two gloriously happy, bright white souls completely immersed in their own company at the end of the bar, she sitting and leaning back against the bar and he pressing in closely against her while standing.

Everything looked different once Robert focused on the couple that he knew hadn't been there prior to the teacher's pointing them out. Now the street was crowded with souls walking about, not just in pairs, but as individuals and groups. The bar was crowded with souls and the light outside looked more like mid-afternoon than the morning as it had. Robert noticed that he was now on the right and not the left of his teacher as he had been since passing through the light gate.

He looked around and the bar keeper was now a middle aged gentleman who passed beer and other beverages over the bar while managing a teen age girl who was making sandwiches and just then passing some hot soup over a counter.

"You're here Robert, you're here." The teacher got up and pressed her hands down on her dress. She made motions that said she was preparing to go.

"What am I to do, Mrs. Delorme?" The smile that came back was the epitome of kindness in any world. The teacher gave an explanation. "You've come to the world that you are meant to be in. When you are a new arrival we meet you at the door and give you some time with things familiar to help you ease over. You did very well Robert, and are ready to find your place here. It's time for me to leave."

Before Robert could ask if he would see his teacher again she was in motion presenting her back to him, dodging a patron here and there. She turned back and with a wave and a smile said "search around, you'll find what you need." When the teacher turned and walked just two more steps she disappeared completely as if walking through a door in the fabric of the air. Vanished. Gone.

Robert turned back to the bar, looked to say his thank you to the lady bar keep and reckoned that with her no longer there - he really didn't have anything to thank anyone for and the feeling was unique. Robert was now alone without his teacher and that did leave an unsettled feeling, but, he did know what the presenting situation, his current status as a spirit of light, as an adult man was where he entirely belonged. And with that, he turned and walked out to discover the destiny of his soul.

Robert strolled out of the pub, down the few steps and onto the street. He looked left at a number of souls moving between shops, then turned right and headed with a purposeful step up the lane way. The purposeful step was particularly odd because Robert had little in the way of an immediate purpose. Nonetheless, he did sense an overall purpose, and was able to think about the strange events that had overtaken him.

First and foremost was the remarkable notion that he had passed through the most feared event in life, death. And while the process of dying was an unbelievably painful and terrifying occurrence, to Robert it now seemed like a lot of the things that are encountered in life that can be somehow managed if a person doesn't see them coming.

They are dreaded with foreboding when contemplated, they are coped with as best as a person can manage when they occur, and there is serenity when they are over and the trauma is done. Robert had hated going to the dentist while alive, that was in a way the same. Dreaded, handled with perseverance while occurring, and seemingly not so bad when it was done.

But now as Robert walked, that is motioned his spirit body forward in a floating motion as his legs figuratively moved, he had a powerful sense that a milestone in every person's fate had been crossed. It was that feeling of something disturbing now being over that countered the other lesser feelings of displacement and basic wonder over what was to come next in his journey of experience.

Those lesser feelings - with all the fear that should have accompanied them, were really not terrifying after all, Robert thought. He was in Heaven, or so he reasoned. Wonder and curiosity were the feelings of the moment and Robert began to draw some local geographic conclusions.

Now then, he thought, after motioning up what seemed a slight upgrade for some time, where shall I find my bearings. The light of day had drawn perceptibly later - it seemed like the latter part of afternoon. The sky was not as bright and seemed a darker hue of blue particularly in the direction he had been moving. The number of souls going about their daily business had definitely lessened.

So Robert decided he should start to ask some questions. Did this place have a day to have business routine for souls to partake in, and for that matter, was there business of any type to be done? Robert came to a sudden stop. In formulating some questions he had come to a very unsettling thought. In life he had been alone, and in death he was now alone.

Robert looked about and saw that he appeared to be at the upper end of the town square that he had been moving about in. He and his Mrs. Delorme had entered the town some distance behind the direction he had been moving since leaving the pub, and they had seemed to walk in square blocks for a long time prior to entering the pub. He was at some far edge of the town square and could see the glowing fields of grass and hills through the open spaces that now appeared between buildings.

To the left were older appearing buildings of brick, with stairs leading up to an elevated first floor with an obvious second floor above. Robert placed his hands on his hips and looked right. A middle aged man appearing soul was looking down at some pages while a few souls sat in front of what appeared to be video terminals. There was a tent covering above them with a fabric wall at the back of the some 50 screens in five rows of ten.

Robert approached the man and asked, "Excuse me, excuse..." and before he could finish the second word the man looked up with an indifferent air. "Yes" was the dispassionate reply.

"Can you tell me what these people are doing?" Robert hoped to start a more far reaching discussion.

"They are looking through the good things of their lives." The man looked down again.

"Just through the good things in their lives?" Robert wanted to sound somehow insightful, or clever.

The man answered as he closed and folded a large paper about the size of a newspaper, in a way that signalled his surrender to the inevitability that he was going to have to have a conversation. "They just look through the good things because it is easier for them than looking at the lousy stuff. So people like to look at happy stuff and that makes them want to come here, and that means we have more customers."

Now there was unexpected word. "Customers?" Robert asked, obviously startled.

"CUSTOMERS, those who want to consume something that someone cares to sell them" was the more than curt reply. The man got up from the high stool he had been perched upon.

"Kind' a new here aren't we?" The sarcasm made Robert think of, home. Rudeness was making this new place seem less comfortable.

"Look it. When you come to where you are now people, like you, have all sorts of questions. Like you they start to look around and begin to sort things out. Most go the central library, with their guide – the person who met them after they cross over – and search the data bases for who they are or have been, and why they are here."

"But my, guide, didn't take me to a library?" Robert felt hurt.

"Well isn't that a bitch, life's a bitch, after life's a bitch, maybe it's all a bitch."

Robert looked down.

There was a period of silence and Robert considered moving on, he looked up and back toward the direction he had come from.

"Do you want to look at the good things from your life?" There was a hint of conciliation in the question styled offer.

Robert thought for a moment and then said, "no", with a slow sense of depression creeping into his consciousness. He was thinking that there wouldn't really be much to look at from his life that was happy. He didn't really want to confront those issues, after all, he had just arrived to a new place and it was beginning to feel just a little too much like where he had just been.

Robert felt an urge, and his desire led to an immediate response. When he looked back at the man, who was now seated on a video terminal table, he had his hand outstretched with a coffee cup from the top of a coffee thermos, and steam rising from a hot brew inside. The man poured himself some from the thermos, into an older looking, stained, café styled glass white cup.

A few sips seemed wonderful, reinvigorating just it had for the past few years in life when depression seemed to get the better of day. The man looked at Robert in an inquisitive way. He hadn't expected to see the hurt in Robert, and that had intrigued him.

"Well sit down for a spell and take a load off." The advice was meaningless in the spiritual environment that Robert was in but it sounded like good advice all the same because of the emotional strain Robert was feeling. There was more than a hint of kindness and Robert sat down on a table adjacent to the man. He sat without a sound, wondering with some anxiety for a hint of context, and sipping the very good taste of the coffee.

The man stared back in silence for a little longer than a few seconds, not signalling any rules that would suggest context. The awkward moments passed. "I know, I know." The words came out with a sigh. "What is it all about, what is this place, what am I to do, what will happen to me? Where will I go?"

Robert surprised himself by jumping in and cutting the introspection short. "Most of all, why am I alone. What the hell is this place that there is no, kind of process, nobody to say go here, or go there, or sleep here, or go work there?"

Robert had sat up a little, his chest moving up and some courage finding its way to his larynx, pumped up that way by frustration. The frustration that comes from knowing line ups, queues for this and that, accepted but disliked in life.

"Well funny enough, the answer really lies in you. Yes, in you. The mystery of this subtle realm is that everybody is in the experience, but few in the know. It's an intermediary place that beings come to before going to the next place. I know, I know, what is the next place? " The man's body shifted a little from side to side. "We all arrive in this place displaced from the world. Heck it isn't easy, one minute you're trying to earn an honest life in the touch and feel world, and the next minute your hit in the back of the head with death, and you end up here trying to sort it all out."

"We souls in the Subtle Domain get better at knowing ourselves, that is to say our spiritual...true...to blue essence. We know we're going to go on somewhere else, that we are going to grow somehow somewhere, so we get familiar with what we know, or like, or feel comfortable with, and then after a while, we sort of slide into where we go next."

"Where are you going next?" Robert liked this conversation; he felt that he was getting somewhere.

"Don't know, ain't really sliding yet, I suppose." Robert heard a hint of melancholy. "I've been here a while. For a while, but, I haven't really started to work with my teacher. Oh I mean that we do talk and stuff, but I know that I haven't started working yet. Not really, not like I should, or will." The last two words sounded like a self-proclamation.

Robert had to interject; he sat the near empty cup of coffee on the table beside him. "But my teacher left me, I mean almost right away." The man piped back, "oh no, that was, she was a friend. I mean somebody who bridges you over. She's not your teacher. "

Robert shot back, "But how do you know, how can you be sure, maybe something went wrong for me when I came through?" He didn't quite finish the sentence.

"Oh, oh no, it doesn't work like that. No, not at all, first, you see, you're to new. You won't work with your teacher until you're ready, until you start asking."

Robert started to push the next question out as he was startled by the coming of a figure to his left from where he was sitting facing the man. He looked up into the weathered, bearded face of an equally bright and white soul body, but who looked quite a lot older than he and the man.

"Thom, Thom, my dear Thom, trying to get it all out, without giving our new chap even a second cup of coffee?" The voice was British, not quite aristocratic, but definitely of an educated class. The figures manner emanated kindness and both conversationalists stood up slightly, resting their spirit backs against the tables.

"Hi Adam, uh this is Adam, the man gestured a hand towards the figure and back towards Robert. " Robert moved a hand out to invite a hand shake and offered "Hi I'm Robert."

"And this is Thom" said the figure back completing a tri introduction that obviated that the two conversationalists should probably have crossed this ground all ready.

"And you are our new chap, the coffee lover. Welcome to the subtle domain, as Thom calls it." Adam smiled a broad and welcoming smile that showed large and numerous teeth, but, that surprised Robert as not all being in good health - some appeared dark which was unusual. Robert prepared a question but couldn't spit it out in time.

"Subtle domain Robert because the answers here don't pounce out at you exactly, do they. They come slow, and because of your questions, help you to know who you have been, who you are now, who you are going to be, and who you have always been."

The last comment caused Robert to look up from his newly poured second cup. Adam had taken a seat off to Robert's left and Thom's right, both other men sat back up on the tables, it signalled they were the juniors and giving way to the advice of an elder.

Adam crossed his left leg smartly across his right and crossed his hands on his lap, indicating a refined nature. A flap of wind seemed to move the cloth tent like top above them.

"Well Robert. The soul is the driver of its own destiny. It isn't fate, or pre-destiny, or divine wisdom, or somebody's master plan, what moves the soul here is determinism. Same on the Earth plane, we determine the circumstances of our experiences, shifting the sands of material and spiritual landscapes to fit the scene of what compels us, what moves us; and, God willing, to what will eventually complete us. "

Adam went on "When on the Earth plane we decide from moment to moment, from day to day, and from life's experience to life's experience what we want from our lives, and when we do, we create reality. You'll come to know in time here that the physical universe is a great field of potentialities; it shapes from energy at the sub-atomic particle level when we decide on what reality should be. So, directly, we decide on the existence we want and from the choices we make we see those desires achieved in some form of completion. And we share them - harmoniously woven together in synchronicity – one soul to another. If it weren't I am afraid we'd all find ourselves alone within our own realities."

"A beautiful harmony then" Robert said, hoping to sound, if not wise, then like he was getting it.

"Oh not at all Robert, actually, it makes for wonderful chaos, but, chaos is in itself a harmony of synchronicity because cause and effect is what it is all, all about." Adam rose to his feet in a way that appeared laboured, and again, Robert thought the presence of a hint of frailty was out of place from all that he had seen.

Roberts comfort zone suddenly shifted, he had become relaxed talking and learning from his new - were they friends - yes, his new friends he thought. When a person has felt in trouble and then it turns out to be alright, a sense of release is felt, perhaps because the fight or flight mechanism of adrenalin lapses, and calm returns. Robert sense of relax had given way to the anxiety of this conversation possibly ending. Adam's words transformed those emotions just as quickly.

"Oh come boy, I'm not leaving you. It's not my idea of fun to sit in Thom's shanty all day watching souls delude themselves by watching the utopia of happiness from successive previous lives." Adam had motioned his hand towards the half dozen souls sitting before the video screens as he rose and took a few steps. Robert turned his body to the right and noticed them with some detail for the first time.

As he, Adam and Thom began to walk away from the tent he kept his head turned back to the screens. He peered a little closer, able to catch the visuals on the screens. A woman was looking at a young girl chasing a cat in what looked like an old 16 millimetre home movie. Roberts mind quickly wondered why technology in Heaven would be second rate.

The woman was looking at the screen memorized, a wide smile on her face, eyes shifting with the child and cat running on what looked like a suburban lawn. He noticed a man, rocking back and forth in his seat with hands cupped on his lap, on the screen was a naked male body heavily engaged in sexual intercourse that appeared to be the last stage of the event. Robert muttered a non-judgemental "Ok" as he ducked under the tent roof flap and followed the others.

Adam was leading, and the three brightly lit white souls turned right and down a wide paved road way with lawn area on both sides and buildings, with souls moving about. Robert had thought that he was near the edge of a township when he walked into Thom's area; however, he now saw quite a lot of enterprise stretching off to the horizon.

Then it occurred to him, the changing surrounding of buildings and souls moving about had nothing to do with location at all, not geographically moving from point to point. Rather, he was moving about sub-planes of the subtle domain, progressions it seemed to him, from what he experienced when he first arrived following death, to the coffee shop and shopping area with Mrs. Delorme, and the pub. They were all responses to his progression of experience and understanding in this subtle domain. Perhaps Mrs. Delorme, then, disappeared in the pub because she must have shifted her consciousness to another bit of business, to another affair, and so she shifted to whatever that plane was he reasoned.

Robert liked this set of conclusions as he walked briskly behind Adam and abreast Thom. His thoughts pressed on, when he went up the roadway to Thom's he was adrift, and so the surroundings had become sparse and, well older and a tad shabby. Adam had called Thom's tent a shanty. Interesting, he thought, and he looked across at Thom, wondering where he was going, why he was walking with such apparent purpose, somewhere.

"Come on lads", Adam said, implying a purpose. "Just up here, just ahead." Robert had no discomfort in following Adam's lead along a walkway that had given way from what appeared to be multiple dwelling residential buildings to three story smartly adorned buildings. They were new looking, with glass that seemed to shimmer with light of their own and independent of the sky.

The sky Robert thought, it seemed mid-day again. He liked that. After all, he didn't know where he would sleep, or even if he should sleep. Did he need to sleep, probably if I determine it, he mused, with a little impolite sarcasm towards this new host world.

Adam wielded right and up a flight of twelve stairs, doors flung open, and up another flight of stairs, round a stair well corner and up another. That left the three standing on a tiled floor in what appeared to be a business club. Adam looked left and right as if to decide which way to go, then turned right brushing Thom back as he marched down the hallway. He stopped in front of the third door to the left, sighed, then twisted the handle and walked in. Thom and Robert walked single file into the room in behind him. It was an upscale lounge.

Adam moved passed some empty tables and chairs to a table near windows overlooking the walkway that they had just come down. He lifted his outer Nehru collared robe off and let it drape across the chair behind him. Robert and Thom sat themselves down and waited for more cues as both looked obvious to be in a fog as to what they were doing.

Adam looked up at the bar to a smartly attired man with a red cloth across his arm who approached the table. "Scotch and soda Ian, scotch and soda for us now and for Andrew over here." The bar keep turned for his bottle adorned wall behind the bar and a fellow a few tables away rose from his chair, folded a bright newspaper and made his way over to the table the three shared.

Robert was amused and comfortable. He sat with arms on both wings of the studded leather chair and propped himself smartly up against the back. A gentlemen's club he reasoned, an upscale gentleman's club. Robert wondered if there was a pool table and he looked around but did not see one. He felt a bead of sweat across his brow from the walk, and it startled him to think that he hadn't float walked to the club, but rather had walked briskly, had to keep up, and it had caused him to sweat and he reached for the cold glass of liquor that had just been placed before him and the others.

"Ah, now that's determinism." Adam jutted his lower lip out and drank in the scotch and soda placed in front of him in a long suction creating surge. When Adam looked up from his frosty glass he smiled at the gentlemen sitting themselves down. Robert looked up to, having placed his glass on the table top, placing his elbows astride it and moving his hands together, left hand cupped by his right above the glass.

Robert noticed that the gentleman sitting opposite was portly, a fine bright white soul persona emanating towards him, but large in the middle section and large jowls beneath a full chin. A different crowd he thought, looking at the few souls in the facility, apart from the bar keep who busied himself behind the bar with his back to the others.

Adam was nearing the bottom of his glass while Robert and Thom politely kept up. The portly figured gentlemen sitting had smiled at the two new comers and now turned to Adam. "Well what do you make of this business about classifying new building imaging constructs, bit stuffy isn't it, almost a bureaucracy I should think?"

The question invited a reply that was favourable, as Andrew and Adam were friends, and so the speculation coming back was on mark. "Couldn't agree more Andrew, whose business is it under any circumstance that a soul might construct this building or that, because the next logical step is that someone on the council wants to say no to a new building imaging construct."

"Yes, I'm afraid it seems that way. Well, now what do we have here with these fine young chaps." Andrew invited Robert and Thom to the conversation. Robert reached a hand forward saying "I'm Robert, I'm a…" the words hadn't reached his mouth when he realized that he was struggling for a new definition of himself as a recently dead guy. Thom filled the verbal open space "I'm Thom, I'm the tag along, really."

"Well then, friends of Adam and so friends of mine. What sort of business are you in, just resting, or getting ready for something new?" While the ice was being broken between the souls Adam was motioning for more drinks.

"Well I'm Robert, and I came to your world just a short time ago, after a, after a heart attack, I think, although no one I guess has ever really told me, that."

Andrew raised a hand to sweep in Robert's comments in a motion that was welcoming. As he did the new drinks were arriving and the men set to inhaling them in. "Well my boy, the body ends in all sorts of ways where you came from, and they do for everybody and everything there. But make no mistake, this isn't our world, it's very much your world, and it's really the real world." Andrew kept on "These things get talked about and soon you understand - that's where helpful beings like Adam here help out."

Adam was three quarters through his second drink when he joined the discussion "Well, you know the absolutely funny thing about the physical world is that 100% of the energy spent by all living things is to maintain status quo equilibrium. It might be in search of food, of shelter, in reproduction, but still it's to maintain the essential life force. And, the ironic part is its futile 100% of the time - ultimately."

"Oh quite right" added Andrew "and not just for animated matter, but for all physical manifestation in its entirety, ultimately. Even the stars themselves expire over time or become cold lifeless matter. Their entire experience only destined to be futile in the final analysis of observers of the physical."

"It's this world, this side as you know it young dead fellow that is the real threshold of our true existence. The difference between this world, its planes and those of the physical is vibrations at the quantum level, we shift back and forth between planes here, and the physical plane, but no death really occurs. Physical matter shifts to other forms, and our true self, our spiritual foot print travels on."

Andrew had seemed much more intense in these last few words; Robert knew that and had listened intently. He was definitely drinking in knowledge of his new environment and each new bit added to Robert's sense of comfort and almost gave a feeling of well-being.

Adam darted back into the conversation "You see lads we arrive over on this side to consider our real essence and to take stock. That means, where have we been in our evolution, where we should go next, or, should we not go anywhere for a long, long time. Should we work with a teacher to answer these questions, should we not care for a while, or should we just be with friends and think it all through. It's a lot like that, we work through our understanding here and we decide."

Adam's voice rose with some passion "...and that my friends, is the journey, not being in the know, but being in the mystery. "

Adam was busily ordering more drinks and the conversation shifted here and there. Robert asked Thom to tell his story and where he was in this journey the older souls referred to.

"Well, life for me was kind of frustrating." The others roared with laughter and without words the implication said well, who the hell hasn't had a frustrating life; perhaps even several of them!

Thom went on, despite being slightly embarrassed. He had been a high school graduate in a suburb of Philadelphia and had played some college football. In the 1980's he had started using cocaine and ran with a tough group of friends. In his early 30's he managed a strip club as a part owner with some mob and drug dealer types. His life was dark clubs, late night parties, and no connection with life or a meaning of any type.

Thom was short for Thomas, and Thom had come from a good family of Swedish decent. Thom new that somewhere he was in real trouble, that his life had been something with promise and that he had squandered it; trading it for something degraded and evil. But, the end for Thom hadn't come from a drug deal gone badly, but from something stupid.

He had been drinking one night after hours and had slipped on a spilt beer, falling backward and hitting his head irrevocably hard against the brass railing of the bar. Not quite dead on the back drop, but by the time his head had hit the floor his life was done.

Thom said that after he had arrived in the subtle domain that he had felt lost for a long time. He eventually had met Adam who had helped him find some context. Some meaning when he was so desperately short on any of it from his life. Adam had helped him reason that his only occupation had been in, sort of entertainment, so, with the help of some others they had used their vision to construct the structure that Robert had wondered upon, where Thom let souls view the good things in their life.

He felt rewarded doing that although he had found no comfort for himself in understanding what would come for him next, and what he viewed as Heaven had been lonely and cold. That is why when Adam came for Robert that he was happy to join along in their walk, of sorts.

Two more drinks had come while Thom was telling his tale. Andrew had listened quietly, smiling and nodding in agreement with Thom's confessions of having spent a meaningless life and having drifted that way to the subtle domain. He knew that Thom was searching and needing to find some bearings.

Adam had smiled largely showing that manicured demeanour of his – his hand tapping slightly on the left arm of his chair – using a ring that glimmered light occasionally to clap against the studs along the outside of the chair. Robert noticed an odd yellowish oversized tooth in Adam's stately smile.

Robert listened intently and sipped his drink with the most recent arrival now stacking up behind the near empty current drink, still in the progress of being emptied. As Thom's words caught his story up to the present, Robert had a feeling that came on all at once, and that sent him back against the seat of his chair with an amused grin that spread to a full bellied laughter. Completely unexpectedly, without warning or cause, and surely without some higher spiritual manifestation as to why, he had to pee.

Robert turned from side to side in his chair, signalling a need to break into the conversation. Adam paused mid-stream in a drink after having recognized his new arrivals sudden shift in character. The sensation of needing to urinate wasn't in isolation, Robert mused that he was half way to corked. Pissed in Heaven, "...who'da figured..." Robert muttered to himself with a sense of self-reassurance as he pushed himself up from the chair.

"Where in Christ's the lieu boys?" Robert placed a hand across his stomach area and rubbed his hand gently. Adam was still pulling on his drink as he used his other hand to point in a direction behind and to the right of the bar. Robert set out from the table, shifting his feet slightly to catch up with the kind of pace someone not drinking spiritual alcohol would keep.

He crossed in front of the bar and turned to his left and down a long white hallway. It lacked the crystal clear white light of most of what he had seen in this domain. The light was still there, but it lacked some lustre in places giving the impression of being somehow older. Almost like you would expect in an establishment that has had many visitors pass its way over a long period of time, and if in the real world needing some paint.

Robert came up to a wooden door with gents written on a door plaque. He pushed it open feeling as if he really did need to tend to himself at a urinal. His senses were confused, owing mostly to the notion he had that the subtle domain did not require physical maintenance of the body. As he presented himself in front of the urinal he pushed aside his pant garment and looked down to see a bright white stream emerge from his soul body.

As he did, another soul entered the washroom and took up station next to him at a second urinal. Robert smiled politely but impishly at the figure, a taller soul who seemed indifferent. As Robert looked back at the process he was evidently quite in need of, judging from the duration and intensity, the other soul belched as if it had to be, tucked himself away and left the washroom. Robert wondered where he had come from.

Robert finished to and went to wash his hands. He ran some water from a tap that sparkled as if having a life of its own over his hands, and he turned if off. He looked up and saw himself in the mirror. The sensation is always a funny one, either in the physical world or in the subtle domain, because it's a moment when we are alone with ourselves, in introspection. Robert had hated it, he always self-judged, but at this moment, and for this moment at least, he liked looking at his glowing face and the health that appeared in his hair, his skin, his teeth, and he moved his face left and right. He felt contented and with no worries. He knew he was in a good place.

Walking back out into the sitting area did produce a surprise, Adam had slid his chair back in-line with Roberts, and Thom and Andrew had shifted to the left to make way for two more tables to be joined in and upon a quick count, five new souls had joined their table. Other souls had taken up a table a short distance away and introductions were being made. He saw the gent who had taken up station in the bathroom next to him in the group.

Andrew was politely bowing to a soul and as Robert approached he said "And this is Robert who has recently joined up. Robert this is Claude, and across from you and next to Adam is Meeshanda, Clair here next to me, Paula and Anna."

Robert nodded to each but was more interested in taking his seat. Another drink had been delivered and took its place in behind the one already on deck. Robert considered that this process was getting a little ridiculous, and Heaven or not he was going to slow things down, especially with new guests and all.

"How are you" came a sweet voice to Robert's left. It was Anna.

"Well I'm here with all you good folks and feeling a little tipsy but other than that fine, for a ghost." The last word slipped awkwardly but the table assembly hadn't seemed to notice or care.

"Oh being here with Adam will do that for you, you have to watch him you know." Anna smiled at Adam who was in a discussion with Claude and didn't seem to care to register the missive comment. "Not to worry, it's Heaven you know, you never get a hang over here."

"What do you get here, then?" Robert had answered back reactively.

"Well, either tired of it after a time, drinking that is, or eating for that matter, and so some do it a lot because it takes them more time to get tired of it, or they just feel bored and decide to do something else. " Anna smiled slightly, raising her glass to her mouth for a polite sip. Her beautiful form shining clearly through a deep aura that set about her long perfectly cut, thin black hair.

"Can I ask you a question; I know I don't know you, but it's kind of a deep question." Robert had purposely deepened his voice to accentuate the word deep, in a sort of drawl. "Why when you drink sometimes do you have to go pee?"

The table went silent for a moment and Robert sensed the sudden stoppage of chatter. Just as suddenly the souls turned back to their conversation. Anna leaned over as if to be private and softly said, "It's because you thought in this type of situation that's what you're used to. You don't really need to use the little boy's room; you just do because that's something that would be normal to you, in the other world."

Robert seemed satisfied and sipped at a drink while hearing Paula tell Thom that she had visited his kiosk tent, which seemed more like placating than genuine consumer interest. Robert listened to the others but gradually he used the goings on of the conversation to catch glimpses of Anna; her hands, her hair, the brightness of her eyes and the shape of her breasts that were evident behind her spirit robe, to notice that she was a fine figure of a woman and more.

Anna sat upright and smiled in her chair, legs crossed, and polite enough to know that Robert was catching glimpses of her, but not embarrassing him by letting on in a way that women seem to instinctively know how to do as part of their unique refinement of character.

Adam was debating what seemed to be a hot point with Claude. "Visual structural constructs are an essential element in anyone's conditioning this side to a feeling of permanence, of belonging, of entitlement. I fail utterly to understand why you should want to regulate that!" The words were emphatic.

"Now Adam, Adam, no one wants to regulate any bodies thought constructs. But isn't it reasonable that if I should vision a lovely house on a nice road with light pink cherry tree leaves dancing about, and you come along and want to vision create a Mexican hacienda, that we need some balance, some unity. I mean does our existence here stand for chaos…"

The last words were unfortunate and required an immediate intervention by Andrew to head off Adam at the argumentative pass.

"Now, now no one is implying chaos, not at all. What I believe our dear Adam is saying is that who is to choose. Who has the right, who will one day say, you are not able to envision that building design construct and hence your own power as a creation capable being is subject to this soul's approval or that ones; some higher power, perhaps?"

Robert leaned over towards Anna and asked "what are they talking about, what is Adam so passionate about?"

Anna hesitated a moment to allow Claude, Andrew and Adam to resume their conversation so that she could speak quietly to Robert. "Well, one of the very settling things about the subtle domain is the ability to create your own home, or business, something that allows you to feel your creative nature and to make something real from it. Most people, well, souls, create a nice home that they can tend to, like on the physical plane. They have a home that they remember, with a garden, or an office, or maybe a workshop."

"So is there a problem then, with this creative construction?" Robert looked over to see Adam politely but emphatically tapping his index finger on the table to make a point to Claude.

"The trouble is that souls like to be close to each other, but everyone has different tastes. Some like to create a beach house next to an ocean, but want to be next to their best friend who likes to have an apartment in a setting, say, like downtown Newark. So, letting everyone be creative and seek out their area of contentment isn't that easy, when someone's contentment bumps against someone else's."

Adam had noted the conversation and spoke loud enough to take the discussion floor of the table. "And that is why we have a multiversity of different planes. If I want a disco and my neighbour wants an opera we simply modulate the frequency of our planes." A moment of silence and Paula, who Robert had barely noticed said "…well, then you wouldn't be neighbours anymore would you."

Anna offered Robert a few frames of context. "We can habituate in any number of planes that suit us, and we do. We think of where we would like to be, and where we would like to go, and we are there. The secret of the Subtle Domain, really, is that it moves at the power of thought."

Andrew had been listening in and was looking directly at Robert. "It just takes time young soul, it just takes time. You have to put some time in thinking about your circumstances. Now, I've got a wonderful sea side cottage a short distance from here. A nice little journey and you'll have some time there to collect your thoughts and see if you're ready for your teacher. "

Robert felt a little stunned and had a long drink from his glass. What did the offer mean; he didn't want to go anywhere. A sense of foreboding came over him and his soul body posture reflected the unease. Anna reached across and touched his left hand in a kind gesture.

"Oh I know the place; it's by the Sea of Chasms. It's a nice little cottage and there are lots of friendly people who love the country. I'm sure that Andrew will let you go when you're ready and you'll know when you are. "

"Ah, but beware the Sea of Chasms, a nasty mess to fall into." Adam was beginning to look drunk. That explained a little to Robert about how Adam looked, he was choosing to be a little gruff, a little "off" including having an apparent spiritual interest in alcohol.

Thom asked the question that Robert would have in a moment or two. "Hey, I haven't heard about a Sea of Chasms, is that real? Why wouldn't you want to fall in?"

Andrew took up the explanation. "Pure energy gentlemen, it's the demarcation point between the sub-planes of the subtle domain and the energy that feeds the turmoil, the disasters of the physical plane. It's the energy of cataclysm, of misery and of doubt. But, Adam is kidding - you can't fall in."

"Oh that's not entirely true Andrew." Shot back Adam. "You can't fall in, or over the cliffs in the sense of gravity, but, my friends, the plight of the living and of those souls who wander the dark under planes is ALL about falling in somewhere one shouldn't. "

"And that, so this repeat performance lecture about the meaning of life and life after life goes, is ALL about choices. Choices we have made, will make, have made and are about to make. Like this one." Anna was speaking and as she did she rose to her feet. "And my next choice is about dinner!"

The group seemed to agree with the statement by virtue of action, and Claude, Adam and Paula joined Anna by taking to their feet. Robert and Thom looked somewhat out of sorts in that the script to be played out hadn't formally included them with an invitation to a role, but all the same, they sensed they were along for the ride and so pulled themselves up.

As the group began to shuffle past a few tables towards the door Adam and Andrew turned towards the bar and waved thanks to the bar keep, Paula and Claude were leading the procession and Anna politely held back to pull Robert by his left forearm forward. Bending slightly she said "dinner time, and the Casino!"

Leaving the gentleman's club the group headed down the stairs without a word. Robert shuffled down the stairs, turned the corner to the lower set, with his knees a tad weak from the scotch drank upstairs. He sensed it, but the alcohol also made him to not really care, he felt a glow about him.

At the bottom of the stairs Robert crossed the entry way with the others noticing the light in the window frames set in the doors, which swung outwards. But as Claude and Paula swung the doors outward, and the group poured onto the landing outside, Robert was presented with a sudden shock. Immediately upon reaching the outdoors the light of day was gone and it was night. Not the dark of deep night, but the bluish dark of late evening. Sudden and unexpected, but so then was the complete change of setting of the surrounding buildings.

The air was as fresh and crisp as Robert had ever experienced. The night was brilliant and alive, the lights on buildings giving off a wonderful hue that seemed to have shards of light emanating from the centre and casting a sort of kindness onto the street, and moths and gnats danced about the light.

Arriving at the street the group paused with Andrew looking about the members as if conducting an inspection. Robert leaned back – taken aback by the culminating surprises as they were unfolding - as he noticed that Andrews dress was now formal. As was Claude's, and Paula's.

Andrew motioned with a hand to signal Anna and in a gesture towards Robert and Thom, saying "ahem" politely but impatiently. Anna reached forward and touched each man's shoulder, her head bowed slightly. With that, Robert and Thom were presented in brilliantly clean white formal evening apparel.

Robert cast his hands out from either hip and looked down in amazement, and as he had decided not to ask for an explanation, he was left with nothing other than a need to laugh full heartedly. Thom was turning from side to side and inspecting his appearance. Robert thought the light of clothes, apparel in general in the subtle domain was a wonder to behold; but the formal attire, smart and close fitting to his new spirit body cast an especially fine aura. He felt sharp and it emboldened his confidence.

Smartly dressed the assembly headed down a grand boulevard in floating motion with their legs motioning forward more for appearance than necessity. Other groups of souls were also headed up the same well adorned road way, some as couples, others as groups as large as ten or twelve, some with children. The boulevard had rich green full height trees and lush tropical plants. Large poinsettias with great leaves and bright red flowers, and many other smaller flowers that moved with the light that was cast from just above ground level landscape lamps.

Robert had the sense that a dinner hour was being called at some great establishment and that the souls were taking muster to the event at a pre-appointed hour. Crossing an arched bridge the group reached a large promenade.

Robert's night of surprises continued, as Anna moved a little closer into him and slid her left arm inside Robert's right arm, which he instinctively bent at the elbow to accommodate the welcomed gesture. The two glided towards a great hall that was domed, much the way a Mosque looks. Great pillars supported a covered entrance to the hall itself. The group moved up marble stairs into the hall which was also marbled.

Robert was stunned. The great hall was enormous. He looked up at the interior of the dome which was ribbed although not coloured. It sloped down to a marble ceiling that gleamed due to the fineness of the cut outer surface, which appeared to be golden granite with speckles of grey, black and silver. The walls had large plants in clay pots that were fifteen feet high.

The floor had a pattern set out in it created by different coloured marble stones and which appeared over polished in their gleam. Soft piano music played dimly behind the sound of hundreds if not thousands of souls. The sound emanated from the far side of the great hall, and in the distance Robert could see a fountain with a single spike of cascading water that curved at the top, falling back upon itself so that it looked more like light than water. Robert could not make out the pattern on the floor as at the centre of the hall was a long central table that he took, when getting closer to it, to be a buffet.

Robert had taken Anna's hand without really noticing, as he had tilted his head back to look at the ceiling and walls of the hall, his body gyrating left and right. In order to keep her hand on Robert's arm, Anna had let her hand fall into Robert's large palm and fingers. Robert was aware of it now, and while he was resisting an urge to squeeze Anna's hand a little tighter, thinking it might be so suggestive as to be inappropriate, he felt quite at home being so close to this soul he had met just a short time ago.

"We'll fetch a table you lot, won't we Andrew." Adam was tugging at Andrew who seemed willing to follow the plan. The two made their way towards the fountain and beyond, nipping at a table of wines poured into long necked glasses, with colours of rouge, and white, and dark red. The two seemed giddy as they made their way across the sheer marbled floor surface and disappeared down a few stairs heading to the right.

Paula and Claude were chatting intently and walked toward the centre buffet table. Thom wandered close behind, looking upward in a manner that seemed to be neglectful of where he was going, and evident that he hadn't been in the structure before.

Anna and Robert glided towards the centre of the buffet table. The table spanned nearly the entire length of the halls width, and had foods of an incredible variety - arrayed amongst plants and vases, candles with sharp bright flames - and each presented with a brass plate and engraved name in front of the platters and containers. Robert drifted a little to his right down the table, seeing smoked fish, artichoke dips, salads that were bright green and leafy, vegetable plates that cast aromas that matched their colour and quality – tomatoes, and cucumber and shredded carrots.

There were meats to, large grilled pork chops that were wet with juices, prime rib roasts with slices carved off for the taking, pinkish in the middle with a large moist reservoir remaining uncut. There were racks of lamb and a variety of ribs. Chicken that was barbequed and others that were baked, and turkey platters with one half sliced neatly on the left and the bird intact on the right. As Robert looked further down the table to the right he saw lasagne, any number of assorted pasta's with sauces set next to them and stews beyond those.

There was a light breeze in the air and the sound of the tinkling of serving forks and spoons against plates. The entirety of the multiple sensory inputs was the atmosphere of extravagance – like the resort Hotels in Hawaii or Bali on Earth - a scene of absolute splendour that would impress an Earthly prince.

Anna had moved off to the left and as Robert gazed that way he saw her returning with two large plates that were larger than normal, but not quite a platter. Anna reached for Robert's left hand and as she pulled it up she slid one of the two plates onto his outstretched palm. As she did she smiled playfully and motioned her head in an invite to dig in.

Robert moved to the table and reached for prime rib. He had two near simultaneous thoughts that both seemed overwhelmingly strange and surreal, which, really they were. As Robert reached for the sliced prime rib he had noticed a cavernous hunger that had erupted in his mid-section.

The first peculiar thought was of when he had last eaten, as sometimes happens when someone is hungry. The answer, he realized, was early morning in his apartment before getting on the bus in a place that was literally a universe away. Since his last meal , a simple breakfast of poached egg, bagel, and cheese he had died, crossed through a tremendous void, and come to make his way to this buffet table in an entirely new world.

The second peculiar thought was of the experience of eating in such a place as he was now standing. His food choices were limitless, his company fashionable and affectionate, his own appearance stellar, and there were certainly no health issues to worry about if he were to indulge his appetite. And so he did. The sensation was that perhaps he really was in Heaven.

Robert and Anna filled their plates amply, although Roberts was both higher in its stack and filled with a greater variety of food types. Mostly meats, juicy grilled pork chops, the prime rib, sautéed prawns, and a rack of short ribs. Anna's contained more greens, well garnished and with a thick browned piece of salmon.

The two made their way passed couples meandering in the area between the buffet table and the steps to the fountain. Anna led the way and as she neared the steps swung to her right and swooped down slightly to signal Robert to scoop up a glass of white wine off a table covered with a white linen cloth, which he did.

As he followed, Anna stepped gracefully down the stairs in a kind of side step that showed her long and slender right leg. Robert noticed it and how in the light of the fountain and surrounding table area that she looked radiant, hair flowing back and right hand holding the white wine upwards to keep from spilling it.

As Robert cleared the last step and walked smartly across the cobbled deck area he felt the glances of souls sitting in pairs and foursomes to his left, and more alongside the main building wall to the right. He didn't feel self-conscious or nervous though, more of attending a coming out event where he was being presented to a new group of people.

He sensed indifference from the assembled diners as opposed to judgement or friendliness, and that suited him fine. He felt comfortable in his soul body, how he was dressed, how he found he was handling himself in the kind of formal elegance if not grandeur that he had never known in life. He felt as much entitlement as any soul present, and that satisfied him.

Stepping off the main deck onto a lower deck Anna made her way across to a table with Adam and Andrew seated. The table was nestled alongside a stone railing with criss-cross exes of stone underneath and low spreading shrubs providing the sense of a wall demarking that deck and an even lower deck. The main building cast considerable light as did low lamps positioned every so often along the lower decks, and beyond them, amongst the shrubs leading out towards the glimmering water.

As he waited for Anna to sit herself in the outer seat he placed his plate on the clothed table, pulled out his chair and slid himself in. As Anna remarked at how the two gentlemen hadn't yet made their way to the buffet Robert rested his left elbow on the stone railing and looked out over stone cobbled walkways amongst tropical plants, lamp posts, and eventually down a short distance away to the ocean gently rolling in.

The water had moonlight upon it, bright in the centre and lessening into sparkles cast up by the slight waves rolling in, but with no moon in the sky. It was a beautiful site, and Robert looked out for a time until Anna pressed his right arm saying "Eat Robert, eat. You must be starved." Robert bothered for a moment to wonder why Anna assumed he was starved, but, as he was in complete agreement, replied "Yes, yes I am."

He hesitated for a moment, looking up at Adam and Andrew for a signal to dig in, and noticing that both were engaged busily in a cocktail, took their warm smiles as permission given. He unrolled his cutlery, raised his wine glass to Anna's and then toward Adam and Andrews and had a healthy gulp. He then set about dismantling his food selections, pulling here and cutting there until the plate began to empty.

A white coat clad server appeared and poured sparkling water into table glasses. She had fine features and black hair pulled back at the base of the neck and held by a ring, allowing the hair to spread out again to the length of her upper back. She held the bottle with one hand, the other supporting its base and asked "Are you gentlemen ready to order."

"Yes, yes, of course, I'll have the Cornish game hen please my dear." Andrew rubbed his chin slightly with finger and thumb, "...with sweet potatoes and green beans I should think. Perhaps a little apple sauce to the side as well my dear."

"And I'll have that wonderful steak you served me last week Angelina, with baked potato...and carrots in butter sauce". "...just like last week." The server had finished the sentence for Adam. She turned to Robert and Anna - the latter of whom sat upright and impressively stoic as she ate indicating solid table manner refinement - and asked if they should like anything else. Robert was caught in a wave of plate plunder as the question arrived and he could only manage a shake of his head indicating no as he pulled his white cloth napkin across his mouth.

Anna took her wine glass and singled that she was fine, and so the server nodded and moved on to another table. As Robert and Anna were tidying up their lips with napkins, which Robert had to do periodically between swallows given the sauced meats in his selections, Andrew began a dialogue.

"Well then Robert, how have you found your first 24?" Robert looked to his right at Anna and then replied as he moved his napkin from his lips and swallowed the last bite down. "Are there 24 here?"

"Just an expression my boy, makes us feel back home in the world."

"It has, been, uh, a lot of things really. I mean day and night here has been a new world. I came here and was greeted, and came to know all of you, but I..." Andrew spoke cutting him off "...but you don't know what it is all, supposed, to mean. You're thinking what am I to do and where am I to go."

Adam shot in whimsically, "Well the Casino would be a damned good choice." Robert remained focused on Andrew's words and bi-passed Adams. "Yes, exactly, where am I to go to, what am I to do, what will my job be, or, well, my purpose, what comes next?"

Andrew leaned forward to reveal light cool blue eyes that lit up moving into the light cast from the main buildings overhead lights. "You need, my boy, to find the deep blue horizon of the mind." The way the words rolled out had caused all to take note. There was seriousness in the words; there was meaning and wisdom, but also the hint of a threat as implied by the presence of a challenge.

The Vast Realm of the Self

After dinner had been served to Andrew and Adam the two souls had made what was obviously the evening pilgrimage to the Casino. The two had enjoyed an evening smoke of cigar that Robert had immediately craved with its sweet aroma that had wafted across at him.

Robert had quit smoking in life and hadn't had a craving during the last few months of his life. It was nonsensical to think of health concerns in his current environment, but he hadn't asked for a cigar out of respect for Anna. He had no way of knowing that if the odour had been something that she felt offensive – she wouldn't have sensed it at all.

But Robert had found a way to feel full in the subtle domain, having made a determined second visit to the buffet and a side trip to a desert table that included dishes made in a flaming alcohol. A single desert dish had been shared between him and Anna after the gentlemen souls had departed for the Casino. They had carefully sculpted a large wedge of chocolate ice cream cake with a rich cream in the centre and puddles of liquid chocolate on the sides.

Robert had continued to rest his arm on the stone railing, and Anna sensed a desire in him to walk along the shoreline. They made their way off of the lower deck, past some smartly attired diners and on to the cobble stone walkways to the ocean.

When there, they turned and walked toward a hill a long way off in the distance. Robert felt a little uneasy as they walked, moving a little to the right occasionally to avoid slight waves rolling in. Robert knew why he felt uneasy during their light conversation, realizing that he wanted very much to hold onto Anna's hand again.

Anna's mood had become very jovial, and she acted like a young women perhaps eighteen or twenty. She laughed with occasional playful shrieks as she stepped quickly to keep from having water run up against her stylish shoes. She turned to slip them off, and collected them up into her left hand next to Robert's right.

As she did she said "Oh Robert look" turning his shoulders to the left so that he could face the ocean. Off in the distance was a reef that the ocean occasionally, rhythmically, smashed into sending up a spray of glittering water illuminated by the energy that permeates everything in the subtle domain. The scene made Robert think that even in this place nature had motions of power that seemed greater than the will of men, or their souls.

As Robert turned back to the direction of the walk, Anna had placed her shoes in her right hand, and reached to take Roberts to support her as she carefully negotiated large pebbles along the beach. The walk seemed to be painful to Anna and so she pulled Robert a little further from the water and on to comfortable sand. Once there, Anna did not remove her hand from Roberts, but turned it a little so that the two met at the palms and fingers wrapped across the back of each others.

The two walked for a time without words, negotiating an easy path for Anna's feet amongst pebbles, sand and rock. Robert asked a question that had been in his mind since dinner. "Anna, what did Andrew mean when he said the deep blue horizon of the mind?"

"Well, when you think of a horizon, like a horizon on a great plain of the prairie what do you think of?"

"What do I think of, what do I think of?" Robert mused a little. "I think, of, I think of what might be over that horizon. I think that the sky is big and that what lies out in that blue where the sky meets the land is what might be. Possibilities, I guess what I am saying is that the horizon makes me think of what possibilities and what is to come I can't yet see."

"Bravo" Anna emphatically shot back. "Very good Robert, because that is exactly what Andrew meant, or, what I think he meant I should say. What we come to look for in the subtle domain is what lies across our own personal horizon. What mysteries, what discoveries, what lessons, and what challenges. What is possible for us and what should we seek as our own discovery of need? The deep blue horizon of the mind dear Robert, is your place of discovery."

Robert slid the hand not holding Anna's into his pants pocket, while looking skyward, noticing that some stars had appeared and looked truly like jewels in the sky against a black background that met a deep blue horizon and then the sparkling ocean. He sighed slightly as he kept his gaze skyward.

"What's wrong?" Anna had placed a little concern in her voice.

"What is MY place of discovery, where does a person find his place of discovery, why isn't there a book to help you understand…" Robert was unable to get the final words out as Anna pulled his hand so that his form came square to her own. She placed her hands just above his waistline and pulled him close.

Her height matched Roberts almost perfectly elevated by a slight rise in the sand. Her black perfect hair reached the small of her back as she arched her upper back to move her lips to those of Robert, and she kissed him with an open mouth.

The two remained in the embrace for two minutes or more, both passionately answering a wealth of questions that most human beings carry for the vast majority of their lives and on into the next. Am I loved? Am I special to someone else? When the answer comes back from someone that we have invested in emotionally – even briefly - as being favourable for the first time, it is a tremendous affirmation, and it carries as much energy as the Universe can muster. It is the elixir that drives the continuation of the human form.

For Robert and Anna in the subtle domain the coming together of their two spiritual forms was an elixir that allowed them to reach some of the answers they needed to point towards purpose.

When the embrace ended Robert held Anna and rubbed the lower area of her back, across an open skin area and down towards the material of her dress, both spiritual energy rather than material form. Robert felt an enormous restoration of energy from his closeness to Anna and was able to easily sense that she too was energized, and the two transferred energy back and forth to each other.

Anna looked into Robert's eyes and said "Maybe it's time to go home." The words took Robert by storm and were a great surprise and a great relief – that souls in the subtle domain do have homes! Robert's relief was signal enough, and Anna led them towards the hill they had now approached, a good distance from the dining complex.

Robert struggled up a sandy incline to stand next to where Anna had moved to, and with one word she asked "Ready?" Robert shrugged his shoulders in an honest query of "for what" and with that the two disappeared from the beach.

An instant later they were standing in what appeared for all purposes to be an older apartment building. Anna shook her feet gently and sand fell to the floor and sparkled in a dance of light before disappearing. Robert slipped off his suite coat, which along with all his spirit clothes now seemed completely out of place.

Anna led the way into the apartment, into a living room that was classically designed and to the right through pulled back white sheer curtains that demarked the bedroom area. She sat on the bed that was a single mattress and headboard with a modernist look sandwiched between two blonde wooden night tables with shiny metal looking reading lamps.

She slipped off her dress in one motion to reveal a transparent bra and panties that did much more to accentuate the soft curves of her spirit body than to hide them. Robert seemed unaware of the actions that he should take, and Anna motioned for him to slip off his suit clothes in a manner that an adult person knows to be permissive but without words.

She spoke as she slid her body up onto the bed, gently sweeping her glowing hair to one side so that her head did not compress the hair. "I know moving about through what appears like thin air is hard to get used to."

Robert was folding his coat across a chair and had shuffled his shoes underneath a chair with web laced netting making up its seat. "Yes, when I first arrived my old school teacher Mrs. Delorme had just, disappeared on me."

"Well, this place isn't like when we were alive and back on Earth. It is a big place because of these literally thousands, probably millions of planes, each a fabric woven by the desire of those of us who live here. So when we wanted to be in my home we simply moved through an open door that took us into the room of what we wanted."

"If we had wanted to have gone to the Casino like our two pals we would have just walked through a doorway that is really, a slight change in the frequency of energy – and poof, you are in an entirely new reality."

"How do you know these things?" Robert asked.

"I live here Robert. OK, I mean I exist here; it is really my home, because this is the real nature of existence you know. Well, and plus you can take seminars to learn these things." Anna had stretched out with her hands folded across her tummy. Her energy level had remained high and Robert could sense it, she seemed to resonate with slight pulses of energy that he instinctively took as being desire for his presence next to her on the bed.

Robert removed his pants and threw them on top of his suit coat, he removed his socks, and he unbuttoned his shirt. He sat on the right edge of the bed, and with one motion laid back on the bed while rolling onto his right side. He placed his right hand under his right cheek, propping himself up on his bent elbow.

Anna looked over at Robert and as their eyes met the two moved their bodies closer on the bed. Their legs touched and Robert placed his hand on Anna's hands as they rested on her mid section. As he did, Anna moved her hands allowing his hand to rest flat on her stomach, which she then covered with her hands one on top of the other.

Remarkably, as Robert's hand made contact with Anna's stomach a swirl of energy began to form near Anna's skin. The motion was circular and quickly grew in energy until it became a constant movement that radiated out into Robert's hand. The feeling was very warm to both and Robert felt compelled to rub Anna's mid section, increasing the radius slightly with each pass, causing the energy swell in Anna to increase in response.

Both knew that something remarkable was happening. Robert felt a swell of energy in his groin that he found came upon him so swiftly that he could only distract himself from it by stretching out, and as Anna turned slightly so that her lips met with his own. Both adjusted slightly again so that Robert could move his left leg onto Anna's legs stretched out together with her ankle atop the other leg's shin.

Energy in Anna was now building from the area just atop her groin and to the pit of her stomach. The energy had travelled up Roberts left arm and as he motioned in circles his own groin and mid section became absolutely alive with pulses of vibrant and irresistible energy.

Robert changed his motion from centric circles to an oval movement that began to touch Anna's left breast and downward to the upper edge of her pubic area. Anna reacted by arching the small of her back and moving her lips with more vigour into Roberts and offering her tongue to the edge of Robert's mouth.

Robert had shifted his lower body closer to Anna's with a slight rhythm but as Anna's legs were crossed at the ankle and shin he couldn't comfortably perform the manoeuvre and had rested his legs back down to the bed. He had become more energized though, through Anna's stronger kiss and had moved his tongue into her mouth to engage her tongue. As he did, he moved his hand to cup Anna's full breast underneath her transparent bra, which fell aside.

After a few motions across the breast with increased pressure as fingers caressed Anna's nipple, Anna moved her legs from being one atop the other so that Robert was able to move his left leg between them. The motion set off a cascade of pleasure through both spirit bodies with energy literally pulsing to the edge of each other's outer edge and where they touched, the energy crossed the boundary of self and engaged the energy of the other.

Robert had become overpowered by the desire to thrust his mid section closer to Anna's and he began to moan slightly as he kissed Anna on the side of her lips and then onto, and into the centre of them. The kisses were deep and Anna began to motion her hips in unison to Roberts.

Robert moved his body back slightly to provide a space where he could move his hand from Anna's breasts, both of which he had engaged, down to Anna's pubic area. He did not hesitate at the outer area, moving his hand under the spirit garment which he moved upward as his finger found the opening of Anna's vagina. It was wet with energy and accommodated Robert's advance.

After a brief and ever deeper penetration, Robert motioned his hand down to remove Anna's transparent panty. She moved her hips upward to accommodate and the garment slid away from her long and slender legs. Robert then sat slightly upright to allow his shirt to be slid from each arm and away from his back. As he looked down the energy in his torso was bright with blue and white hues, powerful and brilliant, turning like a galaxy turns in space, with countless thousands of points of light.

Anna too was consumed by pulsating energy, although hers was more pronounced and moved up to the edge of her being and then swam back into the centre of her body.

Robert moved fully atop Anna's body and as he did she moved her legs apart to allow his body to settle over hers. Both bodies were radiating, swirling, energy pulses. The energy pulses began to slowly move in unison as both pushed their hips together. The energy ran up to the surface of each body and cascaded back down. A good amount of it was beginning to spill across the boundary of self and it seemed to intensify as it moved first into Robert, and then back down into Anna.

The energy exchange brought about a complete devotion to the act that both were now engulfed in. The sensations seemed to urge each beyond the limits imposed by intellect. Each was overcome by the sensation of their energy pulsations. But it was the exchange of energy one to the other that caused them to believe that they had absolutely no control over the sharing of event.

Robert moved into Anna and he felt incredible warmth - he felt energy begin to emit from the end of his penis. It began a feeling that was entirely pleasurable but unpredictable, as the rate of energy spreading out increased a little with each motion to be deeper in Anna.

Anna had moved her legs into an arched position, bent at the knee. She placed her hands on Roberts outer hips and pulled him tightly insider her, and in doing so moved him in ever deeper. She was receiving Robert's energy as he moved inside her and she loved the sensation as being something that had absorbed her mind and thoughts.

The energy between the two where their bodies met, legs, hips, sexual selves, mid sections, chest, shoulders and hands on shoulders, and at the mouth was beginning to cascade. The brilliance and sheer number of energy points was as if in the human body where trillions of cells exist as their own points of life and consciousness.

Their bodies were alive in the spirit world with energy that was both overwhelming in its sensation and growing power - created, intensified, dominant in the self and then thrust at points of contact back into the other where it was further intensified by the host before being shared back yet again.

A hue from the energy began to engulf the two, casting a halo of bright white light as the blues turned white and grew in intensity. Robert had arched his body and moved his mouth, his head upward from Anna and she had turned hers to the side.

Both concentrated on the events that had overcome them and struggled near the edge of comprehension to contain the feelings. Robert was now struggling to hold on to the sensation of energy moving from him deep inside Anna. Simultaneously, Anna, still holding on to Robert's hips and upper buttocks moved him inside her with greater rhythm, moaning as she wanted more than anything to receive all that Robert sought to hold back.

The moment arrived. Robert cried out and electric shock waves of energy shot out from his body at the penis deep inside Anna. He felt his entire being - being cascaded from his body into hers. Again and again in great waves of energy within waves of energy.

Anna's pelvis and outer vagina became engulfed in the waves of energy that Robert's body had sent, and she could not, nor did she want, to contain them. The waves of energy and pleasure had swept up her vagina to her core self and were now radiating a cascade of emotion and sensation. Her mouth was open to gasp for air when the moment came that Robert had sent his cascade of energy deep inside her.

That moment was sensationally catastrophic, as Robert's energy release inside her was super heatedly warm and carrying energy that shot through her essence to every point of light, of every cell that gave her selfness. She had moved her hands up to grip Robert's back with tightened fingers, and fingernails etched into the fabric of his soul's back.

The event of arrival had also been a point of climax for the energy that had swam back and forth during their love making. First from one, then into the other, then back, and as it did so, the light created and shared between the two had reached a brilliance and intensity that had completely outshone all the other energy exchanges.

It had consumed each body's outline so that both had become the glowing brilliance of one. It had consummated two souls so that both had become the glowing essence of one.

As Robert and Anna held onto each other exhausted, Robert felt himself diminish out of Anna that felt most natural. The light shared between the two began to fade – between intermittent pulses of brilliance that then settle, like ambers in a fire that flare up when raw carbon encounters oxygen. The pulses loosing intensity and becoming more infrequent as time passed and the two reached a more relaxed state.

Robert eventually settled next to Anna, taking her hand in his as she rested her head on his shoulder and her flowing hair onto his torso. He gently rubbed her shoulder and down her back with his hand and the arm that cradled her against him.

For a long, long time the two rested in silence without saying a word. What they had shared had in some way, silently known to both, changed them. They had experienced something they could not understand in its beauty, intensity, passion and spirituality.

Eventually, Anna said with a hint of wonder in her voice, simply "the vast realm of the self" and both then fell into a very deep sleep.

The Sea of Chasms

Robert awoke in what was to him, an undetermined time later. The first sense that came to him was of light flooding in through the open windows that overlooked the street outside of Anna's apartment. White sheer curtains were being blown back into the apartment by a welcome breeze.

Robert propped his head up by his right arm with his hand behind his head. He didn't immediately worry about where Anna was – he instinctively knew that she must be in the apartment somewhere. Such was the level of comfort that Robert now felt with his surroundings and new found friends, especially Anna. He wondered about what had happened between him and this spirit that he barely knew, but felt he had always known, and who he now felt he knew more than anything or anybody else by way of their exchange; but, strangely, without really knowing what had happened between them at all.

He hoped Anna would have the answer, but for now, bending his legs upward and down in a stretching motion that spread to engulf his whole body, and yawning deep into his soul, he felt relaxing in Anna's bed was all he could want. He felt rested to the very depth of his soul body through every cell reporting in centrally a deep level of contentment, as if represented by a collective consciousness.

Robert noticed some motion in the outer apartment and saw a figure in a sheer, silk robe with flowing black hair. The sound of a sink facet turning off was followed by the whistle of a kettle, then the pouring of water as it filled a tea pot. A moment later Anna appeared at the entrance way to the bedroom, her hands holding a steaming cup of tea that radiated a pleasant camomile odour.

Anna's face was radiant and she had a wide smile as she met Robert's eyes and sat on the edge of the bed, with one attractive leg exposed at the knee and upper thigh as she curled it under her.

"Would you like some tea?" The words came out entirely politely, which at times can seem odd when people share something so much more than politeness to early in their relationship. Robert just shook his head to indicate no, as he returned Anna's smile. He reached out and took her right hand in his own. He moved down a little on the bed so that Anna could comfortably take his hand.

"Anna, do you know what happened between us? It was the most incredible feeling that I have ever, I mean ever known. I didn't expect that was capable of happening, I mean I am glad, very glad that I did, but..." Anna's words cut the sentence short "...no Robert, I don't know exactly. I mean I have heard of souls having sex in the subtle domain, but I had no idea that it could be like that. I am not even sure that it is like that for everyone, I guess we'll have to ask."

Robert squeezed Anna's hand as she had uttered the word "we'll" because it implied a couple. Something that Robert had not thought about himself as being for a very long time.

Anna sensed Robert had a number of questions forming in his mind. She could sense the computations behind their construct and decided to answer them as she felt them. "No, Robert, I haven't had sex since coming here. I haven't wanted to meet any one, at least for most of the time, but, I felt more recently that I would like to have someone in my world here, and, well…here you are." She laughed a little as the words trickled out.

"What do you do here Anna?" Robert thought of the next logical question develop quickly in-behind the last. "How did you come here Anna? How did you die? When did you live?" Robert had become excited in his not knowing these things about Anna.

She drank a long drink from her cup of tea and smiled at Robert. She heaved a sigh and looked towards the window. The hesitation was palatable and Robert began to think he had pushed too hard. Anna turned her gaze back to him and said "I was a teacher Robert, and in the 1980's I died of cancer. I hadn't married, or even looked for a husband, I was only 33, and one day my Doctor had called after some tests on my cervix. The cancer was linked to another tumour in my breast and by the time they had proposed a treatment they had found it in my liver to. It wasn't long, and it sure wasn't pretty."

Robert mustered some words "Anna, I am so sorry." He had propped himself up in the bed and the words came out seemingly shallow, although the emotion behind it was genuine, and Anna knew that. "Well" Anna said, "I suppose everybody here didn't get to this side through very much nice stuff happening to them."

Her thoughts turned to Robert "…and you." Robert's response was very flat "heart attack, I guess, but nobody has ever really said." Robert thought back to his last moments of life. "I guess it was really quick, but it was terrible, I couldn't breathe and it ended pretty terrible."

Anna had walked over to the dresser next to the chair where Robert had flung his suit clothes. She collected a hair brush and returned to the bed. She smiled widely and ran the brush through her hair. With each stroke energy seemed to buzz about her brilliant hair, pulled back and out of the strands, and twinkling with light as the energy fell downward but disappeared before hitting the floor.

"As to what I do Robert, I teach. It has been the great passion of my life; well actually as I have come to learn, of my recent lives. I teach children, and others, but mostly children at the great hall where people come to learn."

"That is what I want to do Anna; that is what I feel I need to do now. To learn about what I am about in my existence, to know where I belong. I feel it very deep Anna." There was the presence of insistence in Robert's voice.

"Well Robert the learning that you are seeking is something very personal. Some of it is found in books, in lectures, in becoming aware of the universe that you are a part of, but really, knowing yourself and the mission of your being, if you will, well that is something that is very much your journey."

Robert was confused. He thought out loud. "But how can that be, how can we have shared what we have shared, but you not be here to teach me when you are a teacher?"

Anna reached out and touched Robert's leg with a soothing rub. "I don't quite know what our being together has come to teach us Robert, I guess we'll find out in time. And yes, I can teach you some things, like you will teach me, but you will know your teacher when he comes to you. You will know it throughout your soul, and that isn't in a classroom."

"And you Anna - have you come to know your teacher?" Robert was pressing again.

"Yes, Robert, not to long after I came to this side I met a teacher who has spent quite a lot of time with me. But, to be honest, I haven't really been ready to take my next steps. I have had a lot of pain, and I want to just spend time doing things I like. Like teaching, like dinners, like painting, and, I think, well, frankly meeting you."

That was enough conversing for the time being. Anna settled back onto the bed and Robert readied his body to accept her head on his shoulder. He cuddled her, and both gently caressed the other, silently wondering about the mysteries that had created a fabric around them, and between them.

Robert lay alongside Anna for a long time and watched white billowy clouds float by as if painted as a three dimensional object against a patient blue sky. The kind of sky that makes one feel tranquil on a lazy late summer Sunday afternoon.

A sense of peace because there is a feeling of being reassured that no one nor any thing will break into that tranquility. A late afternoon when it seems that every living thing needs that tranquility to rest against the tasks of the coming Monday morning.

Robert looked left at the spirit clothes he had worn to the dinner and then down at his spirit body without clothes. Anna had sat upright on the edge of the bed and allowed a slight wind to pour through the open window and run against her face. She noticed Robert's emotions and walked over to the clothes draped across the chair.

She bent slightly to the right and collected up the pants and coat in one motion. She pulled back several garments hanging in an open closet and effortlessly hung the suit. She leaned forward and picked up Robert's shirt and hung it to, while guiding his shoes into the closet and under the hung clothes.

Anna turned and reached for Robert with outstretched hands. He rose to her invitation and stood before her, putting his hands in hers. She pulled him close to her silk robed body and engaged Robert in an embrace. Anna ran her hands down Robert's bare back and on to his rounded buttocks.

As she drew away Anna pulled her hands along Robert's waist as if drawing a robe belt together. As she did bright white clothes draped themselves down upon Robert's spirit body. He was clothed in a Nehru shirt and belted pants, and sandals that fit comfortably to his feet. The texture of the clothes was that of soft white cotton, like in India.

Robert brought his hands upward and pushed his arms outward to signal his pleasure with his new attire, and that he was clothed again.

Anna looked into his eyes and with a crooked smile, but not quite a smirk, saying "You know you can do that yourself." After a moments silence she added "…its one of the things I'll teach you."

Anna turned her back to Robert and toward the closet; she pulled a drape on the right side of the closet toward the left and pulled a summer dress out and slid it over her head. Her beautiful back and feminine curved backside disappeared under the spirit cloth. She wiggled her hips and moved her hands downward against her thighs so that the dress fit snugly against her spirit body.

"I like to do it the old fashioned way" Anna said as she turned toward Robert and smiled. "Come on let's go get something to eat."

Robert and Anna held hands as they bounced down a set of stairs found just outside Anna's apartment door. As they reached the street Robert looked back at the building and saw Anna's suite was in a two story low rise coloured in a darkish brown pastel colour.

Robert felt energy surge in his body from the warm sun that drenched the street. The day no longer felt like a lazy late afternoon, but rather, one charged with the possibilities of a new day. The two bounded down the street, parting hands as they crossed smaller objects, a child's head in one spot and a cart left unattended in another.

Robert knew that he had crossed another barrier of sorts in his afterlife. He had arrived at a place, another successful transmigration, and this time into a place where he felt the questions that pressed themselves upon his mind would be reduced, and, where he felt someone wanted him to be.

That more than anything else was responsible for the teen like glee that he felt running through his spirit veins. In life Robert had been alone and when he crossed over he had been frightened that he would be alone in the life that follows life. Now Robert felt such a belonging, and his soul was singing the emotion to the world around him.

Robert and Anna made their way past a number of shops with Anna pausing occasionally to look at fruits outside shops in bins here, shoes on racks there. Anna was leading their expedition and had a sense of purpose in her step, and Robert sensed he was being led to some special place she had in mind.

At the corner of two roads, Anna reached out and grabbed for Robert's hand, and wheeled him up a long alley way. Her actions were playful. Near the end of the lane way Anna came to an abrupt stop and Robert's motion carried him a few steps further – with Anna's arm full stretched able to hold him in place to turn and look at the treasure she was presenting.

It was, of course, a specialty coffee bar. Robert was delighted, the timing perfect. It showed in his face as he turned and smiled broadly at Anna, his face warm with affection.

The two made their way to one of the outdoor tables that were placed in a brightly lit area on cobble stones demarking a patio area. Other shops and a bakery completed the lane way's end, and the air was full of the smell of fresh bread intermingling with the vapours of strong coffee percolation.

A pretty server appeared and the two ordered. The server returned to the shop and Robert could see her dutifully managing the process of pulling leavers and then applying steam to milk. The blaze of action subsided and the server returned with two large mugs with steam rising from the brims.

Anna found some pastries close by out front of the bakery and collected them up with some butter and jams on a tray.

The patio area was sided by two, two storey buildings with the coffee shop being in a three storey building to the left side of the end of the lane way. The open side of the patio was the lane way leading back from where Anna and Robert had come.

Robert had noticed that the apartment building that Anna lived in, and the road way that they had walked down to the lane, was one block up from a beach.

Robert could see the brilliant blue water beyond the busy beach between buildings as they had walked. His sense was that he was in a sea side village, in an inner harbour. He wondered if it had a name.

The two sipped their coffee and prepared their pastries without talking for a time. The taste of coffee seemed to restore energy and vitality, but only because Robert's thoughts counted on it to do so - given that he already had all the energy that pulsed in the subtle domain. The long draws of liquid did though, surely increase the already existing favourable mood.

"So what shall we do today Robert?" The question left Robert searching for some context, and to do that he had to start what might be a long process of asking questions. He was always so very full of questions. His reply was logical, appropriate to find a context. "What are our choices?"

"Well, lots of things. We could walk through the town and shop for a marvellous dinner to make together, or we can walk to the library and find some good books, or we could…" Robert cut Anna off in mid-sentence. "How long does a day last - will it be night again?"

"Day lasts as long as we want Robert, and if we decide that night might be more fun, or suite our moods more, then we will have night."

"So what happens really does depend on our moods then." Robert's question was rhetorical.

"Yes Robert, what suits our moods decides our day. Some people love to play all the time while others miss the tasks they knew in their working lives and decide to do things that are familiar to them. So they work, or they study."

Anna added "Most people don't realize how much their working lives do to define themselves - they really need to work at things, especially creative or purposeful things to keep centred and to know themselves."

Robert felt pretty sure that he wasn't going to need to work at mall security to define himself. After all, how much crime could there be in Heaven, or how often would the lights go out because of circuit overload with some fuses needing to be changed out. He chuckled a little to himself.

"Anna, I think that what I need to do is to find out about me - about my soul. I told the guide who met me, and old teacher of mine, that I didn't find a lot of purpose in my life. It was, well, kind of empty, and I…" Robert hesitated "…I don't like the idea of living without a purpose."

Anna smiled widely and very kindly, reaching out a hand to place in Roberts. Her eyes gleamed and she looked deeply into Roberts.

"Don't you see Robert - your life was not at all empty, because it has led to your search now for meaning, to find the soul of who you are - even if that means who you will become, if you decide to go back to life. Whether you go back to life, or stay in the subtle domain for a long, long time, or move forward to the light realms and no longer take to life, you will find who you are because you want to *search*. That is what your life gave you!"

Robert sat back in his chair as Anna's words had come to him in such a strange way. They seemed to reinforce notions that Robert had had in the back of his mind, but in a way that they had not yet been thought of yet - but would be. More than a precognition, a sense that the thoughts the words would invoke were an eventuality, pre-destined to exist and now the package was being opened.

Robert felt that his meeting Anna and the strong emotion that had built between them was to be. He knew that he would come to love her in the deep way that comes through so many shared experiences. Like an ingredient in a recipe that acts as the elixir, essential to the eventual outcome, and reaching its real potential with time.

Robert sensed that his search would eventually cause him to be confronted with decisions about whether to return to the pursuits of the living, or to earn greater spiritual growth through seeking knowledge; or perhaps whether he would seek to move away from the appeals and pains of the flesh. Those were all choices across the deep blue horizon yet to be reached. He began to understand.

Robert asked "Anna, what happens to people, to souls, when they no longer want to return to life, to the living?"

"Robert that is such an over whelming topic. In time, the physical Universe draws the desire of souls to yearn for its return. The need to return, to feel flesh and to reward the ego becomes so strong. Souls go back, and back, and back, to fill the sea that is their wanting, always wanting. And with it, decisions both good and bad that make cause and affect one."

"Karma" Robert declared.

"Yes Robert. But, after so much living and time in the subtle domain - through this dance of and with the self - a time comes when the ego begins to wane, and the meaning of all that exists drenches the soul with query."

"With query?" Robert wondered about the use of the term.

"With query, wonder of what exists beyond the life of the ego, because when it passes the soul is free to discard the physical Universe, and the desire for a body and its pursuits."

"Discard your body? Why wouldn't we want a body? What is the sense of not having a body?" Robert's portrayal of confusion was real.

"Beyond the subtle domain are realms where existence is in the pure light of thought. " Anna's voice was soft and instructive. Robert's mood was contemplative, he thought of seeking meaning on a higher plain, and it made him feel purposeful, mature.

After a few moments Anna again took his hand and smiled with a slight blush "You know Robert, what happened last night with you makes me think that I won't want to give up my body for a very long time!" Both rolled their heads to the side with laughter, and when it subsided, they kissed.

The remainder of the day was spent wandering through shops and in to the interior of the town square where Robert recognized where he and Mrs. Delorme had drank beer. She had said he would find what he needed, and that prediction seemed to becoming truer with each passing experience.

It occurred to Robert that in this realm progress was not measured with the passing of time, but with the passing of experiences. At least at the pace he seemed to be setting.

In time the two desired evening and their dinner and as evening approached Anna led the way to a few grocers near her apartment and she picked out items for a dinner to be made and shared.

Once in the apartment the two cooked fresh pasta, prepared a tomato sauce with garlic added to the mix. They cut leafy wet lettuce into chunks and further reduced them by hand. The salad and meal was completed with a cucumber so fresh that its aroma filled the air, a bright red tomato, and shelled peas. Anna prepared a dressing with oil and vinegar ingredients from her cupboard.

The two sat down to their meal with a brisk merlot.

"When do you work Anna?"

"Like any of us, when I want to. I found though, that I was getting more and more absorbed in teaching. It was becoming my whole life here and I decided to take a break. Children who have crossed over to early are always so eager to learn! They can own your soul with that eagerness to learn!" Anna went back to working her pasta with her fork.

"Oh how sad" Robert said as he ate his salad "yes, of course, the children died too early and didn't become adults, do they become adults here?"

"Well they could of course if they wanted to, but more wait to see their parents and then go on living with them until they go back to living. There is a very, very strong tug from the physical plane for children. They almost always go back to finish learning how to grow up – often to reunite with a parent who goes back first – setting the stage for another try at the learning, and loving." Anna sat back, sipping her wine.

"Do you have relatives here Anna?" Robert began to think of his own.

"Not my immediate family, my parents and brother are still alive. I look forward to their coming through, and I do plan to meet them. I have an aunt and grandparents here, but they aren't focused on the life they had with me in it. They see themselves in a different time, when they were young in their own lives. About the 1900's or something, but way before I was born into the family, anyway, where and when they feel isn't me.

"So they live there, I am not sure that I understand." Robert shook his head slightly from left to right.

"Yes, that is right. They live in a plane where the buildings and clothing is what they knew and loved growing older together. They have fine clothes, and servants, it's like the, oh, what do you call it, la belle epoch - the golden epoch in English. You know, when the rich had everything, a time when exploration around the world was important and unfinished, and privilege for the few. Well, they like being the few."

Anna sounded like a person who isn't that fond of their relatives and if selection in the relationship was an option, would opt out. Anna did sound fond of the time in history. Robert had done some mental calculations and said "But Anna wasn't that time to early for them to have lived?"

"My grandparents were children at the turn of the century and they loved that era, they yearn for it, and to live it again. They know that I am part of the later part of their life but my being around; well it just reminds them that the good old days gave way to a bunch of really painful times, and then they got old. So, the whole lot like being where they were when they were young and like to live it as if they were adults and they would have had a chance to grow up with all the splendour intact. And that life sounds and feels a lot better to them than having to go through a couple of world wars and a depression."

Robert and Anna finished their meal and afterwards found another bottle of wine in Anna's armoire that also contained cheese and breads. Once opened and glasses refilled, the two ran hot water into the sink and washed the dishes. As Robert dried the plates Anna made a pot of tea and the two went to the sofa to sit down.

Anna lit two candles and placed one on a side table and the other on the sofa table. She sat back against Robert cupping the hot steaming tea in both hands as if to warm them up. Robert shifted a little to provide a comfortable space for Anna to lean against him.

"What are your plans Anna, what are your goals for life in the subtle domain?" Robert asked to start some conversation, and the question contained the hint that the two had only known each other through a few experiences.

"Just like this Robert, just like this. I had started to think about meeting someone. I found that teaching and visiting with friends to start to be lonely and not, well, very satisfying. So I looked to meeting someone in my mind, and, to be honest, on my way to the club yesterday with the gang I was sort of excited, 'cause…" Anna had drawn out the word for effect "…I, started to know that I was going, to, to meet you." Anna smiled widely, the ear to ear blushing type.

Robert reflected for a long time and didn't respond. He had thought that he was searching for answers to how the subtle domain functioned, and not about how souls date. Robert thought that romance seemed like a very strange thing to have happen after dying. While Anna had found her way to needing romance and companionship in the subtle domain, to Robert, it seemed half way to being crazy, or at least, surreal.

"Surreal" he thought to himself, "…how on Earth could considering how people meet in Heaven be anything but surreal." The words played in his mind and the actual definition of the word seemed to slip from reason to mysticism and on to insensibility.

All the same, Robert thought, Anna is precious and meeting her is a blessing, whether in life or in the subtle domain. Robert had wanted a partner in his life, and he had had a terrible void being alone in life, and now he wasn't, that was enough. He pushed his head to the left and kissed Anna on the top of her head near her brow.

Robert thought that he knew that somehow that he was meant to be with Anna, right at that very moment. And as he relaxed his back muscles into the couch, he thought, that he loved her. Sometimes, he reasoned, love doesn't need time to incubate, it just arrives fully prepared.

As the couple cuddled they both thought of the bond that had grown between them, of the powerful event of the night before - of the magic that had seemed to flow, and of the energy that had been theirs to share. Magnificent and triumphant, unexpected, and beyond what they felt was of their own control.

The candles burned down, and the light flickered, leaving shadows dancing on the walls, until they extinguished. Anna took Robert by the hand and led him to the bedroom. They undressed and fell into deep sleep.

In the following days the leisurely process of rest, shopping, sipping coffees throughout the afternoon and making dinners together repeated itself. Anna and Robert had long talks late into the evenings to complete their days, and they found their sleep and dreams to be shared - often remarking that they had had very similar vivid dreams – they type that come in deep R.E.M. sleep.

The long talks between Robert and Anna grew in intensity, as they discussed their beliefs, experiences in life, likes and hurts. Most conversations about the nature of the spirit realms ended with Robert asking, almost longing, to know more about the higher realms, as they were known, of light.

Anna explained that while light realms existed where souls cast aside the need for bodies, there were also dark realms where underdeveloped souls, and those with primordial natures that caused them to do evil things, lurked. Sometimes these dark realm energies drive their way through the barriers to the physical Universe, where all involved, suffer.

In time, Anna said, even these wretches experience the slow creep of enlightenment, the gift that is the ability to learn from experience – to improve, even if it is for entirely self serving reasons. But through those minute steps that leads towards less friction against the fabric of the physical and darker realms, slow progress allows for love of another, of caring, of selfless acts to draw the soul forward in its development.

Souls find their way to kindnesses in life, the ability to give and receive being the electric charges that begin to negate ever more parts of the ego, until, over time, the subtle domain – that gift to souls who have lived decently lived lives - sets the stage for the important steps in learning and awareness Anna said.

As Anna guided the discussions, Robert thought of the many planes of the dark realms and of the subtle domain and its many thousands, if not millions of planes- all constructed by desires. He had come to grips with an understanding of the planes described to him, and that he had seen in his own experience. But the light realms seemed beyond his ability to grasp, he could not touch them with the focus of his mind.

He thought of the light realms as the steps to nirvana, a place of ultimate enlightenment. Beyond that - what an ultimate place of enlightenment meant - he wasn't so sure. In fact, he had no mental image of it at all, and that left him perpetually straining for a definition.

The closest that Robert could come to a definition of the relationship of these realms was that they seemed to be organized in a hierarchy, with each successive level a little more elevated than the previous. And he thought, "...why should there be a hierarchy in Heaven?"

Anna felt that more and more Robert was coming to the time when he needed to explore the many questions that she could not answer and that maybe even sub-consciously he was asking to meet his teacher, proper. So, one afternoon she struck out with a proposal.

"Robert maybe we should link up with Andrew and Adam today and you should take him up on the offer to go and stay at his cottage, near the Sea of Chasms."

Robert looked up with slight hurt in his eyes, thinking that maybe Anna wanted him to go away – she saw it and responded. "No my love, you would go for a week, maybe a month, maybe an afternoon, but I think you need to answer some of the questions that burn inside you. It is entirely where you need to be, because I feel you have grown so much through your life and now here, in the subtle domain."

Robert took the advice in as a sort of unexpected heavy wave that suddenly crashes in on you when the sea seemed calm. Once Robert had a few moments to reflect, he straightened himself inside and recognized what Anna was saying. He was a mound of clay taking form and the answers to his endless questions were the hands that might shape and craft the final form.

Robert began for find a sense of determination. Anna was right and that began to excite him. A feeling of resolve was sinking in, and Robert thought of what tasks and challenges may lay ahead of him. He liked the feeling, because since the time of Mrs. Delorme's meeting him, he had wondered what his role, his job, his place was to be in this new world. Searching for his meaning, that was the job. He was ready to sign on.

Robert was ready to learn the lessons of the destiny that was his alone and that is the treasure trove of experiences destined for all souls. That destiny that envelopes all thinking entities like oxygen to a burning ember, those that burn in life and that continue to be aflame after life itself is extinguished. The destiny that guides hinders and challenges souls until they find communion with each other in the high, light realms.

Anna said that Andrew and Adam were certain to be at a sea side café in the inner harbour. Robert had learned some geography in the subtle domain plane. He knew that the cafés and shops of the inner harbour gave way to the town square that he and Mrs. Delorme had been in, and beyond it the long meadow that Robert had arrived to. If leaving the town square to the right, one passes through stretches of farmer's fields on rolling hills, and on to the coast, and the Sea of Chasms.

Robert had the general sense that the subtle domain plane was like a peninsula and he instinctively knew that the tranquility of the restful place he was in was likely to give way at this Sea of Chasms. He would come to find that to be true.

Anna and Robert found Andrew and Adam at the expected location and politely joined their table. As souls long steeped in the ways of the subtle domain and its occupant's comings and goings, they were able to predict well enough why the young couple had joined them.

Robert sat quietly and somewhat nervously listening as Anna and the two gentlemen conversed over the latest news of mutual friends. After a few minutes Andrew broke off the smaller talk and with an enthusiastic tone of voice and turned to Robert.

"Ah my young fellow, so I think you have come to be ready for some time by the sea side then. " Andrew chuckled a little as he spoke, but only to show a spry interest. Robert noticed that Anna was smiling widely with a proud air for his decision.

"Yes Andrew, I guess it's time to do some work here, and settle some of these damned questions. I guess that sounds, pretty juvenile." Robert felt suddenly like a junior again in the group.

At once all three picked up in unison "Oh no". Anna quickly added "Actually Robert, you're a way ahead of us, you're the brave one." Robert looked back at the three a little stumped, how could he be in any way further along than these three long time residents of the subtle domain?

Anna provided the rationale. Adam had died during a raid on the English city of Covington during World War II. He learned after his death that the British government had known in advance of the German bomber raid but had not headed it off or warned the citizens to leave to protect the secret of having broken the German communications code.

Adam was still bitter in his journey in the subtle domain, having being taken away from his young family – a pretty wife and two lovely young daughters, just six and eight. That bitterness had led him, at least currently, to reject the purpose of his soul's last incarnation; of a structure that implied he should search for anything beyond what he wanted to do each spirit realm day. Especially if it related to government, to organized thought, or lack of, as it was.

Adam had decided to age gracefully in the subtle domain to the time when he would have been a grandparent, sipping at gins and scotch and watching his grand children play and supporting his daughters through their time as young parents. He did not want a young prime physical appearance for his spirit body, it would resemble to closely what he had lost in life. And he was in no mood for searching for the next purpose - he was waiting for the heart beats of those loved ones still in life to fall still and come back to him.

As for Andrew, he had been a University Professor at Oxford who excelled at mathematics and physics. He had died in 1958 in an automobile accident and had crossed over quickly and painlessly – even quite blissfully. Death was all that it was cracked up to be; a loving light, a tunnel, a trumpeted arrival, all that a well programmed Christian belief system could choreograph for him.

Andrew relished the continuation of a refined life where the fine wines and colourfully adorned and food laden dinner plates could match the quality of conversation and academic debate. It was all here for him. His essential family had crossed over, and the days were spent in pursuit of the mysteries of the physical, meta-physical, and spiritual.

Andrew just wasn't at all ready to take all that learning and intellectual and social refinement and trade it in for a whole new set of life's experiential lectures, so to speak. He was too fastened to the questions related to the properties and attributes of the physical, in its quanta minuteness and astronomical greatness, to allow him to drift into the barrels of a brace of spiritual pistols – that is the lessons to be faced by rolling the dice on life again. Simply put, he was spoiled by his lifestyle and fearful of what walking away from it to life would mean.

For Andrew, the joy of purpose was to set the stage for others to courageously walk the path to enlightenment, and he would manage the trifle details as a good and sound shield to detract from his own, eventual assignment. He preferred to think of his facilitation of the spiritual journeys of others as a charitable bus ride for passengers headed for destination eternity. In at least some part, his assistance to others - his assistance to the spiritually inclined to finding their own path – was to use them as co-dependents to his own spiritual apathy. It was avoidance of having to select his own spiritual path to growth.

Nonetheless, Andrew's actions were those of a spiritual Good Samaritan and not just those of a selfish procrastinator avoiding the tasks demanded by fate. Andrew genuinely cared for those he helped to find their path, and Robert was a good example - the type Andrew could see easily from afar via the aura about their confused souls.

Andrew did admire Robert, though, because he was so new to the subtle domain and so evidently needing to find the pathway of his search. Anna felt the same pride, as she sat supportive of her new found partner about to set out on that path.

Robert knew that Anna was dealing with her pain and finding slowly where she should go next in the subtle domain. He knew she needed a rest from teaching and that she had looked to find someone and now he would be leaving her side.

Alarm swelled in his mind and he grew uneasy, he felt suddenly selfish that he was so ready to search out his own answers. After all, in doing so he wasn't he neglecting Anna and her pursuits and the question of what the purpose was of them finding each other. Wasn't that a key question too? Wouldn't that answer many of his other questions?

Robert looked over at Anna and his feelings were written in the lines that had appeared on his brow and above his eyes. His eyes themselves became wet with the tears of affection that reached out for Anna's thoughts. He felt leaving Anna even for a short time was a risk, although he didn't know why. Perhaps, it was because just so much had happened emotionally with her in such a very short period of time. Experiences like those happen for souls who pass through life's miracles and tragedies together – and that bond them so tightly.

Anna, true to her generous and nurturing nature, reached back to answer Robert's gaze and concerns. "Don't be silly Robert, you're not leaving me, and neither am I leaving you. I'll be with you in my thoughts until you come home. "

Anna reached out and brushed the hair on the side of Robert's head and then took his hand and squeezed it tightly. "I am very proud of you Robert."

Andrew rose from his seat, his considerable paunch extended in the strange badge of honour way that some refined older gents have to show pomp and privilege over many years. The time had come. Robert and he were to leave.

Robert rose from his chair and moved it backward so that it cleared a space between him and Anna. He leaned over and kissed her on her lips with his hand in behind her head that showed a lover's affection, and then on the cheek in a way that showed a lasting partner's affection.

Robert had always known the means to steel himself for a task and that kicked in now. He felt resolve again in the pit of his stomach as he straightened upright and moved from the table. Just before leaving arms reach of Anna's outstretched arm, he turned back, squeezed her hand tightly and said "…see you soon then." Robert though, had no conception if the statement as spoken was likely, baseless speculation, fantasy, or an outright lie without knowing.

Anna turned to watch Robert and Andrew go in that funny way affectionate people do as if to glean every second of contact from a parting. Adam sat smiling and resting back in his chair, hands in his pockets, rising one out with palm presented to state a good bye, and a look of wise contentment offered to reassure all.

"Well my boy lets walk together and I'll see you out to the road. What you do is to follow the road along to near the cliffs of the coast. When you reach the sea you'll see a carted path that leads up a slope to the cliff and a lovely little cottage. That's for you my boy and you'll find everything you need there, all so neat and tidy."

Andrew's voice was a little patronizing but caring and reassuring – sounding the ring of experience that had reassured others in the same situation and that guesses at the concerns the traveler might have.

The two walked together through the town square. "Are you sure that I won't get lost Andrew?" Robert knew he wouldn't, he couldn't imagine anybody loosing anything in the subtle domain, let alone themselves.

Andrew chuckled a little "This is all about being found Robert, not about being lost, you'll find your way sure enough." Andrew was always jovial, Robert found himself liking that fact about him. "You'll see plenty of farmer folk, you know locals there and they enjoy having visitors in the area, gives them something to talk about. Oh, and let them know that I sent you of course. "

Near the edge of the town square Robert looked left to the meadows he had arrived to, and from, and their brilliant hues and shimmering energy. Andrew stood back a little to Robert's right and moved his hand out in a sweeping and inviting motion to a gravelled roadway leading off to the crest of a hill, and beyond it another hill crest and so on. The road ahead, it seemed, led through gently rolling hills.

Robert felt like he had plenty of more questions and suddenly regret that they hadn't been asked of Andrew. Andrew sensed it and looked back at Robert with those cool light blue eyes and said "Go ahead young fellow, you'll find what you need."

Robert wondered how it was Andrew was parting with the same words as Mrs. Delorme had parted with. Robert thought back to that moment in the pub when she had left and how he had found what he needed right up to this moment, and as he turned to face the road as it stretched out ahead, he knew that the unknown down its length would likely hold much of the same.

The funny feeling though, down deep in his gut and at the back of his mind was, did he know what he needed? In a way weren't they the same thing, finding what we need, want, and desire and what fate does to spell it out for us. All lessons written into a binder, successive year books recorded for a class of one. We the observer, the scientist, the experimenter and in equal measure, we - the result of our actions.

Robert shook hands with Andrew and as he drew away he noticed an almost sly smile from the portly man, with the ends of his lips curled up slightly, and nodding his head in an inviting manner to proceed down the road. As Robert headed out he heard Andrew's voice "...and not to worry, you'll find plenty of food in the fridge and a good measure of port in the cupboards. Travel well my boy. Travel well."

As Robert set out he felt himself float walking simply with the will to do so, his legs gently moving forward and back with the same token motion. A gentle breeze swept across his face and against and through his glowing spirit garments. Anna had created a new set for him; again a white Nehru shirt and loose fitting baggy pants and sandals.

As Robert moved along he saw green fields to his right and left, the grasses not always brilliant in places the further he went. In places the bright long green grasses moving with the breeze gave way to scrub grasses – the variety that takes over when growing conditions aren't as favourable.

The foliage was low in lustre and brushed up against fences made of wood that had seen better days. By virtue of age the sections seemed to be ever swaying toward the ground, commanded by some unknown force of gravity. The landscape reminded Robert of an Irish landscape drawn out in the texture of solitude. Quiet, unassuming, and patient as if he were the only creature to have ever crossed it.

After a time Robert came across quaint buildings that emerged after he crested a rise of a hill, a small farm house and out buildings. As he passed them he noticed others further off on the other side of the simple road. A stone main structure with older wooden buildings off behind worn by the passing of time.

As the scene repeated along the winding road Robert came across souls busy about their days work, or at least as busy as a simple rural life demands. Men dressed in woollens and plaid shirts, caps, one leaning against a stone fence work smoking at a pipe.

The gent waved a playful hello at Robert who signalled back by motioning his hand against his forehead as if to tip an imaginary cap. Robert thought it might indicate he understood the leisurely fabric of the rural lifestyle should the figures turn out to be neighbours he would eventually gab the day away with.

Women seemed to be more focused on toil, pointing at a bucket to the attending gent here, pulling emphatically at a rake there, hanging linens on lines, or working something with sleeves neatly pulled up the arms. The tenants of the land were exclusively older, of the retired variety, held to the land by tradition, loyalty and love and nowhere, were there children. It seemed that the business of grand parenting wasn't on the chore or wish list in this place.

On one farm Robert saw animals for the first time, cows either grazing the more colourful and so glowing areas of grass or meandering towards areas of shade although it wasn't' hot. He saw pigs competing for scraps of food and chickens roaming about in farm yards freely pecking at the ground. He wondered if these animals provided food to places like the great buffet but decided it probably wasn't necessary.

Along one fenced field was a wood bench and he sat down on it. He felt relaxed and at ease, gone or at least postponed were the feelings of anxiety about his newly decided upon mission - the fear of leaving Anna and of all of what might or might not come.

He closed his eyes and let his head fall back, the warm sun against his face. He let the sensation creep in and warm his being. He drew a deep breath and opened his eyes to watch the grass dance left and then a little back right, and then more to the left and then just stay still. He looked down the road as it stretched away into the distance. This time though he noticed that thicker, heavier clouds, a little darker were above the horizon in the direction he was headed.

A farmer came down the road in a cart pulled by an old and tired horse. Knowing the routine, or perhaps some psychic animal politeness, the horse came to a stop where Robert was seated and let out some breath as he came to a standstill, headed nodding up as if to adjust the metal and straps at its mouth. Robert rose to greet his road side guests.

"Good afternoon" Robert smiled as he spoke. The reply was an uncommitted nod. "I'm looking for a cottage somewhere around here, at the coast I think, belongs to a fellow named Andrew?" A silence followed.

The man was smoking a pipe and as he puffed it moved up and his lips tightened, as if pipe and face were one attached for a hundred or more years, and his face unshaven but for the most formal of kin events. The farmer took the pipe from his mouth with his left hand and tapped it against the side of the cart knocking its contents to the ground with a slight wisp of smoke still rising.

When the man returned the pipe to his mouth as a place holder he gestured his head to the left to invite Robert to mount the cart. Robert did without really knowing why other than to satisfy curiosity and to appear friendly.

The farmer said nothing as the cart made its way down the lazy road, swaying a little as its wooden spoke wheels rolled over the uneven gravel and larger stones. Robert mimicked the elderly gent's body style, allowing his stomach to retreat into his lap and hunched over with hands cupped together out in front of his knees. His emotion became flat, although not out of submission to any will, but only to fit the boring routine of plodding down the road way.

After what Robert figured was two hours of the silent journey he heard the faint sound of ocean - the sound of rolling waves and then the smash of the bigger ones against a rocky shoreline. The sound instantly spiked Robert's emotion and he felt excitement that the subdued cart scene would give way to his eventual destination and whatever the experiences to come.

A few more hills and distance were crossed and the sound of ocean heaving and meeting the coast had become loud. Robert looked up at the changed horizon with dark clouds and the clap of thunder in the distance. He expected a rain squall to overcome them from the coast, although the sky directly above them and over land was still clear and warm with sun.

Finally, at the top of a long gradually sloped hill Robert saw the powerful rage of the ocean he was approaching. The water moved as one in heaving motions with white capped windswept waves skating across the top. Robert couldn't make out the actual shore line yet, but he could now see the sky above the water clearly full of rage - electrical energy, bright lightening and resounding thunder mingling, then competing and overcoming the roar of the waves.

The scene was one of power, of nature. Nature, with a will of its own and whose rhythms are power is greater than those of men, or even of their souls. True it seemed, in the physical world and in the spiritual beyond it.

Robert felt compelled to say something to express his awe and to satisfy his urge to verbalize the emotions that the omnipotent scene had raised in him. "Well, that, that looks like a lot of bad weather out there." Robert's voice cracked and was a little raised.

As the cart came down the hillside the cliffs of the coast line came into clear focus and approached rapidly. Robert could see how the road turned from the direction they had been travelling to right angles so that it could follow the coast. Where the road turned ninety degrees to the left there was a cart path that led away to the right and led up a hill to the cliff side.

Robert sat straight in his seat on the old wooden cart bench and strained his eyes to his to make out the details of a cottage. At the cart paths edge the farmer tugged right on the reign and the horse pulled obligingly to bring the cart onto the rutted trail with grass growing in the middle. The cart wiggled its way up the slope and as the cottage was reached, the horse came to a halt.

Robert gave a quick look over the property. The cottage was made of stone blocks and was a good size, its roof made of wooden planks grown grey with time. There was a solid wooden bench in front of the cottage and to the left of the doorway and out back a fenced area surrounding a garden.

Robert stepped down from the cart and as he did he looked face on to the cliff some 15 to 20 feet away and below its edge the turbulent ocean. Above it, the angry dark clouds with rain squalls pounding down in places at varying distances, powerful lightning bolts and, as he looked down the coast line powerful crashes of waves against rocks throwing up columns of spray.

Unexpectedly the farmer broke his silence as Robert took in the direct view of the ocean and sky. "That's the Sea of Chasms lad, the most unfriendly and ungodly place there is…" Robert looked up at him. "…that's the storm of pain and suffering boy, make no bones about it. That be cataclysm and war, and all that be terrible on God's Earth. "

With that, the old fellow prompted his horse to move back a few steps and then turned his cart around, making his way back down the cart path, and on down the coastal road. Robert watched until they disappeared into the distance.

The Tidal Pools of the Past

Robert looked out over the coast line and the ocean's relentless fury, driven as if by a purpose of its own. He didn't feel cold from nature's dark environment but the black clouds and rolling ocean made him sense lateness in the day and that he should take action to settle for the night.

He turned towards the cottage and although he felt a little playful glee now that the time had come to check out his new digs, his mind did wander to missing Anna and he was concerned about being away from her, and why she hadn't offered to come along on this adventure. Somewhere inside he knew that this was his journey of exploration. He was at this place for a reason and for whatever was to unfold.

With a little exploration Robert found that he had plenty of fresh vegetables in the garden out back of the cottage, and in an ice box a large bowl of fresh eggs. In the cupboard a few loafs of bread, cheese and a container with dark chocolate, all of which appeared to be fresh.

Also in the cupboards were bottles of port as promised and a number of bottles of wine, all with dust collected on their necks. A dark container had a powerful scotch whiskey inside and a few others with aromas that Robert could not recognize. The taps worked and poured out glimmering water. Food and drink enough, Robert supposed.

The cottage interior was one large room, with the kitchen closest to the ocean and the living area towards the garden. The centre piece was a fire place made of large round river rocks set into masonry. The floor was wooden that had coloured with time and was nailed down with small finishing nails.

The kitchen had a wooden table and two wooden chairs set close to the window looking over the cart path and roadway along the coast line. Opposite the table was a sleeping nook with a single mattress set on a built up sleeping platform. It had a single sheet and plaid blanket that was red and black, and a single pillow.

Above the bed was a window with four panes of glass divided by a wooden frame painted white and small curtains. Outside the window stood an old multi-branched oak tree and beyond it the hill as it rose to crest hiding the cliff below it. Above the window was a set-in book shelf with a number of thin and worn covered books, each with a plentiful coating of dust, as if they had never been read.

In the living area was a single comfortable sitting chair set to the right of the fireplace and a whisk broom for sweeping in the far corner.

Robert went outside and sat on the bench for a long time, looking out over the turbulent ocean. The fading day looked grey and the ocean and sky ever darker, but he sat quietly all the same. The scene was so terribly angry, out of sorts for the subtle domain. The face of nature was sour, waves of water and of thunder pounding their protest against the unyielding coast.

It did seem though that the rain squalls out over the ocean, each at varying distances, the winds and the lightening did not have the ability to affect him in the subtle domain; and so, perhaps he was looking at something other than the subtle domain? Robert was certain that whatever the nature of the Sea of Chasms - it was separated from the world he had come to after death.

What was it the old farmer had said, Robert thought, "…the most unfriendly and ungodly place there was." Strange, he mused, perhaps the Sea had some connection to the physical world, or the dark realms Anna had talked about; a place where energy transfers, and if so, maybe there is a place where the energy of light also transfers.

After considering the implications, or lack of them given an absence of any real information, Robert decided that a rest was in order. He went into the cottage and lay down on the bed nook. His body just fitting so that the soul of his feet could press up against one end and he could fold his elbows to allow his hands to press up against the other end.

A claustrophobic person might have felt as if they were in a box, but for Robert it made him feel comfortably set and he nodded off for a time. When he awoke from the brief sleep he breathed in deeply a few times and stretched out his legs so that his feet pressed tightly against the nook bottom wall, then curled his legs up in a cosy posture.

Robert looked to the left at the interior of the cottage and placed his hands behind his head. His adventure pleased him and being alone reminded him that he could do whatever he wanted, as little or as much as he wanted.

And what he wanted was some nourishment. He went to the cupboard and took out a long loaf of bread that was crispy and brown at the top. Someone had garnished it with butter before placing it in the oven to bake. He broke off few chunks and put them on a plate. He opened a bottle of red wine that was hard to uncork – having to twist the corkscrew tightly five or six times – and poured the brisk liquid with its strong aroma into a large clay styled cup, narrow at the bottom and wide mouthed at the rim.

He broke off a large piece of hard yellow cheese and took the plate and cup of wine back to the nook. He took several bites and gulps of wine, then placed the plate and cup on the floor to be snacked and nipped at.

He reached for a book from the narrow shelf above the window on his right side, his fingers finding a thin volume randomly. The books were roughly the same size in thickness and were coloured red, none having text either on the cover or the spine.

Robert looked about and saw that the light had faded considerably. He looked about and noticed two lanterns sitting at either end of a wooden shelf to the right of the fireplace. He went over to them and collected one, it felt heavy with oil. He looked around the kitchen for a match, and when finding none, looked over the rest of the cottage. He saw a rack with neatly cut and stacked pieces of wood, and next to them a box of matches.

Robert returned to the nook, pumped oil into the mantle and struck a match, holding it under the glass protecting the mantle until it lit. He pumped the throttle a few more times to increase the air pressure so that the light became bright. He needed a platform for the lantern, and so took a wooden chair from the table to use as a base.

Finally, he settled back into the bunk to read the book he had selected. He opened it mid way and began to read. He read for an hour, then rested his eyes, and then read some more. The story was about a boy who had lived a life of poverty many hundreds of years ago, in India. Robert reckoned sometime before Mohammad in the fifth or sixth century.

The boy's father had been in the service of a merchant and the son had been sent on a caravan as a tending servant. The caravan had become lost in the blistering heat and come to catastrophe. The boy had died of dehydration as had many others as the traders had traveled in circles under a blazing sun by day and fierce cold at night.

The book seemed purposeless. He selected a second. It was a more interesting read, of settlers in the new world near modern New Hampshire. The story was of the family of an iron-smith and their suffering through starvation in cold and unforgiving winters. All had perished the fifth year of their life in the new world, of influenza, including the young daughter who had lingered for days with a fever before succumbing.

Robert completed the book and felt a little bored, so decided to make a fire. He placed the neatly chopped pieces of wood into the fireplace, helped to combustion with plenty of kindling Robert collected from the scrub around the front of the cottage.

Robert went back outside to shore up his reserve of wood and kindling, finding a fair amount in back of the cottage. Outside it was night proper, and above the shore were flickering stars, with the storm of the sea still offshore.

The fire had crackled to life, and the flames sent out a soothing wave of heat and plenty of dancing light and shadows against the walls of the cottage.

Robert repositioned the living room sitting chair to face the fireplace. He poured more of the red wine into the cup, and selected a third book to read by the fire, if only to make him ready for a night's sleep. The fires heat was good and warm and Robert rubbed his feet - less the sandals - together to collect in all the sense of contentment presented him.

He opened the third book and began to read using the light of the fire, book slightly dipped forward. He read for a time and reflected that the story seemed very sad. A story of a father who lived with his family in the polar region of North America – about the turn of the 18th to 19th Century.

The man was of aboriginal descent and had died out on a flow of ice while hunting for seals to feed his family. As he died, his thoughts were selfless, worrying about the well-being of his wife and two children.

Robert felt somewhat restless of the pointless short stories and drank back a few more glasses of wine as the fire danced upon its stage of brick in front of him. The bottle's contents emptied, he applied himself to opening a second and as it made its way next to his chair, and hand, and cup and mouth, he felt a little playfully drunk.

He sensed and caught the moment of the feeling, and pouring a full cup of wine he thought "…well Christ, who wouldn't get a little drunk – one more bloody depressing book and I'll look for a radio or TV!"

Robert selected a fourth book and opened it a little further past the middle. He read about a man who lived a lonely life that didn't seem to have much purpose. He flipped page after page, skimming the words for some passage of interest, but found little to none.

He sensed a little discomfort in the words, and focused his eyes more and more intently on the passing words. They seemed a little, and then very, familiar. A sense of panic began, and spread throughout his soul body, and he sat upright on the edge of the chair, back rigid.

He flipped feverishly for the last few pages; they bent under the force of his intent fingers. The tale ended as the other books had, with the man's dying on the floor of a coffee shop, early one morning. His death bed witnessed only by strangers and those he barely knew.

Robert threw the book to the floor and he covered his mouth tightly with his right hand as if to hold back, or in, his sense of dread. A bead of sweat had broken out on his brow.

The books that he was reading, that were on that shelf, were his lives.

Robert looked over at them. Testimonies to his own suffering; book after book, covered in dust and sitting there not as tales of the living so much as they were the tales of the life of a soul.

Robert focused his dread to understand it, and it came to him. It wasn't so much those books of suffering that sat to the left of the Robert's life and death book that made him so fearful, it was those books to the right. Those were future Robert lives.

He sat at the edge of the chair, looking to his left at those books as the light of the fire danced mockingly upon the book spines, lined up one after the other. Was his fate to be that he would have to live those lives, one upon the other, and did they catalogue a journey and quest for meaning – or lack of it –that was to be his?

The thought of what those book's pages would chronicle horrified Robert and he recoiled from them.

He looked to the shelf again – books and books of suffering that he had endured, and that perhaps he would have to endure yet. He looked at the books in sequence ahead of the story of his most recent death. What would they hold?

Robert felt confused, the thought should have been "what will they hold", but, those pages were already written without the lives having been lived! So he thought.

"Is that it?" Robert shouted out loud. "Is that my whole destiny, just to go back and die and die and die!"

He fled the cottage and took to the bench, running his right hand up through his hair as he leaned forward, frustrated and full of anxiety, but not quite panic. He was wet with sweat and it felt cold against his skin in the open air. He breathed in heavily for a few times, and he began to settle.

He thought of Anna's kind words – that all things are a blessing, and necessary. Had he not found a great peace through the pain of his death, and he was on a journey to find answers and now they were coming, some would be good, some would be bad.

Robert found some determination filling his being and it soon felt like courage. He thought of his decision to find answers in his quest for meaning - of the who, and what that he is, was, and will be. "Well..." he thought out loud "...some of them are inside the cottage on that shelf."

So perhaps, not so terrible and in a way, maybe their being there was even convenient.

Robert sat up through the remainder of the night and well into the next day pouring through as many books as he could. The lives varied greatly, and while some endings were of peaceful older souls satisfied that their lives had been lived and ready to take the hand of death, most were of lives ended prematurely.

A twenty year old who was well placed in a powerful Maori family who died in a boastful cliff dive. A fisherman who drowned on the Caspian Sea fishing for Turgeon who stayed out on the waves to long protecting his precious cargo of caviar while the clouds grew dark and menacing. A soldier in the Great War who died with many others in a senseless battle - with the smell of cordite and death thick in the air on a hot afternoon that was dreadful.

Many of the life and death experiences related in the books surrounded conflicts both small and large - sometimes as a combatant, often as a civilian caught up in the terror, plunder and vengeances of greed and hate.

Stories of life, often mundane, mostly in poverty, lived out on all continents and land masses, but not in sequence after all, and none lived after the Robert life as far as he could tell. Maybe he had lived his last life on Earth, Robert began to ponder.

As evening drew on the second day at the cottage Robert made a dinner of eggs, bread and cheese with fresh vegetables from the garden he washed in the sink. He sliced tomatoes and fried them with the eggs. He ate quietly and followed the meal up with a few cups of tea.

He took the third outside with him and sat on the bench. His mood was contented and as the day drew to night he felt little motivation but to sit and stare out at the turbulent ocean and curious commotion of nature. The sky tormented the ocean relentlessly; pounding at the surface waves mercilessly with rain squalls, the waves in turn heaved and slammed rhythmically against the shore line.

Far off lightening periodically cast a glow against the distant dark horizon, its thunder proclaiming the range of that distance and completing a symphony of calamity as the ocean's rise and fall and crashes against the shore completed the harmony.

Eventually Robert roused himself and walked beyond the cottage, past the large old oak tree and up the incline. He stood at the crest and surveyed the coast as it led away to what he took to be north and then turned back to view the cottage and the coast as it led away to the south in the direction of the cart path and road as it traveled along the coast line.

A wind seemed to gain its way onto the cliff bluff and presented a cool breeze through Robert's hair, and he didn't know if the source was off shore or from high above the subtle domain. He did know that the air against his face and gently pulling at his garments had a little foreboding with it; not so much a source of fretting, but like a fall wind that tells someone of a far northern climate that a change in season is forewarned.

On the way down the slope to the cottage Robert collected more kindling and carried in three stacks of the split wood out back into the cottage. The amount more than sufficient for a long fire, or even two, but a way for Robert to reassure himself that he had his environment well prepared for. The wood was stacked with a precision making a neat, narrow, high row to the left of the fireplace.

Robert stood for a time in the kitchen and looked out the window at the cart path, and the grass that grew between the ruts. He might have felt bored in any other rendition of the scene, but his mood suited him and he felt at ease.

Anna made occasional appearances in his reflections, and he thought back of some of the funny stories and laughter they shared, or the conversations, the deep sleeps, and the closeness.

He fantasized about future times they would have together, leisurely spent shopping days, maybe sharing books on lazy afternoons, the way people in relationships do – especially when the experience is new and the togetherness gives so much energy. New love is a powerful elixir – eliciting the release of endorphins like a powerful narcotic that makes the human form more upright in all regards.

Robert opened the cupboards as if to expect some favourite snack food to pop out at him. He opened one and closed it, then opened it again and then another. He decided on a bottle of port, and took one out of the cupboard. Just before closing the cupboard door he decided to take another – the two nestled by the neck tightly between his right hand fingers.

He opened the knife drawer and found an old style bottle opener and with it, headed back out to his bench. He uncapped the first bottle and moved through the contents in a matter of five minutes. His stomach protested by sending back some of the swallowed air, but otherwise tingled warmly the way initial ingestion of alcohol arranges.

The second bottle ran its course and Robert repeated the scene by un-stocking two more bottles from the cupboard. The emptying process slowed into the third and fourth bottles, and Robert's mood was proportionately lightened so that he felt a little playful as he transitioned through his thoughts and reflections. The bottle held at a loose angle in his right hand, his right elbow on his upper right thigh, his left arm outstretched with his palm on his left knee, and back lazily arched given the relaxation of muscles.

Robert hadn't spent very much time reflecting on his life now past, but having read through so many of its counterparts, he trained his random port sponsored thoughts to focus on the life most recently shed. He strained his thought a little, and wondered what common themes were there in that life that now seemed so distant.

He realised that the Robert life seemed to him to be him, the defining him. Not surprising he thought, the other lives were of people he couldn't remember or recall in the first person, but the Robert life was. And after all, he certainly had a spirit body that was comfortable as it looked and felt – like him.

Robert thought back to his life for themes. He reflected on tragedies, little sorrows, and trivial things; important events in his family life, his parents, his brother, and his triumphs. It occurred to him that what he considered triumphs were those events that he could boast about to others.

It seemed sad to him that the measure of success in life had not been the merit of his actions as good deeds to others or as accomplishments large or small other than the reward he felt by seeking approval from others. At first Robert felt shallow, but then realized that his need for approval just reflected his own insecurities.

He hadn't felt appreciated by his father, or wanted, and he might as well have been from another world in terms of his brother's interest in him. Robert leaned back against the bench, sighed and looked skyward, and with a little smile said out loud "…well imagine that, I learned something about myself."

Robert had been doubtful of himself throughout his adult life and his emotions had been conflicted due to the self-recriminations that he subjected himself to. And here it was - he was insecure because people didn't treat him well, and that meant he could be forgiving of himself. A sort of self-nurturing was in order, something never indulged when blood and flesh enmeshed with his consciousness and that was now newly – at least partially - liberated.

Robert sat with his head back for a few minutes, his mind ran silent; he was gathering in the environment around him. He felt real contentment and at ease with himself. He had not been a perfect person in life, but his circumstances hadn't been either.

Only one question seemed to suit such contemplation – what was to come next? Maybe it wasn't so important to consider who he had been, the Robert that had joined recorded history, or the persons his soul had manifested within the books on the shelf. But rather, who it was that he desired to become, the he that could be, the he who was tucked inside.

"Inside what...?" Robert considered out loud. Then it struck him. Anna and the others had talked to him about desire. The desire that lies in each person - whether as a soul or incarnated – to realize a dream, a vision, or a self image of one's self.

An image of one's self that is a reverse mirror of sorts. Robert considered that notion. When one looks into a mirror they see the compilation of their life to date, the stresses, or lack of, the health they have enjoyed, or ignored, the celebration of youth and the health of cells, or the weathering of the passage of time.

But a vision of self is something quite different. When we image in our mind's eye the "who" we seek to become we see a future self, an image of what we seek through time and action to become. That image is the student who seeks a career, the dieter who seeks a more slender self, the spiritual seeker who sees an enlightened self.

That image, caught by the mind's reflection of self, considers the future. Those in the subtle domain remain focused on self, indulgences of the lives that have been lived, pursuits of Earthy likes and loves - whether it be art, eating, dancing, or being the person in a spirit body they had always wanted to be.

The first steps, however, to enlightenment and liberation from Earth and material universe pursuits is the vision of what more constitutes the body spirit – of knowledge, wisdom, and understanding.

Robert's position on the bench outside of the cottage, empty port bottles below him, head back and content with his ponderings, were direct elements of his seeking. He had pursued the question of who he truly was and the place that was his right in a universe of light and consciousness, of material form and of timeless existence.

Robert looked out over the ocean. He thought of the lives he had lived and that were etched into the books on the shelf in the cottage. He thought of the ocean being like time, heaving in great motions like the tumultuous times on Earth. The waves breaking in on the shore - cresting up upon the rocks in high tide and when retreating at low tide, so that tidal pools are left behind.

Were lives like those tidal pools - he thought – with time leaving but small pools from which lives are drawn and played out? Each succinct and individual, until the waves of time crash in and consume the tidal pool of a life back again into the sea of eternity.

And why? Robert breathed in as deep as his spirit chest would allow and breathed out in a purposely long stream of exhalation. Why? To what end does a soul exist, to what end does the Universe exist, to what end was he searching for meaning?

Robert closed his eyes as if to rest his mind from its pondering. And then, he didn't feel all alone; he sensed as we do sometimes the presence of another. He sat upright all of a sudden and looked around him and then down to his left.

He had desired knowledge, and the time had come for it to arrive. At the bottom of the slope where the road meets the cart way was a figure, turning to make his way up the path.

Cresting the Wave to Forever

As the figure approached Robert suddenly felt dishevelled. He hadn't thought of company breaking in so suddenly to his private retreat of isolation and he mussed his hair with his fingers, pushing it over to the right side in an abrupt and nonsensical brushing motion.

He collected up the empty bottles and made a neat row of them on the far side of the bench so that they would not be noticed by the approaching visitor. He collected himself up and cleared his throat a couple of times. All of which were but memories of how he thought he should prepare for a visitor from a life time ago, and that were unneeded in the subtle domain.

The figure approached the cottage and Robert could make out the features of a man, a fine and fitly shaped man of about sixty. The fine shape was not just the physical fitness of the body, but also in the way the figure moved, his manner of motion with arms and legs in tandem, and as he closed the distance between them, the perfect styling of the hair, a solid chin and nose became apparent.

The figure's garments were of a different design and style than Robert had ever seen, the shirt was seamless in the front and hung outside of the pants and seemed to be a cross between a shirt and a mid-length coat, with no lapels. It had an upright collar with a slight opening at the Adams apple and a stripe of dark green where the rounded thin edge met the figure's skin. The pants and shirt were so tightly drawn across the figure's body that they appeared as one, not just complementing the figure's body style, but being enmeshed with it.

Then Robert noticed that the figure's clothing and body style and how he moved was a little strange because he was ever so slightly translucent. It was if the figure was a carefully crafted hologram, not quite fully present in the existence of the subtle domain.

The figure seemed to be existing in a state of pure energy - a very dynamic energy. The level of which seemed to resonate differently than the landscape and occupants of the subtle domain; the difference in luminosity and vibration was Robert reckoned, why he appeared translucent.

The figure was impressive in all regards, and as he approached the cottage and bench where Robert was standing, Robert felt a sense of awe. Robert's sense of social nervousness at the arrival of another he would have to dialogue with gave way. He was now intrigued at this sudden development.

As the figure reached the bench he looked up at Robert and reached out a hand. In most instances such a gesture is accompanied with an introduction "...hello, I am..." but in this instance the calling card was the figures piercing light grey eyes. As Robert reached out with his right hand he was fully engaged by those eyes and he met them by presenting his own stare, full on.

Robert instinctively knew that the grey eyes were those of wisdom and knowledge, and that they carried a blessing to him. He knew that his teacher was upon him and he began to sense a feeling of contentment, as if this moment had itself been etched in time somewhere and that he had always known that it would come. Almost like an anticipated moment in life that finally arrives – like a holiday or graduation for the long suffering student.

The figure met Robert's hand with his own - and as the two met Robert looked down to see the definite difference between the two. The guest's hand displayed a more advanced energy; a pattern that had more lustre, dynamism, and that had that translucence.

The two's hands fell to their sides, and a silence followed the greeting that lasted an unusually long time, perhaps two to three minutes, but Robert did not feel ill at ease. The silence and defenceless stance – without pretentious positioning of the body - seemed natural and necessary.

As the two stood motionless, a slight wind caught their hair and as it did Robert felt as if a passage of time was occurring, like the moment when a youth feels they have transitioned to being a young man. The surrounding changed too; it had become night over the Sea of Chasms, while at the cottage and surrounding landscape it seemed like early evening.

Robert took to the bench on the side closest to the cottage, his counterpart to his left.

"What is your name?" Robert's voice had confidence in it, he was sure he wanted this conversation.

"Raylon Five" was the answer. Another very brief silence followed and Robert shook his head up and down slightly as he queried his memory for some reference to such a name.

The figure reached out quickly and with the back of his right hand playfully slapped Robert's left shoulder front with a flick of his fingers.

"Just kidding, my name is Gordon, Robert, and I am pleased to meet you." The voice sounded aged and wise, but soft and comforting, and gauged to settle any nervousness Robert may have had lurking somewhere in his consciousness.

There was a sense of humour in the interaction and Robert smiled, "…good one…" he quipped. "Where are you from…Gordon?" The question was part small talk whimsical, part serious query and essentially out of context for two souls meeting in a cosmic and spiritual otherworld.

"I am from a time that you would consider your future Robert, many years from the time that you lived on Earth, centuries, actually." Gordon's voice was steady and even.

Robert postponed the enormity of the statement – which he was deeply interested in given the 'past' nature of the self-biographies on the shelf in the cottage – yet he felt the need to settle some formalities.

"Gordon...Gordon, are you my teacher?" "Are you here to guide me?"

Gordon replied. "Yes, yes, that is fair to say. I have chosen to help you find the answers that you are seeking to prepare you for the next decisions in your journey to find self and unity. Your journeys, from here in the subtle domain, as you all like to call it.'"

Robert nodded his head slightly, taking in the words. "What do you call it?"

Gordon's reply was sarcastic "... the subtle domain." Both smiled. Robert sensed Gordon was being pensive and he wasn't annoyed as much as wondering what path to take in the conversation to break through to knowledge.

Gordon looked out over the dark waves with their wisps of white as heaving sea meets moving air. He clasped his hands together and shifted a little to his right to present a more square image of himself to Robert, then moved his left leg up over his right smartly. The contours of his body were very straight, neat and sharp.

"Robert, let me begin by answering some basic questions you have."

Having just met, Robert reflected on how Gordon could already have answers to questions he hadn't even thought up yet. Still, inside Robert knew that his questions were long standing and that he probably was a beacon, radiating queries for all future travelers and truth seekers to see plain and clear. A psychic open book - as it were.

Robert thought though, on how it was that Gordon had travelled to the subtle domain from the future. Had he died and so was from a light plane, more advanced than those in the subtle domain, or was he from the physical world, with a technology that allowed him to migrate to the non-physical, spirit world?

Perhaps the answers to come would connect some of the riddles of the books inside the cottage, Robert thought. Did they imply he indeed did have a future as a living person or was he ready to receive knowledge and wisdom that would allow him to break free from rebirth and re-death?

Gordon was, of course, telepathic as all are in the subtle domain are, and he reminded Robert of that through a reassuring statement. "Well, just ask what comes to your mind Robert. You're asking and my replying by way of being chatty would be polite, don't you think?"

"Yes, yes, reading someone's mind is a little personal isn't it?" Robert presented a half grin.

"Hmm, actually, I don' think that telepathy in the subtle domain is so much about mind reading as it is the fact that thought travels simultaneously outside of the physical world, as this place is not bound or constrained by the trappings of time."

"Everything is known, or at least able to be known, at the same time; past, future, the soon to be, that that just was, they all stand side by side."

Gordon smiled as the last words were spoken and they were offered up without any sarcasm; Robert knew the lesson was beginning.

"All right then..." Gordon said, taking a breath to provide enough pause to suggest a topic of discussion was upon them. "For the vast majority of those living, and here too, time is viewed in a linear way, a line from some beginning to some future end, and our life, and indeed our lives, being points along that line."

As Gordon spoke he stretched out his two arms and twisted them a little so that the palms faced each other. A bright holographic red line appeared between them, with what appeared to be exclamation marks hovering above the line, indicating some random points along its length.

"But, space and time are really both curved - what your scientists called curved space time." Gordon rested his hands on his knees and the hologram disappeared.

"If we think of time like a globe, like the Earth for example, it will help you understand the implications of curved space time." Gordon stretched out his left arm so that it made a right angle with his body, then twisted his forearm slightly so that his palm faced up. A red holographic Earth appeared with the lines of longitude and latitude included, as well as outlines of the continents, all in bright red.

"Where did you live Robert?" Robert pointed to North America "...here, in the mid-west." A red marker looking like the exclamation marks that had appeared over the red line appeared above the continental United States. A red dot marked a place on the globe approximating where Robert had lived.

'And when you lived, you knew that simultaneously people lived in New Zealand, correct?" Robert nodded in agreement. The globe rotated to an area above Wellington New Zealand and another red exclamation mark appeared above the globe, with a dot marking the approximate area of Wellington.

"Now, in terms of perception, you were quite comfortable living your life in the mid-west while knowing instinctively and logically that people also were living at the same time on the other side of the world. While distance separated you, and time zones, and the effects of different seasons, you were quite sure they were living out their lives at the same time you were living out yours."

Robert nodded in further agreement as none of the concepts offered so far disagreed with his sense of things.

"Now let's think of time represented by the same globe." Gordon stretched out his right arm and the same holographic globe appeared.

"You lived at this time in the mid-west, correct?" The 21st Century appeared next to the exclamation mark over the mid-west. "And you lived as a Maori in this year." The year 1775 appeared next to the exclamation mark over Wellington.

"Let's use the North Pole to signify the beginning of time, and the South Pole to represent the end of time." The globe spun end over end to signify the two points with the words beginning and end appearing above the poles.

Robert looked at Gordon with amazement, his arms outstretched, palms up and two identical globes slowly rotating to illustrate the points they had agreed to.

"Robert, the same representations exist for time as for space. Just as we think of two points as locations in space, separated only by distance, but with events occurring simultaneously – we can also think of two points in time separated by years, or millions of years, but where existence occurs simultaneously.

"If we think of your life as a Maori the position of other points in time shift, as your perspective centres on that event – with that life seen and felt as being your paramount or primary existence. We see your position relative to other lives, to the beginning and end of the Universe has slightly shifted, but they still exist as points in time."

Gordon elevated his hands just a little and a remarkable shift occurred, suddenly a vast number of exclamation marks appeared with their dots on the globes surface. Robert peered closely at the globe in Gordon's right hand, then the left.

As he did, he tried to study each point as he knew that they signified places he had lived, and times when he had lived.

Gordon spoke again "It is all about you as the observer Robert. In a life, singular and isolated from the rest, you are unaware of your many co-existing realities. Not just in the physical universe, but in the spiritual as well, in the Subtle Domain and elsewhere."

"In time you will learn to allow your observations to be less restricted, to allow yourself to shift places in time, and, to shift your perceptions of how you and the Universe relate to each other."

This was sounding like a lot for Robert to take in. He reflected for a few moments, then tried to back track in the conversation for more context to aid his understanding.

"So we can move about in time Gordon? Is that how you came here, to me and this cottage, from, the future?"

"Oh yes, and we do, and we are, and we will be, and we always have been." Gordon let out a brief rolling laughter; in a way that said what he was revealing was remarkable, even to him. A little wonder in the Universe that reinforced the eternal nature of consciousness.

"Yes Robert, all things, including all probable lives, events, and occurrences exist simultaneously. Every life, choice, cause and effect in your soul's journey all bound together in a motion that is circular, with ending joining beginnings, and where one event is directly tied to another. Always interwoven in the outcomes that occur from choices and the events they spawn."

"So the only difference between you now, and the always you, and the forever you is your perception – as the observer. There is a centricity whose focal point is your consciousness, and where it sits, is the centre of your Universe at any given time."

Gordon smiled widely. "Whether you are observing the Robert of the past or the Robert who recently deceased, the crest of the wave to forever, is where your mind sits, rolling on…forever, rolling on."

Robert looked out over the waves as they rolled toward the shoreline, relentlessly, persistently, with their white caps heaving spray into the air. What Gordon was saying, the information he was relaying seemed deep and strange - more than unfamiliar – yet at the same time as if somewhere inside they had always been known.

Yet the relentless rolling of the sea seemed to illustrate perfectly what Gordon was saying, a graphic representation of the motions of consciousness within the Universe itself. Formative, relative, powerful and with a seeming purpose that spoke of a higher order one can't quite define.

Robert broke his train of thought and the brief silence. "And I can change my perception to view other times, what has happened in the past, and, what will happen?"

"Wouldn't my doing so, change the future?" Robert looked at Gordon with a glazed look, he was confused.

"Yes, it most definitely will Robert, and in fact it has. Later this evening you are going to ask me to show you other places in time, in curved space-time; and other dimensions of reality – the higher planes, as they are known. If you didn't ask me the questions that you are going to ask me – then you wouldn't do the things you are destined to do. You wouldn't make the choices you are going to make."

"What choices" Robert shot back.

"I don't know Robert, you haven't made them yet? I do know that a series of choices will lead you to your destiny, and I am here to help guide you to them. Then, once made, you are going to create the Universe of reality that will shape you and the others you share your realities with."

"But, as you will learn, the point is that your seeking is a precursor step, a requirement for the actions that are to be. And once your choices are commissioned, they happen. What I hope to guide you in is that those choices and events are occurring 'real time' to the thoughts of you the observer."

"Once your consciousness is liberated from the confines of doubt and disbelief, you will come to see that that the cascade of events has been done - is being done and will be done all simultaneously because of time not being linear. Time is curved and that is important Robert, very important."

Gordon adjusted his seating position to be more upright. "With time curved, and beginnings flowing into endings, and endings into beginnings, and all that is in between on a great wheel – we come to know that something about the structure of the Universe, and of what we think of as being Heaven."

"We see why higher and lower planes of existence, and of the lives and after lives of those who inhabit them, are really not within an order, within a hierarchy of Heaven. They are only relative to the positioning of the perspective of the observer. And that is why our choices are so powerful; we evolve as beings dependent upon our choice to understand more of our own consciousness, so that the place we inhabit in that hierarchy is where our own desire for knowledge and enlightenment places us."

Robert had listened intently, but the issue of time and of all things occurring simultaneously still troubled him a great deal. Gordon was aware of it.

"What confuses us Robert as observers is the concept of the distance traveled in any journey - the space between things on a journey, or the time between events on a journey. It takes me an hour to go the store; it takes me a light year to travel between this star and that one."

"Journeys are, really, only of experience, not of time or distance. Think of the University student taking a four year degree. He or she endures hours of learning and many sacrifices. The journey is one of toil, but not one we think of as having a distance in terms of the space between things. In this case, time is not measured by the passing of days, but as the passing of the milestones of experiences."

"And so when the degree is earned, the relief from the long haul is entirely related to the experience. Another example is the traveler who has journeyed through a thousand miles of wilderness who relates the experience to all as what he or she has seen along the way, the sense of experience is related to the milestones viewed. The distance crossed is the culmination of all the experiences to reflect upon."

"Within a mind where consciousness has been enlightened, freed from the constraints of considering journeys within the references of time and space, the milestones are also the events of experience, and the transactions between souls that resonate with meaning. The journey, is in the experience."

"And we come to seek, then, the points of meaning in our journey that are particular experiences, and we travel between them for growth, reason and understanding. They become the destinations that are sought after, and that are traveled between."

Gordon knew instinctively that he was reaching Robert with the last few comments. Time without an end or beginning was a concept that was difficult to grasp. But thinking of the many points on a globe that were not so much places or events in history, but rather, a series of different experiences that were the things that really mattered to a soul, and could be travelled between, did register well.

So did the notion that the place of souls, of beings of consciousness within the many planes of existence, was not because of a social class, or hierarchy of status within a predetermined order. Instead, the migration between the fabrics of existence had everything to do with the kind of experiences that were chosen by souls, of the choices and their consequences, and of the desire for enlightenment and expansion of knowledge.

Robert wanted some confirmation all the same on that note. He wondered how it was that consciousness could achieve these migrations, and what was the nature of the observer?

"Gordon, how is it that a soul finds enlightenment, how does it become unhinged from the trappings of existence, of life, how does it grow?"

"Well Robert it lies within that decision to pursue the journey of knowledge. There is a special connection between the very tiny things in the Universe and the very big things. From the tiniest elements, the things that make up the very atoms and molecules of matter, to the giant stars, all things resonate with consciousness, at some level of evolution."

"When you think of you the observer - where did you as a conscious thinker live when you were in a body on Earth? Were you in the mind, the cerebellum, the frontal lobe of the brain, or perhaps in the heart? Or, was the observer who was the consciousness of Robert, found in the cells of the body who individually are billions upon billions of independent living things?"

"Strange isn't it Robert, to think that within that tissue was consciousness, even though the constituents of the living are mere potassium, carbon, and other elements. But yet, together they become something more than their chemistry, so that a personality emerges, itself a kind of chemistry blended from DNA that is in its-self a compilation of experiences."

Robert interjected "…and within the form of physical existence there is a consciousness…" and Gordon finished the sentence "…that emerges as physical matter evolves in its complexities. So much so that it migrates away from matter upon matters demise, otherwise, collected wisdoms would be lost, and so the evolution of consciousness, as it has developed one generation to another and so on, through DNA's coding."

Robert thought back to the comments in the gentleman's club made by Andrew and Adam, it seemed like a long time ago "…ultimately the energy for the continuation of life is one hundred percent futile." All living things die, and matter itself transforms as energy migrates from one form to another. Even the matter of stars is consumed and reborn.

"And how does matter migrate from consciousness Gordon, how does it live on?"

"To teach you that Robert, we have to look back to the beginning of the Universe, and for that a man needs eggs and bread at least."

Robert looked stunned for a minute and then realized the message given was not a great wisdom, but a friendly request for a meal.   The two stood, and went into the cottage to arrange it.

Synchronicity after Singularity in the Multi-Verse

The two spirit men made a dinner of eggs, cheese and bread in the kitchen. Gordon moved about the cottage as if he had known it forever, finding the eggs quickly and cracking them into a large bowl. He grated cheese and popped out back to collect some tomatoes of the vine.

After a few stirs he located an oversized cast iron frying pan and proceeded to cook a huge omelette. Robert was amazed to see that as Gordon took eggs from one bowl to crack into the mixing bowl, the supply of eggs in the first would pop into place so that the same amount always existed. This was the first time he had seen a self replenishing food supply!

Gordon said little as he cooked the meal, and then motioned for Robert with a head nod to sit at the table as he had a plate in each hand and a large chunk of bread in his mouth. Robert did, but first, uncorked a bottle of aromatic rich red wine and found two goblets, filled them amply and placed them on the table.

Once sitting, Gordon's head remained down as he devoured his large meal, which was the majority of the omelette. He drank in large portions of wine in between bites and intermittently crunched on bread.

Robert watched his guest with amusement and a slight grin on his face as he politely ate his portion of the food. He considered that Gordon either loved to eat or was ravenous – perhaps he hadn't eaten in three centuries or more. Whatever the reason, Robert would wait patiently as Gordon had his fill.

"I like this soul…" Robert thought to himself "…I would like to know his story."

Once finished his meal, Robert excused himself from the table and went to the fireplace, placed wood in a stack so that the air could get to it and watched as the long wooden match flame crackled to life and gradually was accepted by the kindling and logs.

Robert thought of how a spark becomes a flame, and eventually engulfs the wood and burns through it until only ash is left. He thought of a life on Earth, from conception, the harmony of events that leads to birthing, and rearing, to adulthood, middle and old age, and death so that only ashes, or dust remains.

Kneeling on one leg he placed his hands on the upright knee and watched the flickering flames dance. A young fire burns with such strength and confidence he thought, its purpose and tenure diminishing as time exhausts the available carbon.

This fire was burning with eagerness, and its luminosity caught Robert in that trance that happens when a sentient being stares thoughtfully at it - the face becoming radiant from the light and heat of the fire's tireless journey.

Eventually Robert stood and turned to see Gordon finished his meal with his head back, looking reflectively at the ceiling. As he noted Robert's returned attention, Gordon wiped his mouth with a dish towel that was on the table, and stood, collecting the cutlery and plates and placing them in the sink.

He ran hot steamy water on them and wiped them clean with the dish towel. Robert noted the actions and felt that on Earth his use of the towel for dual purposes may have been rude. He was sure in the Subtle Domain that it did not matter.

Once finishing the frying pan and returning the items to their place in cupboards, Gordon selected two small crystal glasses from a shelf and poured two Sherry's for he and Robert from a bottle that the latter had not noticed. He handed one to Robert that signalled they would sit in front of the fire and talk.

Robert motioned an invite for his guest to sit in the more comfortable sitting chair, while he selected a kitchen chair to sit in.

The second lesson was set to begin.

Gordon brought his hands together and then spread them wide. As he did a vortex opened in front of the fireplace's rock work mantle and its flickering contents. As the air swirled toward the centre it seemed to suck away the visible light within its area, so that the space became a dull grey.

Robert strained his eyes at the odd space that had been created. It reminded him of the emptiness that he had experienced in the void after he had died. It seemed to have an absence, of everything.

Gordon began to speak slowly. "This is the beginning Robert, absolute nothing, not an atom – nothingness in absoluteness. The matter-less void, time does not even exist here, nor space, because a volume of a vacuum is still something – it is a dimension with width and height and depth - like say a cylinder. Here, there is no dimension, no shape. It is not coloured, not illuminated nor dark, it is stark nothingness.

"When something that is nothing has anything added to it, its absoluteness vanishes and it becomes something. In this void energy exists but does not manifest in matter, in something-ness. It is the energy of the zero point energy field, a sea of probability with no catalyst yet to reflect possibility. And two possibilities did exist. One, that nothingness would continue in absoluteness and the other that something would, or could exist."

"Nothingness was so absolute in the void that it created a paradox, it was not logical that it should be complete and exclusive of anything, some something, no matter how minute or varied."

"The paradox implied that an opposite should exist, or occur, to counter balance – or contradict the absoluteness of nothingness. When something existed it unleashed a tremendous explosion of energy, in a magnitude to rival, or mirror its opposite, nothingness. Because nothingness cannot balance, or co-exist with the existence of something; something-ness by virtue of its coming into being would represent the same size as nothingness."

"The fantastic explosion of energy, and all the assembly that followed allowed something-ness to represent the same dimensions as nothingness. As nothingness was infinite, so became something-ness."

"The Universe!" Robert instinctively shot back.

"Yes Robert, the Universe. The resulting something-ness became our Universe, and, an infinite number of others, what is known as the multi-verse. So infinite, that every conceivable possibility and probability could and does get played out in an endless dance of events and experiences."

As Gordon spoke the vortex in front of the fireplace mantle, and the bleak grey gave way to a single spark of light, followed by an explosion that sent bright light outward in a three dimensional shape that expanded like a balloon being inflated. The light was bright white at first then showed other brilliant sparkles of blues and reds.

The colours appeared to coalesce together as glowing gases, gradually turning and appearing as swirling points of light. Robert laughed out in amazement, able to discern what must have been millions, or even billions of specks of light twirling, and he knew they were galaxies, slowly moving away from each other. As they did, the space created by the vortex gradually seemed to expand.

The images presented seemed to be played out in a multi-dimensional screen of sorts, as Robert could see fantastic detail of depth in the small space. He felt an important question formulating in his mind, and it leapt out.

"But what was that something, that ended nothingness?"

Gordon smiled as widely as his spiritual face would allow, the type of emotion that comes when we have long waited for a moment to arrive, and now that it had, there was contentment. His smile revealed his perfectly shaped white teeth.

He responded. "I am."

Robert sat in silence for a time, transfixed by the slow dance of the galaxies as they expanded in front of the fireplace. They seemed to travel outward and proportionately away from each other at ever greater speed. The scene seemed like a supernatural theatre with brilliance and illumination, and that captured his attention so that Gordon's' words were slow to sink in.

"Robert, we refer to the point of origin of the Universe as a moment of singular occurrence, the moment of singularity - a moment when all that exists came into being in the physical Universe that you were part of."

"Unbelievably, all that is was contained in the indefeasible small space of less than an atom – and from it, all that exists in the physical Universe was born. And, not just the Universe that you are accustomed to, but many others that your earthly senses could not observe. Many, many others, as I said, the multi-verse; a multitude of Universes."

"But within that moment of creation, where nothing became something, there was not a material form, but rather, a thought. A single thought, as striking and unpredicted to the observer - the host of the thought - as it would be to anyone else. An unpredicted and unplanned thought, a sudden occurrence that was, simply "I am. I exist.""

"From that moment, a thunderous explosion of occurrence ignited, leading to all that is - a tremendous collaboration between consciousness and the material form that acts as its host."

"Consciousness, resides, co-exists and animates the material Universe. They were born together, and share the same manifestations."

"I am, was a very powerful thought."

Gordon looked at Robert for his reaction and saw the wonder and questioning that was expected.

"How would a single thought do all that?" Robert was formulating many questions, but the words that presented were just those.

"Robert, nothingness was pretty all encompassing, when it became something, well, the new tenant had a pretty big room to fill. In fact, that is what the Universe has been doing ever since, filling that space."

"All of us Robert, all that we plan, intend, desire, and do fill the Universe with experiences. And, quite obligingly, the Universe provides the stage for us to live out our creations, facilitating all the probabilities that we might desire. Consciousness and the Universe have a symbiotic relationship - where the fabric of existence is shared so that our purposes are interwoven."

From the point of singularity, as your quantum physicists call it on Earth, all the matter in the Universe was, and is, combined with consciousness. Albeit minute in some quarters and respects, it evolves with matter, combined and purposeful, as long as we desire it."

Robert drank in the words, they were novel, but somewhere deep down he knew them to be true, and that they had awaited him, as he evolved his knowledge and desired to ask the questions so that the truths could be unveiled to his waiting mind.

But there were unanswered questions too. Robert struggled to formulate them – he focused his mind.

"But why the connection between consciousness and matter, why does that, matter so much?"

Gordon looked down for a moment and took a laboured breath, he looked over at Robert and smiled with an accepting glean that was paternalistic. "Because Robert, the mystery of what is, is an undiscovered country that we all yearn for, in all the realms that exist. It is the grand unifying theorem that consciousness combines with matter at the sub atomic structure, sharing in its births and rebirths."

"The quest is our fulfillment of the cycles of existence, as we live and learn, and die and learn, and exist within and alongside matter, and when consciousness liberates itself from matter."

"We wonder, what is it that we all should learn - and how can we be taught? The Universe is at its simplest design the world of quantum physics where matter can exist in multiple realities simultaneously. The reason that is important is that the consciousness is gifted with the ability to decide, to make choices, to calculate its options and to enact them. That takes a pretty flexible playing field, a stage that can place backdrops for any scene that consciousness decides upon."

"Quantum physics is all about probability, the probability that any number of choices can and will be made, with matter following the lead of the mind, in a dance from the beginning to end of time, and round again in curved space time where all things exist, all at the same time."

Gordon's voice rose slightly for affect as he continued "All that exists is facilitated by a great unseen field of energy. Energy like those waves you see out in the Sea of Chasms. Ever rolling as they do, like the chariots that carry our consciousness upon the shores of endless experience – in whatever manner we so choose.

Robert looked at the hologram again and saw that an elaborate labyrinth of shapes take form, cubes within cubes with a level of depth that reduced in size so that the number of cells faded into the distance of ever smaller shapes.

Robert understood its meaning, at the smallest shape at the centre, was the ability for a soul to make a decision, and the infinite number of cells that emanated from it were the structure of the Universe so that any number of probable outcomes from decisions made could be facilitated.

A choice, to turn left or right, to get on a bus or not, to move to a new city, to return to life from the Subtle Domain, spawns cause and effect, which in turn leads to other events and that touch others, who in turn also make decisions. Governing, perhaps complicating the cause and effect is the elixir of leaning in the Universe, known to many as karma.

Without karma, the soul would not benefit from experience, and the inertia forward in evolution would be hindered, for only karma teaches the actor to make decisions that can lead away from ego and towards enlightened decisions. The Cosmic equivalent of a soul repeatedly running its head into a quantum brick wall until it decides on better decisions to end the pain.

Gordon allowed a pause in the discussion as Robert inspected the labyrinth before him. Then he added "…in the Universe matter can exist in basic forms, like the rocks of the moon. In such a state consciousness is less than primitive, it is almost inert. But, matter can assemble into ever more complex forms, like amino acids that formed early life and on to forms like the human being."

"As the atoms of matter become more complex, and animate life, so does the consciousness that is seated at the very form of DNA. Within matter that becomes evolved is consciousness that becomes evolved, and in time, able to migrate away from the matter that hosted it."

"That Robert is how a soul animates life in the physical world, and upon the expiration of life, is able to cross the void into other realms of consciousness, like the Subtle Domain. And here, and in the other planes, the Universe, the multi-verse, and their dimensions, the labyrinth of the fabric of existence goes on permitting consciousness its stage to experience by making its decisions."

The labyrinth Robert had been looking at gave way to a dark scene, with large dark areas looking like shadows against a night sky.

"This is the end of the Universe that you lived in Robert; it has expanded beyond the time when gravity could exert its influence on stars and planets. Without the inertia of gravity the fire of stars converting hydrogen to helium and the heavier elements has fallen silent."

"Without life the stars have grown dark, and the light of the Universe's billions of galaxies is now gone. The Universe is black, its matter cold and lifeless, with the many billions of years now in a past back towards the beginning of time, and all of the life forms that existed in a trillion worlds, fallen silent and gone. It is quiet, so very quiet."

"But, consciousness that gained a footing in this Universe continues on, it has found self-awareness in many trillion life forms, it took to its feet, it became enlightened, and has moved on to the higher planes. It seeks to be rejoined in those planes to be one again, as it was in the beginning. All consciousness has journeyed through experiences, and seeks to rejoin to make the many experiences a collective. When recombined, the great question is answered."

"What question" Robert logically asked.

"Well, Robert, in the beginning was a single thought, I am. The dance of the Universe and all its manifestations, with matter hosting consciousness that could evolve and move on to experience all that could be experienced, and to combine again in the higher planes, was to answer one question...what am I?"

Gordon's voice had almost grown silent.

"And so Robert, all of we who inhabit and exhibit consciousness are one in our definition of who 'I Am' is, and sharing through our experiences, and eventual rejoining at the end of time, for the knowing of...'what am I?'.

As Gordon had spoken, the dark scene of shadowy worlds had returned back to the brilliant swirling of galaxies, millions upon millions of tiny but distinct points of light showing the light of stars in blues, and yellows, and reds. The electro-magnetic Universe, all tied together despite its immense size and nature.

Robert had processed a lot of information, not just clues, but the stories of creation, the beginning of the Universe, and the journey through its existence to demonstrate purpose. The shared purpose that gives meaning and that binds atoms and consciousness. Yet for Robert, he needed more of a reference point for context and Gordon sensed it in him.

"Remember reading your Bible, Robert, the story of Exodus? Moses had asked God, before the burning bush, who he should say sent him when the Israelites asked. And what did God say?"

Robert couldn't remember, he hadn't read the Bible very much in life, but after a time he remembered the scene from the movie he had seen as a young teen, The Ten Commandments.

Robert looked up at Gordon and said, slowly "God said, tell them I AM has sent you."

"Yes Robert, that is right. I AM represents a definition of the beginning, of the initial comprehension of conscious existence. That is the initial point of oneness of all that exists, and all of those of us who exist. That is something that we all share. It is the point of synchronicity that initiated all that is, that shapes our collectivity and is the road to 'what am I?', that we venture throughout the eons of existence and experience upon experience to answer.

Robert looked at the galaxies before him as they gave way to a labyrinth once more. It was multi-layered with horizontally, vertically, and hexagonally shaped geographical surfaces. He knew they were the shapes of vast numbers of Universes seen in the macro, the Multi-verse.

As Robert looked, the slightly vibrating layers of individual grids would retreat to smaller shapes, to permit an ever increasing number of platforms of existence to come to view. It was the cosmic landscape of a limitless number of separate yet interconnected Universal planes.

Robert pressed back into his chair, his head rolling back slightly as his eyes took in the image in awe. He knew in his heart that he gazed upon the face of existence. He sat in an afterlife with a teacher and guide who had revealed to him a mystery that he had always sub-consciously sought the answer to - perhaps a mystery that all sentient beings seek the answer to.

"What of the journey Gordon, to the end of the Universe, to the, well the rejoining I think you called it."

"Ah, for that..." Gordon said "...we need more sherry."

The Face of the Evolution of All

Robert poured two glasses of sherry and he and Gordon went outside, standing in front of the bench and facing the ocean. He handed Gordon his glass and then nipped slightly at his, transferring the glass from his left hand to the right. The two stood in silence for a few moments looking at the motion of the heaving waves approaching them and crashing on the rocks below.

The men had gone outside as a token gesture to get fresh air, although in the Subtle Domain no such action was really required. But, the changed scene was a convenient way of changing the direction of their conversation.

"Robert as we look out at the power in nature, here in the Subtle Domain and as you remember it in the physical domain, and, as you will come to find it in the light realms, you see the power of consciousness." Gordon took to the bench, sitting in a relaxed fashion.

Robert moved to join him. "The Sea of Chasms is an example of that then Gordon?"

"Yes, the energy that you see out there and beyond the horizon doesn't clash with the physical world; it is an element of the physical world. The energy of the Universe is inter-related and inter-dependent and so energy from one plane can be drawn to another. Like the Sea of Chasms, whose turbulent energy is drawn to the physical as manifestations of consciousness." Gordon sat slightly more upright on the bench as he spoke.

"It is the fate, karma if you will; the intentions of evil and the misfortunes of the world of the living. The great acts of history themselves are like the motions of the ocean below. Great revolutions, wars, pandemics and the like run their course through energies that are fed from the plane you see below. And others, in time, as the generations of souls on Earth select the realities that engulf them."

Robert sat forward slightly, and said to Gordon "…but how do souls of generations in the physical world choose a reality, I mean it seems to be more just thrust upon us. How do we manage such misery that the energy of this place would find its way to some poor soul on Earth?"

Gordon crossed his right leg over his left, he pulled his translucent pant leg down a tad for comfort, and rubbed his left palm over top of his right hand until he cupped the hands together.

"Robert, just as a trickle of water joins another and becomes a stream, and on with others to become a river, and on to the ocean; the actions of souls often cause ripples that affect the quantum field of the Universe and how matter and consciousness represent themselves."

Gordon went on. "An act of random kindness is an incredibly powerful tool. The gift of love between souls, to care for another, to give unconditionally, the person who lays down their life for another; those are as influential to the condition of souls as any monstrous acts."

"And so, the human drama that plays out. Souls incarnate to the physical plane to evolve their understanding of consciousness and the part it plays in the condition of the enlightenment of all. Together - all of us together, we are the painters of the canvass of reality and when we strive for enlightenment, for kindness, for the betterment of others in selfless acts, we paint a better picture."

"The journey of a soul is to find some sense of meaning, from which it will find its purpose. We endure through countless lives in a fog to resolve the question of what our purpose shall be, and in doing so, to learn our true selves. Instead, the ego of the soul, of desires related to physical lusts, greed, addiction, hate, revenge, and one-up-man-ship draws us in directions that delay and prevent our movement towards enlightenment."

"Funny isn't it Robert, knowledge is all around us. The oneness of the Universe means that the central information of why it has come to be, of the journey of souls towards enlightenment, can be known throughout at any given time to any given soul. But, we must first ask the questions that lead us to disassemble the apparent reality we live in and to seek the true reality of a timeless Universe which itself is seeking understanding of its true nature – through repeated experimentation expressed as the experiences created by all that is."

"So, when we have a desire to know, when we ask for truth and set forward on a path to understanding we find the information comes streaming towards us very quickly."

"But the journey is so gradual because of the fog of reality, the ego, which is so telling - that the pursuit of knowledge for souls as individuals and within their cultures and generations in the physical can be very slow, even stunted by great acts of injustice, like wars. Until, a spark within one here, a willingness to be selfless there, a soul with courage to know and another to reach out, makes the subtle shift. There comes a transition in understanding, and so of consciousness to a slightly higher state of being; and in turn, of the human condition to a slightly better state of being."

Robert thought that why shouldn't knowledge and enlightenment be found innately within all with consciousness. He wondered why the journey had to take place at all. Gordon sensed the pondering in his student and spoke to answer the queries.

'Robert, to answer your question about the apparent development of consciousness within the physical and metaphysical, or spiritual realms, we have to look at two important issues. One has to do with cause and effect, as Buddhists have come to reason them, and the other, to do with the misleading concept of time."

"But first, let me assure you, that the journey to determine the 'what am I' question of the Universe, of consciousness, we must remember that the variable of choice - of decisions good and bad or indifferent towards enlightenment - and the many forms of reality that exist - are central to allowing all that is to manifest. The many experiences from which all that can be, does become. Choice, the random occurrence of events that this road is taken rather than that one, that this world is created from star dust and not that one; all are events important to allowing any and all experiences to occur. The Universe was not pre-ordained, pre-determined, for to do so would imply God was pre-determined, knew all that had to be from the outset; but we see, that is not so until the end."

"Robert, remember, we occupy curved space time, not linear space time. We have found the answers to what we seek in the many millions of shared experiences that are occurring even now as we sit here. To you and me, this seat on this bench in this moment is the leading wave of time and of our own consciousness. Yet, if we were to shift our perception to your life on Earth as a Maori then that becomes the seat of reality that you view as your leading edge."

"In order to find the wisdom that comes from the benefit of knowledge and experience, we must walk many, many roads. In doing so, the being of God that each of us represents learns more about its central existence, through our individual growth and enlightenment so does God become a little more enlightened. Our consciousness adds to the overall compilation of knowing all that can be known, all that can be understood and lived, loved and lost, to be re-found again and again."

Robert sat for a few minutes, and then stretched upward before resting back against the bench and crossing his left leg up over his right and pulling his foot in close to his midsection. He leaned slightly forward with his right hand moving back and forth to indicate a horizontal like surface.

"And so you are saying that all this cause and effect is staged by the Universe, so that we can gain a, a wealth of experience from which we as souls, collectively come to know what our consciousness is, what it is all about? And I have a role in that just like the guy next door, just like guys a thousand years ago and a thousand years from now?

"Yes, although sometimes you are those guys a thousand years from now and the guys a thousand years ago, but either way, you, the many who were you and all those other guys are really all existing all at the same time. The only difference is that you are central to Robert in the Subtle Domain and that is your current seat of existence from you the observer's point of view."

Gordon went on "The point of view Robert is that in the physical Universe where you have lived, there is a perfect balance of synchronicities that miraculously came to be so that you could have these experiences. Quite a gift from a quantum rolling of the dice really, a series of events from which one cause led to a particular event and from that, a new series of events."

"Think of it Robert. If the temperature of the first few milliseconds after the creation of the Universe, of the beginning that your scientists called the Big Bang would have been one part in a million-million hotter, the Universe would not have expanded at a rate that would have allowed it to cool enough to permit the formation of matter, and from that, life."

If the Universe did not cool with such a precise unison of action, a harmony if you will of interwoven events, the smallest electrons would not have had the correct electrical charge to allow hydrogen to become helium in stars, then through successive stellar re-births to become the heavy elements of the early Earth, like carbon."

"If the Earth was not a correct distance from the sun early macro-molecules could not have formed, and they would not have converted hydrogen-sulphide into the oxygen that allowed advanced life to develop. All occurred in an exacting balance and correctness so that advanced life could become conscious of itself, and so, for matter to evolve and for its inherent consciousness to evolve. And that is how our stories came to pass."

Robert spoke softly "All a precise symmetry, the symmetry of balance so that cause and effect is played out an infinite amount of times, all of it interwoven in these amazing shared experiences."

"Yes, and a very interesting point to consider is that central to these Universes and realms of light and experience is our very definite need to observe. Matter becomes matter from the sea of energy, the field as it is known in quantum mechanics, when we observe. It moves from an endless sea of potentialities into the particle of being."

"The Universe wasn't created by a Devine someone casually bored one week, but perfectly shaped for us to experience in. Could have been a random throw of the dice so many millions of times that one Universe would get it right and have the correct properties for us to go about our business, but, really, it was from the outset cast in symmetry of logical progressions of cause and effect so that we could set upon answering that one great dogmatic question."

Robert piped up, chest protruded and both feet now firmly on the ground, reaching back with his left hand to place its palm on the bench back "Which is…" he held back slightly for affect in asking the rhetorical question "…the journey of consciousness from the recognition of I AM to, WHAT AM I?"

The two smiled in unison, Robert having crossed his bridge to understanding.

"Yes" Gordon added "The Universe provides this perfect balance, this synchronicity to enable our experience because we need them to evolve our consciousness collectively – to be as one again, in the end of time, time."

"That is the underlying mystery of the physical Universe Robert. Why such an improbable number of events should transpire precisely in unison so that the small quark can take its place in creating an atom, and an atom a molecule and on to become a cell able to exist in the harsh environment of the physical Universe. To become an organism able to reason and so observe its existence and so to become conscious of it and to evolve its consciousness; for matter inert to become living and conscious. And then for that consciousness to be liberated from matter upon death and to survive - so that it may evolve."

"Each soul is an example of consciousness evolving and repeating the process over and over - so that collectively we are - the face of the evolution of all."

"It is our shared purpose..." Gordon said as he rose to his feet and added "…that so many generations could not define. The shared purpose is finding our meaning through our movement in space and time, in consciousness both within the material and the spiritual, answering the question what am I through millions upon millions of individual sparks of consciousness we know as souls."

"Throughout human history this has been known."

Robert looked over at Gordon with surprise.

"The ancient Egyptians believed that the Universe had begun from a great sea of energy, of potentiality and that mankind had sprung from it, from energy in chaos to organization in the form of man and women and the society that manifests their principles. For the Kings of prehistory in Egypt, that is from a time before the Pyramids were built, the notion existed that an afterlife existed that mirrored life on Earth, and the opposite, for the experience of learning."

Robert added some wisdom "I had read that Isaac Newton had believed in ether that the Universe was believed to be in, and that matter was separate. I guess he was wrong about the mysterious ether but I had understood that he believed that there was more to learn that just science. I mean that religion played some role that he was unable to reference – to know. And that he felt that because he couldn't understand the spiritual part, that he was unable to describe everything about the Universe."

"Well Robert, I am impressed. That is indeed very true. Newton and his generation didn't understand much about the energy that underlies the Universe and from which its many planes derive the characteristics of their reality. They did think that a mysterious substance they called the ether was present but that they could not equate in their theorems. "

"But, they need not pout in the afterlife or feel demeaned, because right up until your time and beyond science has understood little about the field we spoke of earlier. Einstein had said that his cosmic constant, a quantity that he added to his calculations to account for the mass of dark matter in the Universe and its influence on gravity, was the biggest mistake of his career. Scientists learned later that Einstein's missing matter is that dark energy, energy that is not visible but that accounts for the vast majority of mass in the Universe."

Gordon went on. "This mass, this dark energy, the field that pulsates with energy, small strings that vibrate the resonance of existence, really is the underpinning of all that is. But you know, mathematics and the pursuits of physics aren't the gateway to real understanding, just, as Newton had said. Religion does provide the doorway to enlightenment, and really, it is spirituality that unhinges the great mysteries of existence."

Robert shifted a little on the bench to be more upright, sensing a need to push Gordon a little further on the issue of religion. "But I have always thought that religion, I mean organized religion didn't ever have much to do with spirituality. At least, not that had anything to do with enlightenment. Churches always seemed to be for their own sake. Judgemental and often causing more suffering than the goodness to others that they were said to stand for."

"Yes, that is true in many instances. From the time of the formation of societies, as much as 30,000 years before Christ organization in society has largely been under the name holder of religion. And when it has served as master of the faithful almost always the lust for power within humankind and the greed of the selfish have caused it to be an oppressor, rather than a freer of souls."

"Organized religion has had much more to do with dogma than with celebration of the spirit within, for sure. But Robert, any reflection that takes the mind from the clutches of the self, that is the ego, and sends it on a path to spirituality is reflection that is freeing and worthwhile."

"Think Robert of the little church that existed in a small town. Think of the charity, the love, the kindness that it brought about by virtue of it being there. In worlds of suffering and torment, a little church could be as powerful as any government, any army – to the advancement of the one, the individual. And for the living on the Earth plane, the kingdom of Heaven is hosted within the Universe of the one, just within the individual."

"But Gordon, how on Earth could a little church be as powerful as an army, say, or Hitler, or Stalin, or someone like that?"

"Because in life the slow walk to enlightenment takes place in the one, an act of kindness unsolicited and given from compassion one person to another, is more powerful to the movement of all of humanity than one great act of cruelty. The influence of Hitler's speeches about his plans for terror did nothing to take those souls forward; but rather to a miserable end – many of them soulfully prematurely."

"But think of the work of a small community Church. The orphaned child who was raised by step-parents after being placed with them by the Priest, the widowed mother supported by the flock so that she can raise her children, the sick and the elderly taken by the hand at the time they pass on; all these seemingly small acts generate more power than all the tyrants and their acts of barbarity."

"For the living on Earth and for that matter those who linger in the Subtle Domain in self indulgence to long, departure from the confining influence of the ego is the task that they are challenged to complete. It is the ego that is the trapping of the mind, hindering the ability to walk a road to selflessness and so in time, and experience, to find enlightenment."

"For those still bound in egoisms, the need for power, control, and whose lives are all about selfishness and materialism, or driven by anger and cruelty, well their minds act as a filter. Yes, a very limiting filter that blinds them from the real truth of reality, of the Universe they live in and the realms they come to after they die. The benefit of enlightenment is to remove the properties of the filter and to allow the real self to begin to shine through to the real reality, and visa-versa - to allow the true reality of existence to become known to the mind."

"And so, Robert, religion is surely an influence that has taken souls forward throughout time, and judge not too harshly those organized religions that were just the instruments of man's selfishness and evil. For all the great philosophies of man, what you have called the 'isms'; communism, capitalism, fascism, and so on – they were all destructive. Some good done for some, but mostly just the rants of the unbridled ego of mankind where rationale was created to serve the few -through the toil and suffering of the many."

Robert took to his feet and shuffled forward a few steps, he placed his hands behind his back and pushed them back and down in a long stretch. He looked out over the ocean for a minute and turned back to Gordon.

"I am on that journey aren't I Gordon?"

He then spoke inward. "I am on that path. The answers that I have been seeking are those that would see me with enough knowledge to seek enlightenment, and so to free me from ego."

The words were no longer questions, but statements that Robert was making to himself - the testimonial of a soul ready to escape the boundaries of the physical plane. A testimonial that all souls are destined to make with the passing of the eons.

The Great Cathedral of Worlds

Robert had gone back into the cottage to fetch the bottle of sherry. He poured generous amounts into Gordon and his glasses, and then held his upright in an invitation to Gordon to make a toast. The latter rose to the occasion and the glasses met with a tinkle.

No words or thoughts were exchanged as the gesture in of itself was telling. Robert felt a sense of confidence brimming inside – part relief from the presence of endless questioning he had had since arriving to the Subtle Domain - and something else to.

He felt that his newly acquired knowledge had freed him, at least to some degree, from the chains that bind others who have not sought out the path to spiritual liberty. In a way he felt that he had earned his place in the Subtle Domain – a rite of passage so that he now belonged in his surroundings. He was no longer a new comer with much to learn; he was now a resident with wisdoms that others had yet to aspire to. He was becoming a veteran in the ways of the spirit.

What was it that Gordon had said; that once knowledge is sought it comes on very quickly as wisdom and knowing is all around us? Yes, that was it he thought, it exists in the very fabric of existence and is accessible when the individual is prepared to seek it out.

Robert poured a second sherry and as he and Gordon sat quietly it struck him that Gordon seemed quite willing to follow along with the celebration. Robert sat back and looked outward over the Sea of Chasms below, and he turned to sit a little more to his left so that he could expand the panoramic view. In doing so, he took in the image of Gordon the way people do when they want to observe another without looking like they want to observe the other. Robert gazed out at the shore and water below and at Gordon from the left aspect of his vision.

What Robert sensed most about his spirit world companion was that he seemed to be utterly selfless in that he did not express any sort of need or personal reflections - nothing about his own journey, needs, likes or dislikes. There he sat - a translucent being of light energy, obviously of an advanced kind given the high resonance of the frequency of his vibration - sipping sherry. As Robert looked at him, Gordon simply sat looking forward, his casual stare fixed outward onto the ocean below.

Robert was contemplative and the subtle movement of his thoughts initiated a number of reflections with accompanying emotions tagging along. He felt gifted that he had received an open door to walk through to the place of wisdom that he had arrived at. That alone seemed more generous than any gift he had received while alive on the physical side of existence.

The next thought was of appreciation for the being of energy who sat next to him and he felt silent gratitude for the information he had so willingly and selflessly provided. Robert knew somewhere inside that his mere recognition of the feeling of gratitude was enough, that the cognition of appreciation was in itself expression enough – and well represented to the witnessing Universe.

The third thought was of accomplishment after having achieved something substantial. Stretched out at the beginning of the journey was the unknown, far off in the horizon was the known and he had been willing to risk to go search it out. And so there he was, at some sort of marker along that journey with a milestone having been reached.

With that Robert looked upward and took a deep breath – and exhaled a slight sigh as the air was pushed out. He took note of the apparent lateness of the night, or early morning – that middle ground where one shifts to the other – and he felt sleepy. He reached over and patted Gordon slightly a few times on his shoulder and said "…think I'll go in for a rest." Gordon smiled a little and he turned his head to the right to acknowledge the message received and Robert's departure.

Robert went into the cottage and stretched out on the sleeping nook so that he faced the dying embers of the long neglected fire. A few moments later Gordon came in and placed a few more smaller pieces of wood in the hearth, and when they took to flame, a few larger ones so that the fire was restored.

Robert lay motionless with his left hand tucked in behind his head and in between it and the pillow. The renewed heat felt comforting on his face and he knew that sleep was not far off. Gordon sat in the more comfortable sitting chair and the mood was subdued and silent, except for the crackling of the wood yielding its carbon to the flame.

Robert shifted slightly and turned his head upward to watch Gordon, the brilliance of the energy within his soul body quite luminous and evident despite its translucence. As the occasional sparks danced out and into the air they sometimes crossed the boundaries of Gordon's spirit body. As they did they seemed to contrast the many points of light within him as if to evidence that he and they were of a different order of existence.

Gradually Robert's eyes become too heavy to receive in the scene and he fell into a deep, deep sleep.

When he awoke the light of day was streaming in the cottage through the window panes and he reckoned it was late morning. He leaned his upper body out of the sleeping nook and pushed his hands towards the door so that he could achieve a full morning stretch. He then curled his legs up and placed his head back on the pillow, so that he could reason out his feelings for the day.

He realized that he had dreamed and he searched out the visions that had been his world in sleep. He remembered being an older man in the dream, perhaps 65 with a trimmed white beard upon his face and matching his white hair. He lived in a sea side cottage but quite different in appearance than his current abode. He was a philosopher of sorts, spending his days reading the teachings of the ancient Greeks - Aristotle, Socrates, and Plato, and contemplating the mastery of mathematics that was the marvel of Archimedes. The dream had seemed so real.

Robert looked around the cottage and saw that he was alone. Gordon was not present and his whereabouts was sufficient motivation for him to quickly take to his feet to determine where his teacher was. He worried that perhaps he had received the totality of his lessons and that Gordon had left. He regretted falling asleep.

Robert went outside the cabin and searched the pathway down to the coast and along the shoreline but the scene was empty. He turned and walked to the back of the cabin and found the garden area empty, he turned and walked past the old oak, and there, at the top of the cliff bluff was the luminous teacher, hands behind his back and looking out over the ocean.

With a few strides Robert was standing next to his teacher who left his gaze fixed out over a blue stretch of water, not breaking it to acknowledge his student's arrival next to him. Robert sensed Gordon's fixed stare and took note of his facial features. Gordon looked distant in thought, with the edges of his mouth slightly curled upward to evidence peacefulness, and Robert looked outward to share in the apparent mood.

He squared his body to the image of the ocean beyond the cliff edge and Robert heaved in deeply, shaking his hands slightly as if to rid himself of unneeded mental residue. He breathed in again, and again, and kept his eyes fixed out over a calm sea as if pressed flat by the hot sun that was gleaming off the water's surface and that felt warm on Robert's face.

Robert settled into a sense of calm and his body was mimicking the peace emanating from his guest and teacher. Robert let the ease of thought and body overtaking him to set his mood and stance as he waited for a cue from Gordon – perhaps out of respect, and more than a little because he was relieved that this soul had not left him.

Robert looked to his right and saw the curve of the cliff as it seemed to head to the north, giving more definition to the coast line. He stepped forward a little and looked the other way down the coast, past the cottage and down the slope leading to the road and the coast as it wound to the south, rising again before carrying further on and out of sight.

Then it hit him, Robert shot back into his previous stance and gasped with excitement. He turned and looked back towards the inland he had journeyed across to reach the cottage. Arms' swaying a little – like a doll's as a child turns it quickly in their hands. He bent down a little at the knees as he turned back towards the coast as if the gesture would help assure him of the accuracy of the information his senses were providing him.

The sea was calm. The sun was hot; it was a brilliant and lovely day. The dreadful storm that had pressed up against the coast and tormented the sea was gone. But how Robert thought, wasn't that storm the energy of the turmoil of the living, the pains, and angst, tragedies and horrors that gave the impetus to a world of beings caught in cycles of despair.

Robert felt cavalier, and turned to Gordon with a broad smile. He swung his right hand in a wide gesture towards the ocean. "Lovely day isn't it" Robert loudly proclaimed. Gordon smiled back and broke his stare and the silence it seemed to command from him.

"Yes Robert, it is a lovely time isn't it." Robert's head jogged a little given the strange insertion of the word time, rather than day, or place.

"Isn't this a good time Robert? You have crossed over to it. You have taken a large and important step. You have decided on enlightenment and walked away from the entrapment of ego, the binding influence of selfishness and the tyranny of the mind focused on materialism."

Robert had a deep down understanding of what Gordon was saying. The calming of the storm was to do with the Universe that was inside him, and that he in turn is within – both a true, shared experience. Robert had migrated from another level of understanding, having walked through a door opened by his own query. The pain of the cycles of life and death could perhaps be safely tucked away in another time of his being. Indeed his environment was attesting to the fact he had experienced a graduation of considerable magnitude in the journey of a soul.

"You don't belong in a world with storms of pain Robert; that plane of existence follows those whose minds are entrapped, and knowledge has calmed the waters of your experience. Come, walk with me."

Gordon turned away from the cliffs and headed at a gentle pace inland. He was completely at ease, and as he walked he let his right hand bristle across the tops of long grass with a crown that looked something like slivery wheat atop light green grass.

Robert followed Gordon just a slight step behind, showing respect, and his junior position. The sun was glistening off the tops of the gently moving grass and the aura from it cast a luminous hue across the landscape that was beautiful. The scene to Robert was one of pure magic. A new journey had begun, or at least, a new phase in his current journey.

Gordon lessened his pace to allow Robert to walk astride him. "Well Robert, the journey then, is entirely a personal one in terms of choices. We progress or not, we regress or not, through our own decision making. Large and little, and adding up in time through seemingly endless variations to the whole of our journey as singular beings of consciousness. Thos variations in experience are linked through, what in time becomes a cascade of shared experiences of others, and so, advising the emerging consciousness of a truer reality of which it is a rightful member."

"Our actions together make a river of experience that we as beings of light and soul also are a part of. Like droplets of water that form a trickle that becomes a stream, and a creek, winding down to join a river, and in time to add to the ocean."

"Like that analogy each of us contributes to streams of consciousness and rivers of thought that sweep humanity and beyond, in this realm, towards great advancements and at times, horrid retreats of enlightenment. The ebb and flow of these experiences is necessary for the growth of reasoned awareness, and so, really there is no good or evil per-se'."

"That is part of the secret dear Robert." Gordon suddenly stopped and clutched at Robert's forearms, so suddenly that Robert felt startled and a little self conscious. "The ability of one good act to spawn another, like the wings of a butterfly that cause a ripple in one area on Earth that causes a weather system in another."

"Like that little Church we spoke of last night Robert, that can cause more of an influence that the great tyrants of the world full of hate and anger and who cause such harm. One unsolicited act of kindness can have as much power and influence as any other thing. It is love, and compassion, and understanding enough for one neighbour to sacrifice for another, one stranger to risk his life for another that are true examples of the great energy of being."

Robert reflected a moment as Gordon released his embrace; the two souls began their stroll again. Robert pushed aside the sudden and dramatic emphasis Gordon had put into his words, and offered an example of what had just been said to him.

"Gordon, in my time, well, a little before my time there was something called the American airlift. I saw a show about it one time. The Americans were airlifting food into Berlin after the terrible catastrophe that was World War II. The Soviets weren't allowing food into the city by truck and the only way to feed the population in the Allied zones was by airlift."

"Really what was happening was a war for the hearts of people and the world was watching closely. One day, an American pilot through gum, or candy out the window of a plane for some children to pick up; and when they did, he kept throwing some out each day afterwards."

"Soon, word travelled and many, many German children came to get candy. When they became hundreds and hundreds, the scene of so many children wanting simple candy was evidence of their suffering under the policies of the tyrants and the Russians had to relent. World opinion had turned against them. The Soviets lifted the blockade and the food trucks came back. One man, one kind offering, helped bring the world back from the brink, as the blockade could have led to a new war with nuclear weapons."

Gordon smiled widely and took his right hand and placed it firmly on Roberts's upper back, where the shoulder meets the shoulder blade and squeezed it a little. "Good Robert good." He turned to the north and continued to walk, heading back towards the cliff that was in the far distance ahead.

"There are so many examples through history Robert. Some so little, like a traveller who on his journey comes across children hungry. He arranges a meal for them with an inn keeper and continues on, unbeknownst to the children. The gift seemingly coming from thin air; just a random act of thoughtfulness and kindness given unsolicited. Later in life, one of the children becomes a philanthropist and gives the gift of education to another whom, in dedication, finds a cure for a disease that killed millions."

"Kindness is a great boundless energy, under which hate must yield, as it gives nothing itself to the adventure of existence which can truly be perpetuated. Great cruelty inevitably dissipates, and life finds away to survive and press on. In time, trickles and streams regain the ground and we take yet another step."

Gordon was walking with a little more purpose in his step. "With the development of great technologies, societies are able to share information more freely, and consciousness becomes more in sync. Wealth allows for more sharing of the ability to provide sustenance and the civilization comes to expect a more charitable standard for all.

Gordon caught Robert's eyes and he knew the coming question. "Yes, some civilizations come to destroy themselves at these times, but so many are able to divert their attention away from simple materialism, greed and ego, and take the next step together towards a higher understanding."

"Gordon is technology then always linked to the ability of a society to take steps towards their own spiritual evolution? Is it a precursor to the advancement of a society, and so of the souls from it - that come here to the Subtle Domain?"

"That is a more difficult question Robert. Certainly much spiritual advancement has occurred in non-technological societies. Think of Buddha, and Christ, and Mohammad, some of the great teachers, who lived during times where spiritual growth was far in advance of technology."

"Yet, within technological societies there is a platform of information sharing and provision of basic need, so that trivial fears and wants can be discarded. The body, the mind, free of mundane toil to survive, begins to look inward. Here advancement takes form through a collective willingness to pursue new horizons of thought, and religion is relegated to an outdated form of mind control, and spirituality shines through as intricately connected to the quantum Universe."

"Consciousness and existence find more complex representation of their inter-relationship. We find we exist for a reason, with purpose. The magic of the fabric of existence becomes known, and it inspires us. The more the inter-relationship becomes apparent, the more that we see that we have a shared purpose, to explore all that is known."

The two souls had come back to the edge of the cliff and had stopped their walk.

"Gordon, when you speak of many societies, are you speaking of those of Egypt, and of Rome, or Atlantis?"

Gordon replied "Robert, there are many millions of societies, civilizations. It has always been so funny that existing alone, in the deep isolated realms of the Universe that civilizations believe they are the sole inhibitors of the Universe. Of course, with infinite resources and a constant inertia for matter to form into more complex patterns, and so into higher forms of consciousness many civilizations have arisen."

"I always wondered that Gordon, I mean, it always made sense to me that we were not alone. So, alien civilizations do exist then - in other areas of space?"

Gordon looked over at his student. "Oh yes Robert, although they are as much a part of the Universe as you, and so, not alien to anything. They exist as did your society on the Earth plane, in a Universe that manifests consciousness and matter. The Universe is a great cathedral of worlds. There have been so many worlds that have been created and, so many experiences that have been created."

"Is it time for me to see them Gordon?"

"Smart boy!" Gordon was smiling widely. "Do you trust me Robert?"

The reply was almost in unison "Well, I can't die again can I."

Gordon took Robert's left hand and slowly walked him toward the edge of the cliff. He slowed slightly as they approached it, and with head bowed almost irreverently, took a step off with Robert in tow. Robert saw a bright flash of light that eclipsed the scene of the Subtle Domain that had been around him for so long, and was gone. The two souls disappeared from the cliff face as if the fabric of space had been torn to thrust out shards of enormous light. It then resealed and the ocean below rolled on - silently as if nothing had ever, or would ever, disturb it.

As the flash of light subsided Robert felt a moment of disorientation as his last point of reference he had of a physical environment was to have been walked off a cliff, and where he should have been somehow artificially levitated in the air above the water and rugged coast line below, or, to be falling head over heels towards it.

Instead, he was presented with an image far more astounding. His eyes took a moment to adjust to a strange darkness. As his eyes focused he made out an ever increasing number of points of light. At first just a vast number in a central area and as the process of optical adjustment continued, he came to see thousands, and then millions. The canopy of darkness slowly retreated to reveal so many points of light, that the blackness seemed just a backdrop or stage on which a Universe might be cast.

Robert realized his soul body was intact and not really perched upon anything; he was adrift with the brilliant illumination of Gordon next to him. In this strange environment his teacher's body was far more dynamic than it had appeared in the Subtle Domain. Its many points of oscillating light seemed somehow in step with the Universe that had unfolded around them. And as Robert noted, his body too was a vast number of points of light, and it reminded him of his first night with Anna.

The two beings hovered in place, as much in motion as any of the other objects in the infinite space they had torn their way into, but with the vastness of the scale, to their senses they appeared to be fixed in place.

Robert said nothing as he was overcome with awe that staggered him completely. There was a silent and great majesty before him, and eventually Gordon broke the silence.

"This is the physical Universe Robert. It is vast and limitless, its dimensions even overpowering in scale to those of us who have spent eons in the spiritual planes. The scale of a galaxy is so great that it may hold as many as 400 billion stars, and, within a local group of galaxies, there are many millions of galaxies. All together in the Universe there are many billions of galaxies, all in motion away from each other, each being a center of the Universe and at the same time moving away from the Center of the Universe."

'The Universe Robert is much like a great balloon, ever growing with its centre out a point of reference to each and every thing that has been created. We, the stars, the galaxies, are as if painted on the balloon's outer skin, and as it inflates each point races from each other. But, because all were together at the point of singularity when the Universe began, each is the centre when compared to everything else – each of which are their own centre of the Universe."

Gordon moved his hand as if to push away from the fabric of space around them and suddenly Robert felt as if he and his teacher were being sucked away from the many points of light, the stars. The sensation escalated and Robert associated it with increasing speed, they were rushing away from something, and stars – appearing as small points of light were racing past his peripheral vision.

Then they stopped, and Robert noted that a calm of sorts had occurred. Some background energy had ceased when he and Gordon had moved outside of the combined points of light. There was a silence of sorts. And Robert gained a visual sense of why. They had left what now became clear as being a galaxy. He and Gordon had been in a galaxy.

In the calm and silence Robert watched the galaxy retreat into the distance. It was itself becoming a distant point of light. Then another passed Robert's left peripheral vision, then another, then one to the right. Then several rushed past.

Robert knew that he and Gordon were in the lonely place between not only stars, but galaxies themselves. They were in the void. So empty of a place, that even the roar of star creation and the thunder of their deaths was unheard. So very far from all that is that even in the many billions of years of creation, not enough time had existed for the sound of the threshold of existence to have reached this point along the expanding surface of the balloon like nature of existence.

The sense of motion stopped and Robert looked about, noticing galaxies at all points of the horizon in a now slow dance away from he and Gordon. Fear came over him and he realized how incredibly lonely the Universe really and truly is - a loneliness where a lifetime of consciousness might be swept aside and forgotten as if in a blink of an eye.

Had Gordon taken him from Anna, from the Subtle Domain, from life on the Earth plane so far into remoteness that he might be lost forever? A cold panic gained a footing in Robert's mind. He felt terror in the pit of his stomach – the kind that makes you want to throw up as adrenalin for the fight of flight instinct demands blood to be routed to the muscles.

Robert knew that he was not flesh and blood and so would not be sick, but all the same, being in spirit and terribly alone was also known to him, and was equally terrifying. He had experienced that just after his death in the void of the in-between of planes, where the veil of transition is starkly absent from form, or light, or the comfort of another.

Robert sought out comfort and turned to his teacher. "Gordon, this void is terrible, I, I am scared."

Gordon's voice seemed without emotion when he answered. "This is the end of existence on the physical realm Robert. This is the time when the force of gravity is so reduced by the expansion of the Universe that star formation has grown silent and dead. There is too little gravity to tug at atoms so that the laws of physics coalesces them into gas clouds. No gravity to ignite their nuclear fuel so that they might provide heat and warmth for life – the gift of a parent star to its worlds."

"The stars have burned through their essential elements and are now exhausted. No more fantastic super nova explosions, only dense remnant cores and worlds that have grown so very cold Robert, and lifeless. And the darkness is complete, no more peering out into a night sky full of stars and possibilities; this is the end."

Robert could feel the coldness, not by virtue of cells with receptors to register it, but rather, with the icy certainty that Gordon was speaking the truth. Robert surrendered to that stark truth.

"Why are we here Gordon?" Robert's voice was strong with determination; he wanted an answer from which he could decide conclusively upon whatever emotions the next lessons would require.

He did not like this place in its entirety and he longed for the Subtle Domain, the cottage, and especially all that Anna now represented. The exchange of energies that he had experienced with her, that spectacular moment now had such a meaning. To share with another – now revealed as such a treasure - and so impossible here at the end of the physical universe.

Gordon spoke, a tone of his former warmth and humour showing through so that an inkling of hope returned to Robert's being. "We are here Robert, to teach us, both, of the gift of the counterpart to physical matter – consciousness. Remember what we spoke of by the fire in the cottage Robert. Consciousness was created with matter and arose with it in complexity, to provide the many myriads of experience that took 'I am' to the place of answering 'what am I'."

"And long before this dismal existence it was liberated through the very process that you have endeavoured with courage to accept and pursue. The evolution of your very own soul and it occurs through every step, every seed that is born, and every life that is lived and indeed with every death that is died."

"Let us be gone from this place!" Gordon had shouted the sentence and with it Robert learned the power of thought in the spiritual planes to travel amongst realities, even to and from the physical. It was desire, and his to leave this void was as strong as any he had ever had.

The void seemed to stretch away into the distance and then contract quickly toward them and the sensation was like being in the bend of one long elastic that had been stretched and then released. Robert sensed being thrust forward, although, he wasn't quite sure if he had been thrust forward or if space had been stretched and then suddenly released – putting him into a different place, or time.

Both were true, his place in space had changed and the time had altered, he had moved back in it. The result was the two souls being put into a much different scene. A scene so profoundly different that the experience seemed like being in two completely different universes - although they were in the same.

Robert felt completely different emotionally. He sensed warmth, the kind that happens when one is reunited with family, like at a special Christmas on Earth. He felt suddenly safe, and the sensation sent love and acceptance through him. He felt the euphoria that occurs when a terrible fear is resolved.

We are in the fellowship of consciousness Robert. This is the life of the Universe Robert, all the outposts of life in the vastness. And as you can see, it is immense and plentiful beyond belief. Life is common in the Universe Robert, it is immersed in life and the same seed, the same code that creates life is consistent throughout.

Robert felt a strong sense of joy, he was overwhelmed. The scene before him was emotional, he viewed the Universe in a large macro sense, and he could literally feel life that burned near the stars that hosted worlds with life of all kinds.

He knew instinctively that he shared the experience of all living things and of the consciousness that lies within each, a gift and a miracle at the same time. There was a brotherhood within this existence, and while nature has a competitiveness that is viewed as cruel, it also has a uniqueness that ties all living things together.

"Gordon, this is so opposite to the void, being there was almost worth it, to feel this, this shared-ness between all living things. It, it is wonderful!"

Gordon smiled back at Robert as the two looked out upon the vastness of stars all about them. Robert reflected that early human life on the Earth might have been something similar – to look out at night and see the glow of fires in caves where life existed.

Robert raised his two arms and shouted "A great Cathedral of Worlds" and then again even louder, "IT'S A GREAT CATHEDRAL OF WORLDS!" Robert was right – a great Cathedral of worlds it is.

Robert's mind gathered in the sense of so many outposts of life all busily pursuing the trillions of experiences occurring each second, in each place. The busy hive of experiences all clattering at once, like the hammering of keys in an early adding machine, ever totalling the collective experience of all that can be, all that is, and preparing the scene - ever instantaneously – of what is to be.

An in the eventuality of eternity that is particular to curved space time, to tally an answer to the query of "what am I".

Robert felt a question form in his mind and then rush into a full-fledged curiosity – the kind that you are compelled to resolve. "Gordon, why are all the places life is found, I mean why is all of life, from the same seed? Why are all things alike?"

Gordon moved his hand in a sweeping motion and the scene changed once more. Robert drew back as if to give range to the world that appeared before him. There was a planet suddenly below him, and then rising in front of him and Gordon.

It was wondrous in appearance. Some future appearing world from what he knew of Earth, with large continents that were crisscrossed with bands of light and other large areas of clustered lights. Robert looked upon them, great cities he reasoned, with transportation systems linking them. He saw periodic beams of light from some, and he somehow knew them to be signals sent to other neighbouring worlds, or perhaps, to some outpost world's great distances away.

"Robert, life is very often carried through the Universe at the molecular level by comets. The simplest amino acids – the building blocks of life, of genetic material – arrive to compatible worlds through star dust, quite literally. In fact, this produces a great irony, because life is often extinguished through the same source. Comets become the giver, and taker of life."

"This was true of your Earth. Life arrived through simple amino acids into the warm pools of the early Earth. There they grew in complexity and over time radically changed the planet when advanced enough as organisms to produce oxygen. However, on several occasions, and two in particular, life was nearly extinguished completely when comets caused great extinctions; the dinosaur's demise being one of the most notable."

Robert went on. "The common thread though, is not just the delivery method of life to worlds to provide a common denominator. There is an inertia that drives matter forward into higher forms from the outset of the right environment for life.

Life, as they say, always finds a way. Life is similar because it follows an effective path to sufficient complexity for consciousness to manifest. Life seeks not just the advantages necessary for continuation in nature; it also seeks to understand some reckoning of its place in that environment."

"That culminates eventually in species that consider the question of purpose, and they indeed are advanced life forms. Getting there, follows varied points but the nature of the Universe, its foundation in the laws of physics and the symmetry of mathematics – the underpinning clues of existence and its roadmap – create sentient beings with foundational similarities, who in time seek enlightenment."

'Some because they understood the connection to spirituality from the beginning. They understood the field that underlies all of existence in the physical and how it ties everything together. They understood the quantum nature of physics from the outset and saw that the Universe exists to permit experimentation by consciousness – and they adopted it as a guide post to the fundamental understanding that enlightenment provides."

"Much as quantum mechanics sought out dialogue with Buddhism in your time to fill in the blanks. Mankind needed to slum about in the dredges of war and conflict which are really just the products of unbridled ego and the manifestos that indoctrinate simple folk to fill in the ranks for slaughter. After a time, science became able to see the true reality, which is the energy field on which the play of life is carried out. A great hologram created by our minds to live out experiences until we can grasp true meaning and purpose – and from it, enlightenment and freedom from the hologram of the physical universe."

"Come Robert, let's explore this world."

With those words the two souls descended to the strange planet's surface, which seemed an instantaneous transition to Robert. They had arrived at the centre square of a great city Robert saw the inhabitants all about him.

"Can they see us Gordon?" Robert's query contained both concern and fascination and wonder.

"No Robert, we are as ghosts to them. They are of the physical and we are of the spiritual. We move in a different wavelength and frequency in energy than they, and so, their minds filter us out – not being in harmony with the true reality of existence."

With sufficient reassurance of privacy from Gordon, Robert began to explore the figures moving about him and his teacher. They were tall and slender. They moved about on large thin legs that provided motion that seemed to cause them little effort. Atop the legs was a slender hour glass shaped torso and long arms.

The neck was many more times as large as his and the gentle motion of the passer by's seemed to suggest that the species was a refined, or dignified and advanced from of life.

He gazed intently at their large dark eyes, each about three to four inches in length and a good two to three inches in width. They sat on either side of shallow nose with small oval nostrils and above a small mouth with narrow lips. The mouth did not seem to contain any teeth per se.

Robert considered that they indeed looked like an alien species on Earth as portrayed in early science fiction shows – although much taller.

"My Lord" he exclaimed "they truly do look so much like aliens."

Gordon chuckled out loud so that his upper torso leaned back a little. He turned to Robert, saying "Well they shouldn't Robert, after all they are human."

Robert gasped and looked at Gordon with disbelief.

"What was there a nuclear war or something? How in…" His sentenced ended as his mind had stopped trying to reason out the obvious transformation from the human being his spirit body replicated and the species set out before him.

"Yes Robert, these are the descendants of human beings who lived on Earth much further into you're last life times future. They are the descendants of those humans who came to inhabit the mid to outer solar system."

"Some centuries after you lived the moons of Jupiter, Saturn and the other giant gas planets Uranus and Neptune became the primary source of minerals and resources, and housed all the great manufacturing facilities. Heavy industry was moved into space environments in the moon's orbits, or on the moons themselves so that the Earth would no longer be polluted and plundered."

"The Earth biosphere was finally recognized for the oasis in space and gift to humanity that it is. The fragile and spoiled environment of the planet became sacred and valued, and an effort was made to allow it to recover from mankind's misdeeds."

Robert fumbled through his mind for context, and none was coming forward. "But Gordon, with all due respect, they do not appear at all to look like humans, other than having legs and arms, and eyes and mouths."

"In less than Earth gravity Robert, the human genome rapidly changed. Low gravity meant that bone and tissue grew in length and became less dense. The human race was then irrevocably divided. Those living in less than Earth gravity

- pretty much everybody who was born in space or on the solar systems smaller worlds, became forever different from the billions who lived on Earth."

"Those millions, who were born away from the Earth, could never visit the human race's home world. The gravity would kill them, much like a whale dies on shore when gravity places too much pressure on the heart, circulatory and respiratory systems."

The inhabitants of space eventually became numerous and over time the connection to Earthly humans began to be strained. It wasn't enough for them to toil for the sake of the Earth species, and they set about being star faring adventures and explorers. They excelled in their technologies and advanced science a great deal."

"Much like the Polynesians on Earth, they set sail in order to expand their sphere of influence, using science as the catalyst and means for their journeys. They flourished and set out on generations' long voyages to distant stars, from which the explorers would never return. Like, say, those who ventured from Polynesia to Easter Island, never to return."

"As with this world, over time the inhabitants were so morphed from their ancestors on Earth, that the home world was forgotten all together. In time, the stories of the species on Earth was less and less important, and then abandoned all together."

This world is small and about one tenth the gravity of Earth. It circles a small star that is a good distance away. As a result, the inhabitants developed large eyes to gather in the available photons of light, their legs became very long and their bodies slender and without stored fats. Being space faring people, they relied on nutrition other than animals, which would consume resources unnecessarily just to provide protein. Having lost their carnivorous nature, the mouth became small and teeth disappeared. In fact these 'people' place little value on eating, as most nourishment is liquid – and placed more value on knowledge, and science."

"Without the complicating influence of animal fats on health and the relatively low pressure on the heart and lungs from gravity, the inhabitants live very, very long lives, some several centuries. That has allowed the race's collective consciousness to develop, to become wise and knowledgeable, compassionate and thoughtful. War, poverty, greed and crime have no place here, as they would unnecessarily hinder matters. In other words, they have no utility."

Robert looked out at the long tall figures effortlessly moving about. "They are truly an advances species then." The sentence was a statement and not a question.

He saw the connectedness of things and he commented on it to Gordon.

"And so, I am here in this time, as it now sits, as my point of reference in the physical universe's curved-space time. It is my seat of consciousness and point of reference. And, this race of beings would not, could not have existed without their first having been an Earth species. Without the cause and effect of my Earth time, and before it the many others, and following my Earth time, the many others – this place would have never been?"

Gordon smiled slightly and said "Come student, lest go look a little closer at this reality."

The visited world was departed and the two souls withdrew quickly from the surface spaceward so that the planet became a coin sized disk and then but another point of light in Robert's panoramic view of star filed space.

There was a period of quiet and the scene remained tranquil for several minutes – the stars gently twinkling in their multitude. Robert's emotions subsided and he grew calm inside – even complacent given the peacefulness of the moment.

The moment of transition occurred so quickly that no point of demarcation was apparent from one reality to the next. The physical universe had given way to the underlying foundation of what it is – energy. An infinite field of energy, not so much pulsating as it is oscillating in the harmony of a vast number of frequencies.

Surprisingly Robert did not feel shocked by the scene – in many respects he felt at home in it, absorbed by it and as if he and it were one – as all things in existence are as one with it. Gordon could not immediately be seen in the enveloping field, but Robert could feel his thoughts in his mind.

"All that is, is born of this one energy Robert. This single wave of energy that provides the source for all the potentialities that existence can create to experience. All that is resonates from this energy and in the frequencies that are played out – like the strings of an instrument as they vibrate sound into the world."

"Think Robert, of a radio wave on Earth. As the signal is sent out from a central transmission point it behaves like the ripples upon a pond as a stone is tossed in. The waves of sound carry out ever further from the central point. A listener in one location here's the sound of a voice, or of music, just as another listener here's the same sounds – even though they may be separated by a distance – even many hundreds or thousands of miles."

"That each listens to the same information along the path of the single wave is extraordinary, that at each point in space and time the same information is encoded in that wave. It is the gift of the electro-magnetic universe."

"As all of existence is drawn from the well of this single source, this singular wave of energy, the same information is always present and available at any given point, regardless of space or time. It is what Einstein called 'spooky action at a distance."

This wave of energy brings forth the processes that cause the physical universe and that provide the context and apparatus for other realities, what some think of as other dimensions and even other universes – and what you and I have called the spiritual realms that are subtle, and of light. The field or sea of energy sprang into existence at the point of 'I am' – combining consciousness and matter into its long dance of experience seeking."

"It is also a well of information available to all those who seek to observe, and who, by virtue of their existence imprint the wave with their story – the history of their experiences. What we are, what we do, is always known here, it is, if you will, the great repository; and creation is but the stage on which the play is enacted. And that stage Robert, as your scientists knew, is but a hologram and what is seen by the eye and mind – but the vibrations of strings of energy and thought to be reality."

Robert understood, the information was so basic at this source level that the truism of it was self evident to him. The world he knew was really this energy, but viewed as the earth, water, and sky that he took to be reality. Not so much an illusion, as it was only a partial view of reality – as the mind made form of some of the vibrating energy – but far less than all.

Robert thought of the great meditates in history. Buddha, Christ, the Tibetans, and monks of many religions, they had trained their minds to listen, to tune into, the many other frequencies of energy that were all about them. Their minds no longer restricted to the vibrations that the dogma of human society insists must be listened to – instead, over time and with discipline, they calmed their minds to listen to the many other harmonies. Like a radio dial, slowly tuned until a single station is abandoned and the multitude of others are discovered.

"Consciousness uses this field to achieve a number of outcomes Robert. Whether a life on Earth that becomes the journey of the soul to the Subtle Domain for reflection on abandoning ego and pursuing higher knowledge – this wave, this field becomes reality to the point of view of the observer – when consciousness decides what it should be. What is a point in time to one may be different to another, what is one location in space to one, can be far distant to another – all existing and co-existing together."

"And it is how all that is, is entangled – the elixir that combines what we are, have been and will be. How the fabric of existence is bound in cause and effect where experiences are interwoven and inter-dependent, and entangled amongst the many. It is the scribe that maintains the history and pushes the story tellers back together so that the script cannot neglect the actions of one upon the self or unto others."

Robert and Gordon's consciousnesses withdrew from the energy plasma so that it seemed to stretch limitlessly in all directions slightly below them. The action was for reference and really was only a mental construct – as the energy of the field encompasses entirety – and so even the point of view of them above it.

Robert felt somewhat confused and unsettled and it had caused the cavalier sense of things he had before entering the energy field to vanish and it interrupted the contentment that he had come to know since the arrival of greater knowledge while at the cottage. A question formed in his mind."

Gordon, how do we know that consciousness forms reality and that it was present from the very beginning, to answer 'what am I? I mean, I sense that it is the truth of things, but, I guess my mind looks for the proof?"

Gordon waved his hand from left to right in a dismissive manner and the wave of energy re-manifested itself to represent the reality that he intended. Robert looked out at a scene from the material universe and a rather splendid one indeed.

In front of him was a great nebula, its gases orange and red, and in places new stars were being born – with the bright blue of their hydrogen cores. Great fingers of dust rose from the centre of the nebula, where other stars would coalesce and ignite into solar systems.

At a great distance there was a spiral galaxy, its star filed arms wrapped at varying distances around its galactic centre. And beyond it, other galaxies, slowly receding in size and Robert knew they must be at enormous distances in the distant past, with their light having took eons upon eons to reach the point that his consciousness was now perched.

"As I have said Robert, in the very beginning there was the point of singularity, of creation. The Big Bang, if you will. Matter and consciousness sprang forth on their great journey. In your time, 13.7 billion years later, your scientists looked back and saw light from very near the beginning of time and space. Your astrophysicists observed it."

"Yes" Robert answered, wondering what the significance was.

"As we know, consciousness is the decider, when matter that exists as a wavelength, becomes a particle. That is, leaves the sea of potentialities and fixes in position to become a 'something'. Well, consciousness did so with this light, as energy from the field, emitted as a wave that became photons of light. They were observed – not just when your scientists looked at them, they were what they are from the outset. They have always been photons of light from the Big Bang – the beginning."

Robert understood. They energy had material form from the beginning 13.7 billion years before his time, his life, and those of the scientists who knew the energy to be from the time of the beginning. Consciousness had to be present then. The laws of physics said it had to be so.

Across the Divides

Robert looked out at the Cosmos in a mood of quiet serenity. He saw it not as a place of great remoteness, vast lonely spaces and barren worlds. Instead, he looked at it as a busy machine, governed by interlocking processes of physical interaction – and all driven upward from the energy of the field that underlies and creates it all.

Each action with a purpose and interconnected to the consciousness that had come to populate it, although, often not even recognized by that consciousness. It was still though, an amazing Petri dish of immense size and its beauty and fury could not be ignored. Robert drew in the spectacle with suitable reverence.

He gazed at the pillar of dust forming its long fingers – twinkling with the young birthed stars twinkling so brightly with their abundant hydrogen. He thought of the great red star that must have exploded to give these new stars the dust to coalesce and gravity to ignite their cores into becoming stars, and what that must have looked and sounded like as the ancient star burst its outer core in the final cataclysmic death throw.

Nature was a superb artist, as if a grand master had decided on history's greatest canvass and thrust forward a series of brushes to craft the scenes that would unfold over the eons in depth and color in a carefully choreographed play. Each scene patiently waited until its predecessor finished its performance, like the super nova setting the scene for the dance of new suns and their accompanying solar systems of planets, moons and comets.

Robert could sense the consciousness that underlies the creation, and he felt its slow rhythmic beat, like a faint drum at a distance, or the hum of an engine far off. It was relentless. He had travelled far enough on his journey to knowledge that he had shifted the essential concept of his own being. While perhaps not yet a master, but certainly an apprentice in the ways of the spirit.

The Universe would never seem the same again to Robert. Its mysteries had unravelled in many respects and its source understood to a reasonable point. He reflected on that, what had seemed so large and unknown was now parcelled out in ways that allowed his mind to manage them. Size and dimension proportioned adequately to discern a beginning and an end; so that they could be adequately reasoned in his mind.

Gordon sensed Robert's transition and maturation had reached the goal that he had set out for the lesson and that it should end. He turned to Robert and as their eyes met the latter understood the signal and nodded his head slightly up and down.

Robert closed his eyes in a submissive way to bring on whatever was to happen next and with a great, reverent, peace in his heart. Part respect and part gratitude for all he had been shown and invited to experience.

He kept his eyes closed and the feeling of reverence became greater. At first he didn't know why, and then he understood. It hit him. He was about to migrate from the physical to the spirit world again; the second time as Robert. It was the transition from the physical plane that the living fear as death – because it represents the end of what they have come to relish as the only true reality and because it holds the fear of the unknown.

Robert had come to know now, that both are not reasonable or necessary for the living. The lack of living was a gateway to the great true adventure. And he had walked that road, and so doing so again from the Universe would be much easier a task, as he returned to the Subtle Domain.

Inside he also knew that his soul had made this journey many times before, as the stories told on the books on the shelves of the cottage described. Nonetheless, the journey deserved reverence as it was to him, a Holy thing.

Robert opened his eyes in time to see a blaze of light – the same as he had experienced when arriving to the Subtle Domain to meet Mrs. Delorme and the same as he had seen when he and Gordon stepped off the cliff side above the cottage.

As the light subsided he was within the familiarity of the cottage and that pleased him a great deal. Next to him was his teacher, and the two stood as if the remarkable events were but conversation over a game of cards. The relaxed feeling Robert knew, was the warmth that comes from returning to a place of fond familiarity after a long journey.

Robert knew the importance of what he had seen though, and he sensed that those experiences were profoundly imprinted on Gordon as well. However, like many returns home, the traveller is drawn into a sense of lull before a rest restores the vigour of the recalling and retelling of the places visited. And as a late afternoon sun sent light through the panes of the window, Robert felt the nook beckoning him and he obligingly answered the call.

As Robert laid himself out he gazed through the little window and up at the quiet patient clear blue sky. His teacher took to the sitting chair and stretched out with his lower back slightly curved so that his legs could fully stretch out while resting on his heels. Both souls needed rest to process the meaning and significance of the recent startling events.

Robert's eyes grew heavy but he kept them open to look over at Gordon whose eyes had shut and his head nodded downward to meet is upper chest, then slightly offset to the right. His translucent energy had noticeably settled into slow rhythms and Robert reckoned that he was asleep. His own eyes closed and sleep came very quickly.

He awoke to a wonderful aroma filling the cottage and the sound of gentle sizzling that he took as being some creation that had been heated then turned down to allow individual ingredient flavours to be drawn out and integrated with the others. Those magical combinations of flavours that themselves are generous, yet only fully completed when brought together with those others for whom they are naturally matched.

Robert mused a little that perhaps souls were that way. Unique and gifted in so many ways, but made complete when joined with another – and only then their full magical qualities released through their togetherness.

He wondered if he and Anna were that way. Had he discovered through his journeys the meaning of the blending of energies when they first met? Had he stumbled upon a key element of his essential completeness through the journey of the Robert life – or rather, the ending of the Robert life?

He certainly felt that the Robert that he now was exceeded the Robert that he had been upon his arrival to the Subtle Domain. He knew that the current essential Robert was a collectiveness of all his previous experiences and would they not be amplified if he were to have Anna's experiences added – mingled in?

Like a life on Earth where two join in a union that combines their lives to form a new perspective. Each person comes from a family unit that provides them a collective history of all those who have come before them, and that they consider to be their essential selves. However, upon finding a partner, and combining their lives, a new perspective is attained and a new family formed.

The lives that are subsequently lived, especially when children are added, create a new chapter from which each member shares an identity. Knowledge and experience from the past are added, and together provide the foundation for the arrival of new experiences – all adding to context of self that is always evolving.

For the couple that have lived together for 50 years, do they not see themselves as more of a single entity that just of two individual entities? They have a wealth of shared experiences that are of the blessing received over the years, and of the challenges and crisis that they have survived together. When one passes, the other is left without context and may be adrift at least in some respects - for their remaining years they have.

While collecting his thoughts Robert resolved to query these points to Gordon and to ask about the meaning of the experience he had with Anna. But, out of politeness and perhaps out of the hunger that had sprung up inside him from the aroma in the cottage, Robert decided he should first explore the prospect of the meal that he sensed was nearing completion.

Robert rolled out of the nook and looked over at a pleasantly set table. A large square table cloth with frilled edges had been placed over the wooden table so that its edges hung down to create four triangles dipping down towards the floor. Two plates were set with cutlery on either side and in the table centre was a candle that flickered lazily close to a vase that had some flowers that were common in the landscape outside the cabin. A dark bottle of wine, uncorked finished off the simple settings.

Gordon had his back to the scene and was managing two pots and a fry pan. In the latter a number of large shrimp sizzled that looked juicy and tender, their tales removed and surrounded by slices of garlic in dissolved butter. In one pot was a tomato sauce with a heavy amount of onion, peppers and assorted seasoning enmeshed and in the other was rapidly boiling water with pasta in the form of spaghetti strands.

Robert felt a rush of contentment that comes from knowing that the cooking meal has reached its zenith and is now ready for presentation.

Gordon turned slightly to take in Robert's standing figure, licking a finger tip and then his thumb. It was obvious that he had been picking at the creation as it was being readied. No truly good cook can resist the temptation to test and sample their creation to reinforce the sense of good decision making along the path to readiness – and to be certain at the point guests are invited to share in.

Gordon seemed to be fully in control of the process and so Robert filled two cups and placed them next to the plates. The dark red wine had a rich potent aroma that in itself was a convincing invitation to settle into a chair at the table. He found two bright white, almost glowing napkins and folded them neatly aside the plates.

As Gordon managed the last few details, Robert lit a fire that slowly crackled to life. He waited a few minutes until the point of combustion was sufficiently engaged so that he could add a few larger pieces of wood. When the flames were fully engaged he turned back to the table.

Gordon had arrived with the drained pasta and had spilt out large portions onto each plate. He used a wooden spoon to gather the shrimp and contents to the lip of the fry pan and then on into the pasta sauce, stirring a few times round and round so that they had become one with the sauce. They no longer were shrimp and garlic, but were now something else, a full, rich and well created sauce that he then spooned out generously on top of the pasta.

Food is a fluid sensation in the Subtle Domain as the aromas carry inviting waves of anticipation. As meals are consumed the tastes are overflowing in sensation and when swallowed, give an amplified feeling of well-being. Like everything in this Heaven like realm, all seems greater in intensity and beauty, giving contentment and peace for those who take but a moment to notice. When noticed, every meal then, is a success.

Robert sat down to the meal with earnest. In-between bites Robert looked up and over at Gordon as he worked a spoon and fork like a grand master of pasta dishes. He gathered up strands of spaghetti as they became intertwined in the fork, poked a large shrimp and then spun the collection within the concave surface of the rounded spoon so that the assembly, sauce included, could be moved to the mouth without spilling a single item.

The process was repeated in quick successive intervals so that the plate surface began to see daylight again from below the heaping, steaming, creation.

Robert's system was much less perfect but enjoyed to the same degree. He tended to the shrimp and past individually and ate much more slowly than his teacher. He preferred to emphasize the flavours in a slow procession of carefully scrutinized bites.

Robert thought that the sauce deserved a fresh bread to dab into it, and as he did Gordon's head popped up with mouth full, and he nodded toward the cupboard and pointing with the single index digit of his right hand extended in an Einstein styled 'ah hah' eureka motion. Robert took to his feet and, opening the cupboard closest to the stove to find a loaf of deep brown bread still warm as if it had just arrived from the bakery.

Silence followed and as Gordon ate Robert settled after a time and he took the cup of wine and held it between the outreached fingers of both hands, elevating it above his near finished dinner plate, in a gesture of victory over it, but really just to reinforce himself that he was satisfied and the eating part of the meal for him was at an end.

He took occasional sips of wine. The moment the liquid reached his lips it was strong and poignant. As it reached his tongue and taste buds it revealed its dry and smooth true character, and it finished with no discomfort of after taste. Whatever it was, it was an aged fine wine.

The quite reflective time, with fire crackling and providing warmth in the hearth allowed him to swirl different thoughts through his mind. He settled on the notion that a long time had gone by since he had spoken with Anna, and a lot of things had gone by to.

He wondered what she may be doing at just that time and he reached out with his mind for her. He thought he saw her interrupted in her own thoughts so that his telepathy might have her reach back for him. He thought it possible and so he resolved to ask her if she had such a recollection the next time they would come together.

He hadn't thought of the next time they would be together for some time, and so in doing so he began to feel that longing that comes from missing someone. The missing that causes a person to resolve that they will soon take the actions needed to remedy the distance apart and bring arms around their loved one very soon.

As his thoughts returned to his place sitting at the table he thought better of a quick return to the town centre, and a premature return to Anna. He had embarked on a monumental journey for his soul that was literally a quantum evolution of his basic nature. This journey, these experiences were perhaps, the' defining moment for his transition to an advanced soul, and he had come so far. There was no turning back he'd have to see it through. He was signed on for the duration, no room or purpose for half measures.

As Gordon's plate was nearly finished, he slowed his bites and took breaks – occasionally sipping at wine and eventually chewing and swallowing slowly as he cradled his napkin in his hands above his plate.

Robert took the opportunity to press forward a question.

"Gordon, when I first arrived in the Subtle Domain, well, a little while after I arrived at the Subtle Domain, I met a soul named Anna. Just after my cross over really, and we had the most unusual experience together."

"What happened, did you get a bill for the buffet meal?"

Robert's eyes blinked a few times in shock at the sarcasm that had leapt out of his teacher. He chuckled out loud a little and smiled, not offended by the remark. It did though, seem out of context from the tone of the discussions that they had taken up to date, and he wondered a little how it was that Gordon had known about the buffet meal.

Did he also know about the shared energy exchange and magic of their love making to?

"Ah Robert, so it begins."

Gordon sat back in his chair, and reached his arms high into the air above him, stretching his upper torso, then settling back in his chair, legs out stretched and hands folded together behind his head.

"Are you ready then, for the great adventure, the great journey?"

Robert looked over at his teacher, somewhat perplexed, had he not been on the great journey? He shifted his right hand outward, palm up and in a horizontal swaying gesture that was to signify agreement with the proposal – in principal.

Gordon took his napkin and ran it across his lips and placed it next to his plate. He took his wine cup and took a long purposeful gulp, allowing it to swish between his cheeks a few times so that the initial poignant taste could unveil the dryness of the flavours, as if the wine had been neglected too much during the dinner.

"Robert you and your companion Anna experienced an event that allowed you to peer through the veil of the Subtle Domain, and into the higher light realms."

Robert was awe-struck; he had that feeling again that somewhere, somehow he had always known that, and Gordon's words were the confirmation slowly drawn in that surreal way they do when we hear something powerful. Like Robert's earlier revelations, it was a package of knowledge that had been stored away by someone at an earlier time - and was now being carefully and eagerly opened.

So many questions began to form in Robert's mind, all needing to be ordered, put into priority. He was getting good at this, to find a pace when events began to reach a cascade and new understanding stood on the horizon.

Why had Gordon refer to Anna as his companion? Was that pre-destined and meant to be – as an eventual universal truth? The veil of the Subtle Domain Gordon had said - hadn't he and Mrs. Delorme said that he had already come to the 'real' reality by coming to the Subtle Domain? Was the Subtle Domain merely another veil to be peered through into another, greater, or truer reality?

Was everything just meant to be an endless puzzle? Robert thought it best to not ponder on the many questions further, he would just let them tumble out, as is.

"How was that possible? How could Anna and I do that, to, peer into the light realms?"

"It is rare Robert but certainly not unheard of. It is an occurrence for those in the physical domain, and the Subtle Domain who seek, to query for true reality. Those with no query in their mind, no seeking, no wonder, and just pursuit of the material and self-rewarding, well, they are as far from truth as a fish is from climbing a mountain. They, are in different worlds, where the vary environment they need to start up the mountain cannot be imagined to exist, let alone be attained."

Gordon went on.

"For those who can desire enough for enlightenment, to forgo the material, the journey to the high light realms becomes possible. The trappings of the material are the trappings of the mind. When we are unhindered by the ego and of the material and power based satisfactions that it demands – the next steps become as natural as stepping out the door for fresh air."

"In some ways Robert, all the planes of existence are real, and should not be thought of as being unworthy or unreal. Each plane is true in reality to the observer who sits within it. He or she is within the frequency of that plane existence – and their understanding of things corresponds, making the experience valid. If unquestioned, it remains valid and true to the observer, however, in time, things become static, and some come to question, to seek."

"The secret that comes forth and into the knowing is that the ego is relentless and cannot be tamed. It must be unbridled, unhinged and ultimately discarded. That privilege is won over time through selflessness and compassion; it is then that we resume our position, or super position, as beings of light, the pure light of consciousness."

Robert remained silent, his head bowed slightly so that he could reduce the stimulus from the surrounding cottage and let Gordon's words swim in.

"Robert, at the end time, we beings of light rejoin, after having ventured into all the vast experiences that are possible while being in a state of being, to share all that has been and can be known, to answer the initial question of the beginning, of what am I. In the end time we know, the mystery sought in the beginning time."

"The beginning time when consciousness sprang forth into creation – and we set out as the creator and the creation both. God, as has been known Robert, is the collectiveness of all that has existed, risen to consciousness, and joined together in the end time. For those who lived in your physical universe, it is the end state of curved space-time that joins round to the beginning state. To those in the quantum reality of the spiritual realm, it is the beginning and the end, and the side by side of all things existing at the same time, in a single state of energy from which all that could be experienced, was drawn to exist."

"In this way each is true, and all points of view the same, but limited in understanding and point of view – depending upon the positional state of the observer. In other words, as might be limited due to their point of view."

"What Anna and you experienced was the energy of spirit in the end time, when we rejoin into the river of light. A oneness made whole again after being many,

many, separated points of light, and that event my friend, is a great sharing of energy."

Robert thought for a moment. Had he really just heard a definition of God in some scientific term? He deciphered the words slowly in his mind. "God is the collectivity of consciousness in an end state, in curved space time." He reflected that consciousness existed in so many forms and places within the Universe, and that at the end of time it had found its way home to be collected up into a whole.

"You and she ventured your energy together in the same space of spirit. A process where you had become one as much as you were two; soul-mates as the event is sometimes referred to. You tasted the experience that is to come for all, just for you and she, you represented that joining together in a sexual experience, which was your own special event to share."

"An entirely beautiful thing to share, powerful and exquisite to the soul I am sure. More joy and love than can be imagined before it is actually experienced."

"Well, you certainly have that right Gordon." Robert smiled widely although he couldn't help but blush a little.

Robert took the words in and the sound of them was welcome, although quite surreal. The words were magical and resonated in him like good news does when something favourable touches a life. The sensation was positive and it reminded him of the pleasure that he had experienced with Anna. Yet, some questions pressed forward.

"But why Gordon, why would Anna and I share that experience. Why us? Was it because we were meant to be soul-mates, was it something that was destined, or, pre-determined?"

"Yes and no" Gordon replied. "Yes because there was an inevitability that you would both venture to the point as observers that you could experience such a coming together, you have progressed as souls. No, because nothing is pre-determined, pre-ordered until the desire for experience works through the many variable occurrences of cause and effect until we arrive at our point of reality."

"If existence were preordained from the outset then there would be no point in the journey, well, at least no practical need for it. After all, the experience is not in the destination, but in the journey that takes us there, isn't it?" Gordon smiled and had moved his arms upward and out from his body in a circular fashion, for effect.

"If existence was preordained I am and what am I would have been known simultaneously. Existence would have been unnecessary and a spiritual mute point. And the point being, it was not preordained and so all that is, had to be.

Something was born in place of nothingness although the two are in an embrace of duality. Something could not have been born without nothingness having been the precursor condition, like a child being unable to exist without its parents."

'The beauty of all of this Robert is that we souls are all entitled. We all are present in the end time to collectively know the final computation of our derivative components. Where a condition of one became a condition of many, to experience all that could be known, round to becoming one again in the end time. And through all that knowing, have we not come to know something of our meaning, and our purpose."

Robert continued to feel troubled about why he and Anna should have experienced a glimpse of the time that souls rejoin, why he and she, and not others. He and Anna had certainly not seemed intent on discovering some final truth about existence when they came together. In fact, Robert thought, they hadn't thought of anything else but coming together.

Gordon spoke to Robert with a kind and soft voice, almost as a father to a son when events provide them a special place to bond, as the gifts of insight are shared.

"Robert, you do under estimate the relevance of your quest for knowledge and understanding, and the influence that it has on your soul. It has been a beacon signalling your soul's point of arrival. The Earth experience that you had readied you for the transition to enlightenment that you are now pursuing. It was as if a trumpet heralding your arrival, to the audience that is truly of self – the collective you."

"You have longed for understanding, and since your arrival to the Subtle Domain, the brief and intense experience you have had has not deterred you from the path you set for yourself. Your growing love for Anna, has not dissuaded you from your journey. Your desire not to seek out the glimmering rewards of the ego – to impress, to taunt, to gloat over others, for gluttony, selfishness and so on, are no longer your pursuits."

"You seek truth beyond all else and it is your place of right as much as any other soul to find it. And so, it brought you, and Anna, who embodies selflessness to a place of greater experience. Your time to come upon the higher realms is near and it closeness helped you and Anna to arrive at its energy level, even while in the Subtle Domain."

"When!" exclaimed Robert, brimming with excitement. "When"

"After the dishes are done Robert, after the dishes are done."

So Bright the Light upon My Mind's Eye

After the simple chore was completed the souls retired to the outdoors. Gordon did not seem content to sit on the bench and as Robert was full of anticipation he followed his teacher's lead, walking down the cart path to the road alongside the cliffs.

Robert was perplexed by the action, walking for no apparent reason. He chose to not question. After reaching the road they followed it along in the direction that the old man and the horse and cart had travelled after dropping Robert at the cottage.

Gordon had arrived at the cottage from the same direction, and Robert wondered if he was retracing his steps, back to the place that he had come from. It seemed strange to him though, that the higher realms should be just over this hill or that. He reckoned that such reasoning was nonsensical, that his journey to a place of greater understanding, of light and of a higher order, should simply be walked to.

Robert had seen enough now of the places of the spirit to know that other worlds were of thought, and not locations on a physical map. He sensed that Gordon was probably just favouring a walk after the large meal, to feel more comfortable.

"Robert, as you are feeling, the transition to the light realms is a journey away from the trappings of the mind. They are realms where the ego has been discarded as an unwanted and unneeded commodity, something that simply slows one down in the muck of the mundane. With the freedom from the burden of jealousy, envy, hatred, and self aggrandisement, the mind is able to explore much more clearly the emotions of love, compassion, reason and selflessness."

Robert jumped in with a question that burned in his breast. "Will I discard the ego now Gordon; will I ever return to the Subtle Domain? Or for that matter the Earth?"

"Your journey has always been toward the light Robert and I can assure you that it is your destination, eventually. But, do not feel too great of haste toward that eventual migration, for your love of Anna remains here in the Subtle Domain."

Gordon went on. "You will be tasked with the decision as a point only on the way to your destiny. And you can't really answer it until you fulfill the weigh points along the journey to eventuality - with all the information that is required for you to evolve upon."

Gordon stopped and looked up at the dark late evening sky. He breathed in deeply a few ties and shook his hands a few times as if to shed unwanted energy. Robert's emotions seemed in tandem and he fell quiet inside, his mind at rest as if in a meditation. Emotion felt far away all of a sudden.

The two stood silently together. Gradually the tranquillity of the surrounding began to give way ever so slightly. The subtle multiplicity of vibrations that construct the Subtle Domain became evident, oscillating the way they do to create the fabric of the plane before them. The cliff side, the ocean, the rolling hills and roadway, all became evident by having their component energies revealed.

As the energies transitioned Robert felt a glow of contentment that swelled to become an all encompassing aura around and throughout his being. A contentment and peace that revitalized him and that can revitalize any soul that has tasted the judgement and competitiveness of the physical plane, now being shed.

The contentment felt was all encompassing and it was simultaneously forgiveness and empowerment, a sense of having had a right to having been a human being with its many faults, and a right to being an evolving soul able now to come home to the kinder, wiser, higher realms. Robert fully surrendered to the sensational emotions.

He searched his mind for a term of reference and there was none. The closest experience he thought of was the time when childhood gives way to adolescence for the first time and the person becomes aware of its existential potentialities. The initial sensations realized are extremely powerful and herald the arrival of a new time in life, or, in this case, of existence.

Robert felt oneness with the Subtle Domain all of a sudden, the place he had found to be foreign when he first came to it, and that now seemed to be a place entirely and essentially his own home. A home now being left, but that was one that had wonderful qualities of acceptance and peace enough, for one to find their place and reason. A place of non-judgement where the cast is set for exploration of the only real motivator, the self, which eventually liberates one enough to take further steps.

The landscape began to break down in its apparent form and complexity. The scene of hills, cliff, sky and ocean became unfocused and no longer had its sharp and brilliant hues. It gave way to a maze of points of light, as if millions and millions of tiny bright lights had suddenly been turned on. Once alight, the landscape of the Subtle Domain became entirely absent.

To adjust, Robert closed his eyes and then opened them to an entirely unified light spectrum, with the individual points of lights making an envelope of blazing light that surrounded him and his teacher. The hue like a bright day where to frequent use of sunglasses leaves the eye very pained to look at the light of day. Not quite a pain, but a definite discomfort hard to manage and resolve.

Robert let out with an instinctual reaction by laughing wildly, although well into the event he realized that the process was only occurring in his own mind. He knew, thought, that he had not been alone in that process. He recognized, somehow, that Gordon had also been laughing in his mind.

More importantly, he knew the event was powerful enough that it had even swept up his seasoned teacher. Robert thought that even a master could not but be overcome with love and the laughter that it inspires when fully engaged.

The light about the two was somewhat like the threshold he had experienced at the gateway between the ether and that had given way to the Subtle Domain. But this experience was far more omnipotent and intense. The luminosity settled to permit limited vision, and enough for Robert to see they were standing on a marbled terrace that led to a few steps and the outline of two Greek styled temple pillars.

He wondered aloud in his mind "Am I in Heaven?" The concept seemed at once silly, after all, wasn't the entire spirit world sort of Heaven?

Gordon, ever the teacher, spoke to Robert's mind. "Patience, we will be met in a few moments." The intense luminosity began to settle as Robert's eyes and emotions began to settle to the surroundings. Greater depth of vision and detail began to emerge.

A figure appeared in Robert's line of vision in the direction of the stairs and temple like pillars. The figure was that of a woman and through the fog like distortion of the surrounding brightness, he could see outstretched arms presented in a welcoming way as the figure approached. He resonated with the strong sense of love and acceptance all about him. An apparently everlasting and quite complete, love.

As the figure arrived to him and Gordon, Robert noticed the woman's fine features. He placed her look to be that of a person about thirty, although her appearance seemed transient between a youthful look that can't quite progress on to adulthood; retaining the beauty of radiant youth. A warm smile spread across her well featured face.

"Welcome travellers, I am Tawna." The greeter's outstretched arms enveloped Gordon in a welcoming embrace that included a kiss to his right cheek. She then embraced Robert, kissing him on the left cheek, and squeezing his right arm strongly as she released him.

As the brief embrace ended Robert looked down at the shorter woman's face and noted the appeal of her shaggy blondish hair, rich full healthy skin, and perfectly symmetrical bright white teeth. Her lips were ample and again perfectly symmetrical, rising in the centre of the upper lip to a crest where the two sides joined at the slight indentation to suggest her youthful sensuality.

Tawna's eyes were evenly spaced and her eye brows were slightly darker than her sandy blondish hair. They presented a lovely contrast to her light, sandy brownish eyes that were sandwiched between the pure whites, and together, they cast a vision of healthy beauty. Her nostrils were smallish and the button of the nose was turned up, just slightly.

Her figure was approximately five foot six inches tall and while her breasts were not large but were well rounded and firm. Robert noticed them as he did the tan coloured skin of her shoulders, arms, and legs beneath a simple short dress that fastened as a collar around her neck, and pleated as it covered her upper chest and breasts and flowed on just past Tawna's waist, hips and upper thighs.

The garment design allowed Tawna's tanned and healthy skin to show along her upper back and perfectly shaped legs. As she turned to lead the two souls Robert saw viewed her shapely figure and rounded buttocks. The package presenting, that was the soul Tawna, was lovely in every respect. He noted her appearance not from a point of sexuality necessarily, but, as evidencing a spectacular example of the human form.

Nonetheless, Robert registered that he was attracted to this soul with her girl next door look mixed with stunning beauty. There was something more though. Perhaps it was the warm greeting that instantly coverts a stranger to being an acquaintance, or the similarity of chemistry that allows someone you just met to be the kind of person you know you are going to invest in to get to know. Or, perhaps, it was that Robert knew that he had just embraced with a soul far more in advance than himself.

Whatever the composition of elements, Robert was charged with energy beyond just being an eager and fascinated leaner in a new place. He felt youthful and full of adventure, once again the novice in a new environment and the sense of mystery of who Tawna was, and what her story was all about, was ripe in the air about him.

Tawna led the two souls towards a few steps and as they mounted them Robert's eyes had fully adjusted to his new surroundings and were now accustomed to the luminosity of the light realm.

Once up the steps and onto the promenade between the two Greek like columns the three walked under and through a covered walkway and onto a larger terrace that permitted a panoramic view of a large city below. Robert gasped, raising his arms up and then letting them fall to his side in a gesture that suggested acceptance of disbelief.

The view presenting was spectacular not just because of the dimension of the city seen below, but also because of the symmetry of the presenting structure. Robert had no point of reference for the appearance of the city, and nature before him.

The sky was a peculiar hue of light blue, almost turquoise. It was criss-crossed by a grid of bright white lines like those of longitude and latitude on a globe of the Earth. The sky sat above a flat landscape that carried off to the distance as far as the eye, or even the mind, could see.

A multitude of buildings could be seen stretching out to the far distant horizon, and off to the right towards what appeared to be a mountain range far, far off. Robert searched his mind for a reference, and decided the scene from his memory that seemed most appropriate as the Bonneville Salt Flats in the United States. The luminosity resonated much like the air above the flats slightly distorting the view owing to rising convection currents of hot air, distorting the outline of the distant mountains.

He wondered why the sky should have a grid set out upon it, but wasn't quite ready to start asking questions, intent instead to use his senses and powers of observation to continue to gather in information about the vast scene below.

Robert looked at the buildings more intently and scanned those up close first, and then the rows that followed in-behind in ever increasing depth. There were squares with trees situated every so often along the main arteries and where they connected. Along the roadways he could see tiny figures moving about, many in pairs. There were no vehicles, just multitudes of figures moving about.

Off the to the left a good distance away was a large round structure that he assumed was a coliseum – and was so large that he thought it must hold tens of thousands. To the right was a large columned square structure that was massive and so stood out. It had an enormous open air plaza and an officious look to it.

Where the three stood was not so much a terrace Robert reasoned, as it was a granite floor set on top of a hill that was topped by those Greek columns and its roof structure, like a temple. An arrival station for souls arriving from the Subtle Domain perhaps, or elsewhere he wondered.

Tawna seemed patient and relaxed with the new arrivals, and Robert did assume his status was as a new arrival, and that his teacher must have been in the light realm before. Tawna stood relaxed, her arms at her side and a slight smile sat upon her face, one of peace and contentment. She looked out at the same scene as the two guests, in a respectful way that signalled that Tawna too was impressed by the vista, even though she may have seen it a hundred times before.

Gordon was the first to speak. "Shall we walk a little? Tawna, I think our friend would like a nice cup of coffee."

Robert's head shot up and he smiled enthusiastically, feeling some dry wit forming in his mind. "Ah, am I that easy to figure out? I like this Heavenly place, you guys think of everything."

Tawna shrugged her right shoulder up and forward to motion the two to follow her in a gesture that did set the three in motion. They walked down a six foot wide series of stairs to the left of the granite platform and onto a path that wound its way through a lovely forested area with a slight descending incline.

After walking under large palms and alongside areas with lovely lush and brilliant flowers of red, pink and yellow petals they arrived to a walkway in front of the first series of buildings.

A few more steps and they were on a large boulevard that headed directly away from the arrival platform behind them and up the slight hill. Robert turned to look back at it and its ceiling visible at the top of the treed hillside, as if wanting to demark a point of reference for future navigation purposes, either geographically or as a point in time when something important had happened.

The three's walking pace was relaxed and the temperature felt almost tropical to Robert, he felt warm and as if a garment or two could be shed. The time of day felt like mid-afternoon when the temperature should be at its height. The style of motion was that of three new acquaintances, moving with respect for the space needed to accommodate each other, in paces that were carefully designed not to infringe upon another, with Tawna in the middle, Robert to her right, and Gordon to her left.

"Tawna, tell Robert of this world, I know he is dying to ask you about the sky grid." Gordon smiled widely as he spoke.

"Well, everything is dying to get here, isn't it Gordon." He and Tawna broke out into a spontaneous laughter and Robert chuckled a little, suggesting that he understood the joke which he did, a little.

He said "I thought that people died and went to the Subtle Domain. I, uh, hope that you don't have to die there to, to be able to come here?" Robert's comment contained a little real concern.

Tawna answered him. "Ah yes, fear of death, of the transition, because of the unknown. Funny, when you think that those on the physical plane fear death because they don't know what lies behind the door of the event of dying? While for those in the Subtle Domain, and for Buddhists for that matter back on the

Earth plane, they fear having to live again, as it too has a doorway that leads to the unknown."

Robert thought back to Andrew, who stayed in the Subtle Domain assisting others to find their path, but not wanting to cast his fate in a dice toss of having to live again. He didn't want to risk his refinements through the potential for the careless circumstances fate can inflict that might lead him to be something less. The twin brace of pistols that karma, and the actions of others, can unleash.

"No Robert, all who have travelled here have lived a physical dimension life at some point, and did so prior to their eventual journey here." Tawna's voice was sweet and genuine.

"The migration to the light dimensions for some on the physical plane though, is direct. They are ready and the pursuits of the Subtle Domain are unneeded because they are unwanted. For those whose journey need not hold them to the desires of the physical body, with its wants and needs, they come to this plane of greater enlightenment and its focused pursuits."

"They have transcended want and need and are best suited to the desire for greater knowledge. All here pursue knowledge in one form or another."

"One form or another..." Robert mused.

"Yes, such as music, philosophy, mathematics, science, poetry, metaphysics, spirituality, and many others Robert. Archimedes, for example, feed from life by the point of a Roman soldier's sword, had no need for a spirit world such as the Subtle Domain with its many distractions. His pursuits are in the interests of pure mathematics. He seeks the truths of the symmetry of the underlying universe. Geometry and calculus, a perfect language whose logic is rhythmic, constant and in itself a great mystery that unfolds in simplistic beauty as it unravels to the curious mind that pursues it. And so, Archimedes pursues it with no Earthly interests needed to interfere."

"In fact, he can be found most days in the Hall of Academics toiling in ever increasing complexity, still using the tools of the ancient days on Earth to measure, calculate and consider."

"Today?" Robert was surprised.

"Oh yes, today. Many of the great thinkers and learners of your time, that is, of the human kind on Earth practise their knowledge here. Lives intermingled not out of any relation to time as you knew it. They pursue associations related to their learning and experimentation desires. For example, Newton would prefer to spend his time in discussion with Einstein, more than a contemporary who only wishes to muse about 17th Century England. "

"Are they here now?" Robert quipped.

Tawna chuckled deeply so that her shoulders pressed forward, and with her wide smile exposed her perfectly shaped, white teeth set behind her plush, full lips.

'Oh, I am not entirely sure Robert, many, many liberated souls are here, but role call isn't on my list of chores I am afraid to say. Well, actually I am delighted to say."

"I thought that those in the light realm had discarded the need for form, you know, human bodies represented in the spirit. But, we have bodies don't we." The question had just leapt out of Robert, and its arrival was out of context to the discussion the three had to date.

"There are many high light planes, or realms Robert. In fact, every level of existence is as it is, having been created from the energy of light. However, as you think of the higher realms, yes, they are of pure thought and in that environment there are the masters who no longer manifest their being with bodies. Not as we see them here anyway."

Gordon joined in the discussion. "Yes, there are masters who have evolved beyond the material and the spiritual, to the place of omnipotent understanding. Their ability to reason has given them the miracle of pure understanding. They are the Buddha, the Christ, and others who meditate in a place of knowledge that has transcended all but the purest of considerations related to existence."

Tawna spoke next. "They are of everything and nothing, for everything and nothing are but one, in the truest reality. As nothing bore everything, the cause is the effect, and so the effect by nature must contain the elements of the cause. You see, embracing nothingness means that you are no longer bound to the servitude of the material."

"Even to the material thing of knowledge as souls on this plane are imprisoned to seeking, is but a pursuit of something and still contains elements of the ego. The beings of the high light planes are contemplative souls, forever engaged in meditation with the peace of being freed from all of the materialism of the phenomena that we call somethingness – that is, the Universe."

Robert thought back, remembering that Buddha on Earth had said that the true reality was nothingness and that existence was an illusion. He remembered that physicists had speculated that the Universe was a large hologram from which consciousness could experience. And hadn't Gordon told him about how the realization of "I am" had caused existence out of nothingness; existence as a vehicle to answer the question of "what am I"?

He made a realization and let it spill out. "I get it, as nothingness is the true reality it is meaningless to occupy oneself, to obsess over materialism, as it is an illusion." He stopped walking for a moment as the realization settled in and he said it again to himself in a low voice "Obsessing over material things is pointless, because in reality the true existence is nothingness."

Gordon looked at Tawna with a little twinkle in his eye, and placed a hand on Robert's shoulder, in part to return him to their slow pace of walking.

"Well, it takes a lot of time to give up the material and spiritual Universe my friend it takes a lot of time. And yes, for the masters in the high light realms they have been able to advance far enough in thought that the only currency of endeavour is consciousness."

Tawna added in. "Robert, your consciousness is in every way as valid as the maters, or anyone or anything. You reason, you consider, you search, you seek knowledge. To love, to live, to like things, those are all valid and should not be ignored, devalued, or make you feel diminished or, well, guilty."

As Tawna finished the sentence, Gordon had turned slightly and with a motion of his left arm and hand, offered his companions to enter into a building. Robert knew at once what that meant, it was time for coffee. He was an eager participant and led the way into the establishment. Tawna and Gordon followed.

Robert gathered in the type of bistro it was and after a few looks to his left and right, placed his hands against his upper back and leaned back slightly. He raised his head a little as if to stretch his neck and he said "hmm" a few times.

Tawna had approached a server and ordered a cappuccino, Gordon said make it two and not seeing any reason to be a rebel, Robert raised his right hand with three fingers stretched out. Gordon had taken a large brownish muffin and placed it on a tray. He noticed Tawna's glance and so placed another on the tray, then a third. Robert fetched some butter and three knives, then a small glass bowl with what appeared to be raspberry or strawberry jam.

Tawna turned and had three large mugs in her hands, topped off with foam. She bent forward slightly as she carefully manoeuvred the treasure as if she might just get them to the table that Gordon and Robert had now taken to. She placed the mugs on the table and slid one over for each Robert and then Gordon; the latter of whom reciprocated by sliding a plate with muffin on it to the right of Tawna's steaming mug.

Robert waited politely until Tawna had settled into her chair and clutched her mug handle to draw the foamy content to her mouth. He then drew up his own cup and allowed a generous amount to spill into, and fulfill the expectations, of his waiting pallet. The flavour was rich and poignant and delivered a full reward.

A second healthy gulp followed and before it was swallowed Robert was swirling he mug to gage how much of the precious content remained to be looked forward to.

Didn't matter he thought to himself, one way or another – in this realm where need was cast away from the manifest of the soul – he was going to have another.

Gordon and Tawna had located the knives and were drawing butter across a half of the divided muffin. Gordon decided upon jam to top it his muffin off, while the hostess had skipped the step and proceeded directly to a first bite. Robert skipped both steps and broke off a large chunk politely and sent it on to his mouth in a speedy fashion that avoided dropping crumbs on the table top or onto his glowing spirit cloth.

Robert ate politely and his mood turned to being jovial. He smiled slightly and turned to Tawna saying "…well, what is there to do in this fine place?"

Tawna turned to him and replied "I'd like to take you both to a group discussion today Robert. There are many, many seminars and talks that occur all over the city, but I'd like to take you to one on altruism."

"Altruism…altruism, interesting." Robert wasn't at all sure why the subject was interesting but searched in his mind for context. What was the definition of altruism - just being a giving person?

Gordon piped in to give some context. "Altruism - as in the principle or practice of unselfish concern for or devotion to the welfare of others and which is really the opposite of egoism."

Robert could guess the relevance to his visit to this higher realm. Egoism holds the soul back from its progress; it is bound in materialism and serves only the self. The ways of the spirit, of consciousnesses development to a true state of being able to understand its true nature is hindered by the ego.

Altruism represented the opposite, devotion to others and their welfare through compassion and giving allows the pursuit of consciousness to be the souls' focus, rather than being a side show. Along with that, the ability to uplift those less enlightened – in a way inspirational to the masses toiling about in their self-interest, at times collectively moves consciousness forward as a whole.

"Ah…the pursuit of altruistic intentions, action, and the change that it makes in others, and so, in us…" Robert exclaimed.

Tawna and Gordon's heads popped up and a slight smile was on both of their lips. Tawna clapped her hands together to show applause and Gordon mimicked the action. "Yes, Robert, yes, that is a lot of what will get discussed today." Tawna lifted her cup and motioned it toward Robert in a gesture of toasting him and then sipped a few times at the brew inside.

"After our coffees we'll wander over to the 'Light in Life' square and join in with the others. Zandu is the guest speaker today and will moderate the discussion. He is a very wise and old soul, and in his last life was an instructor at the University in New Delhi. A fine soul and a good friend indeed and has a love of lecturing."

The three finished their coffee house visit in quiet, watching politely the other patrons and the way new acquaintances do when the initial discussion of greeting and civility have run their course and more in-depth matters await the context of time being shared together.

Robert had finished his fill of coffee first and sat in a reflective mood as his companions slowly sipped theirs. He had a quiet in his mood and felt subdued and content. He reflected upon it and that perhaps this was the traveller resting before the next experience is staged and he was just awaiting the effort that would be required to go and explore it. Perhaps, he considered, he was just content in a safe place with the knowing that he would soon meet others who would impact his journey in ways large or small.

With their cups empty and side plates reduced to mere crumbs the ensemble of spirits rose and left the café. They walked in a manner that was a pace above casual strolling, led by Tawna, and that gave Robert the impression that they were on a time table of sorts. Nonetheless, the walk was by no means rushed.

Gordon had a slight grin on his face and looked as a tourist returning to a favourite destination; and now that the moment had arrived, there was great contentment. Robert couldn't help but blurt out a question.

"Gordon, have you been to the light realms before?" He waited eagerly for a reply.

"Oh, heavens yes, we've been here before." The reply left Robert perplexed and he rushed to inquire further, but Tawna cut in – inadvertently cutting short his line of inquiry.

"Gentlemen, we turn left here." With that the attractive sandy blond rushed across the boulevard and onto an adjacent cobbled road at right angles to the main thoroughfare the three had been walking on.

Robert and Gordon scurried to catch up to her and in doing so were soon at her heels, just slightly behind Tawna's quickening step.

"We don't want to miss Mr. Zandu's introduction to today's topic. I think it important if we are to contribute to the discussion, to make available our thoughts" she said.

A few thoughts were bouncing back and forth in Robert's mind in a sort of intellectual pong game. What did he have to contribute? Especially to a conversation he didn't even really know the topic of let alone and rules regarding debate and dialogue, that is, if there were any. He considered there should be in a respectable higher civilized context. Tawna's comments seemed strange, but he let them pass by assuming further information would be forthcoming.

He turned his thoughts to Gordon's statement. "We've been here before." What did that mean? Was it because without time and space in the spirit planes that all things exist side by side, and all times and events? If so, had he perhaps always been in the light realms – even when in physical Universe and Subtle Domain? Is that what Gordon had meant he considered?

Before he could re-enter the line of dialogue, Tawna wheeled to her left and onto the top of a rounded open amphitheatre. They found themselves on the top step, of many rows that descended down to a half circle speaking platform at the bottom. All made of stone, and with the stone rows doubling as seats, on which many souls were sitting, perhaps thirty to forty.

Tawna led them down a few step rows, and then smiling widely at two souls seated, moved to side step them and take up three spaces for she and her soulful companions.

Robert placed his hands between his legs and rubbed them gently together, palms open, and easily accomplished given the arch of his back sitting on the stone step seat.

On the speakers patio below a few souls were speaking amongst themselves. After a few minutes one of the souls, a large silver haired man came forward and with raised his arms, palms outward, towards the assembly. His face was pleasant and relaxed and showed a wide smile.

"Welcome friends, welcome. Make yourselves comfortable and available for our discussion today, is certain, to be lively and inspiring. We look forward to the journey we will share today together in knowing and understanding."

The soul moved back a few steps and let his arms drop to his sides. Then, with right foot slid back and behind his left, he swung his right arm gently up and back in a welcoming motion towards the two souls standing behind him and who he had been talking to.

"I am Michael, and today I take pleasure in introducing our guest speaker, a master and dedicated teacher, Zandu, who taught us at the time of the Buddha, and who teaches us still."

A polite applause followed, and the introducer gave way to the introduced, and he faded back as Zandu made his way centre platform. He had the dark hair and skin colour of the Indian sub-continent and it contrasted against the shimmering bright, white, of his spirit garments which were Nehru in style. The combination set an aura like glow about the soul and as he began to speak, Robert noted that his figure commanded considerable attention.

An Indian accent, refined with sound pronunciation presented. "And so, my friends, through generations and generations on Earth we have suffered, and struggled for survival. We have taken the whip of the master across our backs; we, the master and the sufferer both in one."

"Why does the sufferer continue to suffer so? For want, for the material things he will suffer, for power he will suffer, and for the illusion of the safety provided him by the surroundings of things. What shall he find instead? The destruction of the material things he sought after, the falling of his power, and the certainty of his death."

"His only safety comes in liberation for the want of material, the belief it will protect him, and the freedom of an enlightened approach to his beliefs so that he can view reality as empty, but for the presence of his own consciousness now aware of the futility of the material."

Robert found that he could follow along and agree with the words as they were spoken. After all, hadn't he heard the same message since his arrival at the cottage and what Gordon had said to him, and the journey they had taken together? He knew that ego was the binding harness, materialism but bait to trap the mind, and eventual emptiness, cold and stark, the certain eventuality of the physical, material universe; and that Universe - but a stage on which the play of experiential existence is enacted out to conclusion.

But why the terrible suffering he thought? Why the countless repetition of cruel acts, either by egotistical consciousness or manifested by nature itself? Why the competition for the small gains of intellectual turf? Couldn't there be a simpler, kinder way forward?

"Our way here, dear friends…" the speaker went on "…is a lamp post for those who travel the dark path of suffering. Our pursuit of knowledge, of reason and compassion and understanding, is the beacon for those still cast adrift in cycles of suffering."

Robert felt a sort of kinship with the words. On Earth hadn't there been the example of teachers whose desire for greater understanding and knowledge, to quest for the betterment of humanity, done so as an example to others? And hadn't their purpose often ended by being quashed by the evil intent of others?

He thought that true not just of the great teaches, the messiahs, but also those souls who did not claim high moral or spiritual origin or inspiration, but ordinary souls – as much as they could be described as such.

Ghandi, Mandela, and Mother Teresa as examples in seeking human compassion on behalf of others: Socrates, Galileo and Newton in science; Bethune and others in medicine - so many examples of those who risked terrible deaths to protect the innocents from the tyrants. Those who sought justice in spite of the face of tyranny - simply to lead the way with the strength of their convictions.

Each in their own way, the lives lived for the betterment of others were indeed inspirational and served as a testimonial to others to take the dangerous path of pursuing liberty for others, in mind and soul. Slowly, the advance of compassion has trodden on.

"Yes" Robert thought "...more so than the acts of evil of the great tyrants, whose energies spent, have only harmed that advance for a time and in the end are burnt embers extinguished by time and all that they stood for but tumbled pillars to the ground."

In his mind Robert could see many historical examples of leaders, teachers, and religious figures – all of whom had given some small gift. And what of the acts of kindness over time never noticed, or that are long forgotten. Had they not all provided a little, or a great, impetus toward the betterment of the condition of the living in mind and spirit?

Examples exist everywhere, like a neighbour who watches over the home of neighbour who is away without being asked or ever their having ever mentioned the careful observation. A stranger in a crowd who notices a child walking alone and perhaps lost in the throngs of others, who carefully watches over the child until they are certain that a parent is indeed nearby and available with an umbrella of protection should the child indeed be lost. The patron of a restaurant who notices a young couple without much means and so quietly pays their tab and leaves unnoticed.

Those acts of kindness, small as they are, may not be the great beacons of light urging consciousness forward along the great path of compassion, but, certainly they are candles lighting the way, through long journeys - and providing shelter against the cold dark nights of cruelty and selfishness.

Robert felt contentment with his assumptions; he felt he was getting "this stuff".

The soul lecturer spoke on:

"And from our vantage point of having advancing knowledge, do we not see in ourselves the ability to gift ourselves by venturing back to the living realm of the Earth plane to teach others? Is not the return to the realm of the suffering the greatest gift of our compassion?"

Robert's emotional self picked up markedly. "Go back to gift one's compassion" he thought hard on the prospect. The notion sparked alarm in him and his back straightened a little.

"My God" he thought "were the light realms spiritual recruiting grounds for spiritual missionaries to the physical planes?" Then, the notion didn't seem so nonsensical or unreasonable to him at all. Souls well versed in knowledge, compassion and the ways of the spirit would indeed provide guide posts to the multitudes of souls who might be enabled to embrace their own spiritual journey to enlightenment.

Robert breathed in deeply and let his thoughts sink in and be felt a little. Were souls in the Subtle Domain really all that different from those on the Earth plane? Not really he reflected, those on the spiritual side were really just displaced living souls by virtue of the absence of being associated – even encapsulated – in living tissue on the physical plane. They were just as prone to being selfish, spoiled, thoughtless, egotistical and inconsiderate, he supposed, as those on the Earth plane.

He understood that souls in the light planes were perhaps nothing more than migrants able to move on in their enlightenment because of their realization that hanging on to petty pursuits of materialism and ego were nonsensical, pointless. Yet, with pursuit of greater ideals, in a quest for knowledge and understanding, there was a meaningful way forward.

Somewhere inside though - he sensed that there must be more to the story of existence of consciousness to be told that just that. He wandered through his thoughts for an inkling of what was troubling him. The lingering thoughts melded together and formed a notion.

If knowledge and the pursuit of the true reality of existence were the goal posts to be reached in the light realms, but souls had to be encouraged to suffer the return to life to share their insights and wisdom, then wouldn't the absence of doing so be selfish on the part of enlightened souls? Would not the pursuit of knowledge be wasted if it weren't altruistically shared with souls still bound in materialism and ego in the physical?

n fact, for those who debated the day away in the light realms – but who were unwilling to share openly their discoveries – could not their entire desire for advancement be considered a selfish pursuit, and even considered an aspect of ego?

Yes, Robert thought, the very nature of seeking knowledge for one's own pursuits would be akin to seeking wealth where the end goal is only a reward for the self.

The teacher's voice picked up and echoed back and forth in Robert's private debating club mind as if taking up the challenge of the debate.

"So, along this journey to a higher self, we benefit from the example of the high masters. Where time stands as an idle and alien instrument, where all things are learned and given side by side as if placed on a great mural. Where to complete the great painting, all brush strokes provide a part of the whole, and where each brush stroke touches the next and the one before it, so that together the final image is drawn together."

"This understanding is known to some, the knowledge is complete, and the whole is complete, as will come to all in the symphony of the final time – in the time of the rejoining; as occurs with you, our new friend."

Robert's head shot up and then from side to side hoping to see one of the unfamiliar faces accepting the role of being the new arrival referred to. No luck, the teacher was looking directly at him and him alone. He felt conscious of the heads turned toward him atop bent, strained necks.

"Come friend join us here on the platform and make available to us your reasoning and its wisdoms."

Robert looked at Gordon to see if he would rise to his feet to answer the challenge just by virtue of his looking toward his teacher. Again, no luck, Gordon's eyes met Robert's with the expression written in them that he was expected to participate – if by no one else – then at least by his translucent instructor.

Tawna too looked over at Robert with a pleasant and encouraging smile so that her bright white teeth appeared draped by her perfectly symmetrical lips.

Robert slapped his palms down on his knees for re-assurance and then used them to propel his torso upward atop his feet.

He nudged his way past Gordon and the two souls next to the aisle so that he could descend the forty or so steps to the speaker podium-terrace below.

Once there the 6th century Master reached out a hand, but, it bi-passed Robert's outstretched hand and clasped around his forearm instead, just below the elbow. Robert returned the clasp in what he took to be an ancient version of the gentlemanly handshake.

After a long moment of single arm elbow embrace the two released. Robert's hand and forearm tingled vibrantly and he clenched and released his fist a few times. He had received a gift of energy, very definite energy, and it launched a sense of enthusiasm in him, almost replacing his natural shyness and unease at the coming dialogue.

"Tell us your thoughts friend, and of your journey." The words were loud, but soft in tone, and kind.

"Well, I am Robert, from, the Earth at the time of, the beginning of the 21st Century."

There was no reaction from the assembly. Robert wondered if his place of origin was unable to register in the points of reference of these other worldly travellers; or, perhaps he was the making of an 'other' worldly amateur night flop. He thought better of it, and took a little caution in choosing his next words. As they emerged, he felt more confident than he had expected.

"My journey is to find the light of meaning, and from which I will find my purpose. I seek the truth of reality and I seek knowledge; yet, I am torn because I do not know the course of things that are to follow, or that should follow, or, really, that I will follow."

"I don't know what the finding of knowledge will mean for me, or what I am to do with it, where I am to go, or be, should I find greater insight present in me."

"Interesting" said the lecturer "tell us more" and with that he stood aside and made a grand sweeping invite toward the crowd as if to thrust forward more thoughts from this novice guest speaker.

"Well, I am curious about, altruism. If we seek knowledge but do not locate it in selflessness for the benefit of others, is it altruism, or is it something else? Is it maybe just a function of selfishness, - that knowledge is acquired with great effort but is then only used to benefit or reward the self?"

A slight gasp filled the air, but more signalling the assembly's note of a profound remark than containing any kind of disapproval.

Robert went on. "Can we not place the desire for knowledge in a similar view to that of materialism?" The gasp returned, a little enhanced.

'Yes, the pursuit of the ego and the material are the pursuits of the self are they not? Distorted, and hindering to the soul. Yet, when knowledge is the sole pursuit, the sole endeavour to strive for, as in this place, but not passed on willingly and enthusiastically by those that have attained it, is that not also a form of the pursuit of the self?"

'I mean, what other context is there? Is such pursuit not the same as those in the Subtle Domain who pass the days away in what pleases them? If knowledge is not pursued for the purpose of the enlightenment of the whole, then it is but for the pleasure of the wholes constituents; surely then, more representative of our divisions, than of our unity."

The words had just sort of tumbled out, from where he really didn't know. Robert just assumed they had been forming in his unconscious as it had considered the context of the lecture, and that his finding of a voice with confidence had propelled them forward.

The assembly grew silent, the lecturer stood motionless for a moment, and then another. Robert suddenly felt that he had gone too far, he looked up toward Gordon and Tawna and found they had taken to their feet, making their way down the steps towards the platform.

He felt exposed to the social elements, then a little angry. Hadn't this group asked for his opinion on things; well damn it, they had asked and he had given. End of story, he trumpeted in his mind.

He took a step back and in doing so Sileas turned to his side, presenting one half of his spirit body toward Robert and the other toward the assembly, as if to middle man the ensuing debate between the two.

Robert's anxiety gave way to curiosity as he looked up again to see Gordon and Tawna reaching the stage and taking up station next to him, a few steps behind. "What is going on?" he muttered to himself, searching for some form of context.

Just then a short and portly soul with a bald head - that rose above two puffs of whitish hair above each ear and joining at the back of the neck - rose to speak.

"Explain to us friend, how it might be that we are so selfish here in the light realm, where we seek truth through reason and through understanding."

As Robert collected his thoughts he saw Gordon and Tawna walk past Sileas's back and take up a stance just behind his left flank. Robert at first considered saying he was sorry and perhaps a misunderstanding existed, where a soul such as he, new to the light realm should observe far longer before joining such a discussion.

To his surprise, he admonished the strategy alongside a mounting confidence filling his belly. He'd been the learner and observer long enough, it was time to have an opinion, to put the knowledge he'd acquired to the test; no matter what may come, Heaven or hell.

"What I mean to say, what I believe…" Robert's words belied the nervousness public speaking can engender at its outset. "What I believe is that altruism is a difficult goal to achieve. At some level we are all selfish if only at a minute level. We proclaim our willingness to be rid of being selfish for the sake of others, but rarely do we achieve it, the lofty perch of true selflessness."

"The great irony, so I have come to learn, is that our surroundings, whether here or on the physical plane, in the Universe, or in the Subtle Domain, cause individuals to pursue something there are interested in - and often it is based on some self-need. I see us hang on to these things as if they are so very precious. The rich man to his wealth, the old man to his possessions, the reader to his books, the writer to his pen, the seeker to his journey, the lover to his partner, the academic to his studies, the intellectual to his knowledge."

Robert thought briefly of Andrew as the perfect example, a refined intellectual unwilling to return to Earth for his own growth and by doing so to put his fine living and vigorous discussions, food and wine, a. To risk the barrel of fate's pistol. Instead, he preferred to aid others along their path, and be co-dependent to their enlightenment rather than to face his own journey.

"Comment?" was Sileas only word. The same soul rose again.

"But sir, you must consider that our true mission is to experience, to learn and realize, through which…"

Robert, to his surprise and to that of all the assembly, cut the portly soul off mid-sentence. "…this sea of energy, this field that underlies all things, all planes, that records every other thing that is thought and done – as consciousness experiences all that it can."

"Well exactly friend." Another, much younger soul had taken to his feet, a few rows from the podium. "We here are seekers of knowledge. Our experience is to seek, to debate, and know that knowledge is an experience in true wisdom. You might learn that." The final sentence was meant to embarrass the upstart guest.

The crowd gave a collective chuckle that was part amusement and part arrogant self-assumption.

It only served to prod Robert on.

'Yes, exactly, you seek knowledge. What is the venue for passing it on to others?" Robert waited a moment or two to pass before explaining his point.

"I spent a life time not giving much, so that in the end I had little. I believe that giving to others is giving to all. How advanced would our comrades in this journey to enlightenment be if the collective wisdom of this place were shared in its entirety to the physical realm, to the Subtle Domain?"

Robert went on. "What mechanism connects the inertia here to the seeking minds there? If they were to join the journey to an egoless existence now, through spiritual enlightenment now, would that not provide a greater degree of experience to be realized? By not doing so, isn't the growth of knowledge and experience necessarily reduced?"

Sileas smiled widely and raised both hands; rubbing thumb and forefinger together he evidenced a point of interest had been reached. He joined the conversation.

"Ah, the challenge we face, the challenge we face - when does the leaner become the learned, and then onward, to become the teacher."

"Many times we have discussed the empirical validity of our assumptions – in history, on the Earth plane and the implications of the science in our physical and spiritual development."

"But as you know, my Earthly journey last was at the time of the Buddha. The great teachers on Earth have not been counted amongst the incarnate for fourteen centuries measured on the physical. I take our newcomers words to heart – thank you Ro'bert."

Sileas spoke Robert's name phonetically suggesting he was unfamiliar with the dialect that produced it.

"I have appreciated your thoughtful knowledge and placing a value on the sharing of that knowledge – rather than solely on its creation, interpretation and storage."

With these words spoken Sileas moved back a few steps and moved his left arm in a motion that swept Tawna and Gordon in toward Robert in a sort of huddle. He then turned and spoke to them.

"My friends, I would like to invite you to lunch in our villa by the ocean, can I count you amongst our numbers this day?"

Robert felt a sudden release in the protective tension in his soul body. He preferred the notion of a sea side villa and lunch to standing awkwardly trying to hold his own in front of a large number of slightly put off, if not out rightly irritated higher beings in a realm of pure thought and light.

Gordon and Tawna signalled their approval to the invitation and Robert moved his hands upward and then allowed them to fall to his thighs in a slapping motion, signifying a happy surrender to the proposed plan.

He had no way of knowing that Tawna was inwardly feeling great honor at the sudden invitation.

Sileas turned toward the assembly and spoke. "Dear friends, we will now take our leave and I must ask your forgiveness for our quick departure; but I beg you to continue the seminar and the discussion."

With that Sileas turned back toward his guests and with arms raised said "So then, passage for three" and with it Robert felt the scene of the amphitheatre and all the faces disappear. As it did he thought "...doesn't he mean passage for four?"

Considering Sailing

Anna ran her forefinger gingerly atop the child's forehead in a long and loving sweep. She looked down at the innocence of the face below hers, perfectly symmetrical large round eye lids covering proportionately the beautiful large brown eyes beneath.

She thought of how wonderful it was, that such a beautiful creation could have been made and how imperfect existence was that such a life could end so quickly on the physical plane. Only nine years old and Anna felt such an obligation towards the young soul to wake her gently from the sleep that helps guide the very young between the physical and Subtle Domain.

Anna quietly heaved a large breath and slowly pushed it out through her tensed, pursed lips. "How would she tell Robert" she thought to herself "how would she tell Robert".

The River that is the All of You and Me

Robert felt himself re-assemble alongside the others, and instantly sought to affirm his new surroundings, still largely unacquainted with travel at the speed of thought.

He made a quick count of his companions and found them to number three and with he being the fourth. For a moment or two he pondered it strange that Sileas was poor at math, but let it go as he was distracted by the surroundings, and they were spectacular.

The group stood on a platform which was actually an upper floor looking over a jagged rocky cliff that culminated in a long sandy beach. The white sand along the curvy shoreline met a darkish blue ocean that rolled in a light rhythm that was neither calm nor rough sea, but rather, persistently vigorous and with a very slight white cap above the waves.

The structure they stood on top of was a terraced building with maybe 20 levels below, each jetting out twenty feet or so further than the preceding floor above it. The architectural design looked like a long rolling staircase ending at the beach far below. Robert could see small figures walking along the beach, moving in pairs or as singles – some away from the beach house towards the far end of the beach, others back towards the building. He gauged the distance from the roof top platform to the beach below to be about 600 feet.

As Sileas began to speak Tawna turned toward him while Gordon continued to look seaward, as if transfixed as sometimes occurs to a sentient being when memorized by the rhythmic pulses of the ocean, or the crackling of a fire.

"Welcome to our villa, a place of thought, reflection, rest and yes, sometimes action. Yes, sometimes great projects begin here, at least in their design and intent. "

"I would like to invite you to lunch and to spend some time in our company. Is that acceptable to you?"

Lunch sounded like a superb idea to Robert and he wondered what type of food would be offered at this place, and for that matter – in the light domain itself. Tawna smiled broadly and Gordon nodded politely and Robert noticed his manner as being almost flat, and then that his energy ebb and flow – that which gave him a distinct luminosity had changed ever so slightly.

Sileas waved his left hand in a sweeping motion toward an entrance way that was concreted and open aired, with what appeared to be wooden frames that sat where the concrete recessed revealing some language or symbols that were unrecognizable to Robert on the wall in which they were etched.

Once reaching the interior of the building a large rotunda appeared with a raised bench against walls made almost entirely of glass providing a magnificent panorama of the ocean and shoreline – the sun reflecting brilliantly off the ocean in the far distance where the sea met the horizon.

In the center area was a round sunken area with clothed sitting benches, topped by soft, attached cushions. A few souls stood and others were seated in what looked to be a casual pleasant discussion, paying no attention to Robert and the others.

Sileas led the party along a walkway that was made of small flat rocks set closely together in concrete leading away from the rotunda, round a wall to Robert's right and with the glass wall and sea on his left. After 20 meters they passed an observation lounge to the left, again sunken with the glass walls meeting the floor so that sitters had the impression of sitting at the very edge of the cliff.

Once past the second sitting area the foursome arrived at a staircase that spiralled down to the lower level. Robert hesitated a moment as the individual stairs appeared to be translucent panels made of a whitish energy. They became only distinct because of their blocking out the view of the floor they were descending to. His initial footing was tenuous, as he had no point of reference for manoeuvring such structures – like a person stepping on an escalator for the first time.

As soon as his footing was firm enough he walked gingerly downward, carefully noting his balance as beyond each stair he could see the floor and furniture below with no beam or hand rail to rest one's hand to prevent a tumultuous fall. Near the bottom, he stopped for a moment and reached his left hand outward, to his surprise, a section of handrail met his hand, glowing with a brighter whitish luminosity, greater than that of the stairs. It felt neither warm nor cold.

The group arrived at the lower level after having completed a full 360 degree spiral from the upper floor. The new level had a luminous appearance uniformly throughout and Robert saw souls sitting at equally luminous tables, being served by pretty female servers, themselves dressed in garments that showed the same degree of luminosity.

The scene was futuristic to Robert's mind rather than of some higher plane. Robert felt that somehow the appearance of an 'other' worldly technology was at play, and the scene appealed to him.

Sileas led the group a short way beyond the first few seated souls and past a dark wooden half-moon divide to a round table with chairs and the group took to seated positions. Robert and Gordon to the back of the table and Sileas to Robert's right and Tawna to Gordon's left and as they sat the two positioned their seats so that they could take in the view offered by the ceiling to floor windows.

Tawna spoke first, and softly. "It has been some time since I have been in the centre and I had forgotten is beauty and complexity."

Gordon nodded in agreement.

Sileas smoothed his hand along the table surface and raised it to his jaw, ever so slightly, with fingers at right angles to his palm so that the presented a platform to rest his head on.

"I have been here for several centuries of physical plane time, after my last crossing in the seventh century. I have preferred to be on the plenary committee as we have prepared informational exchanges for the Master's plane to the light realm and on to the physical plane."

Robert's head shot up a little with his curiosity peeked by some of the words, particularly those about exchanges of information from a Master's plane.

Gordon spoke for the first time, in some time. With a light voice he said "The high Master's plane, the realm of the most advanced souls, who throughout existence have overseen the recording of experiences in the field from which all is drawn."

Sileas, with his hands now gently rubbing together at the palm said "Yes, the plane where everything done, thought, and experienced is mirrored and retained. From it missions are arranged to a multitude of other realms to encourage, to mentor, and advancing consciousness forward - to guide and provide impetus to those beings, those souls, who are plodding toward greater enlightenment."

Gordon looking straight forward and almost emotionless spoke. "This is why you were invited here you stood out from the usual discussion, you understood."

Robert looked at Gordon and pulled his eyebrows down as the skin above his nose contracted – that look that registers being perplexed, if not concerned. Gordon had definitely changed in his oscillation and he seemed almost distant – as if he was phasing out to somewhere else. Robert was concerned.

Then as he looked at Gordon he felt Sileas's hand on his right arm.

"Yes Robert, you stood out. You knew that pondering knowledge for centuries is just rewarding a new phase of materialism. It is still the pursuit of the self, just in a way that collects less in the way of material possessions and more in the way of intellectual possessions."

"Our craft here is to receive, shall we say, suggestions from the highest realms and to see them delivered, as needed, in the physical realm. We are the conjurers of magic and mystery on a thousand, thousand worlds - slowly plodding consciousness forward. And, at times, we return with the Masters to ncarnations that are intended to provide large impacts in overall progress."

Robert mused a little and said matter-of-factly "Like Christ and his disciples."

'Oh yes" Sileas said "That is true, but ones like the disciples were those to be uplifted; and Simon Paul and the others were fellow journeyers who, through the inner peace they were available to find, assisted others to shed their stubbornness and allow new ideas to sweep in to their consciousness. And in turn, they shared insight with others, and so on."

"The veil of incarnated life blinds us to those true realities so that the obsession of ego has full reign to dominate and plunder. Much effort is required to break down that veil."

"But why is it so Sileas" Robert said "Why must the ego be given such a wide berth to have at it with creation?   Why couldn't all things have an equal footing, even opportunity for growth?"

Sileas shook his right forefinger toward Tawna and with a smile said "This one is a good one Tawna, this indeed is a good one."

"Yes, I was with him as he crossed" she added, smiling widely.

Robert reacted as one does when they realize they are the object of external scrutiny and they focus on the attention being paid them.

Tawna went on "His query and desire to seek the reality of his own purpose is unique and enduring. We felt that when he and the other joined together in the Subtle Domain."

As Robert frantically blurted out the words "do you mean Anna" Sileas suavely turned his forefinger and thumb as if turning a button into its hole, in front of his lips. The effect was instant, Tawna settled back into her chair rather than offering the words she seemed just about to say.

Sileas filled the sudden gap in communication. "And now, for the refreshment, I believe it has arrived."

As the last words tumbled out two pretty luminous servers appeared and rounded the half moon blind each carrying a plate in each hand. One was placed in front of Gordon and then Tawna by the closest server, while the other placed a plate in front of Robert and then Tawna.

Robert looked down at the plate from one direction and then the other, his head sifting to give the impression of "what on Earth is this?"

The plate's contents contained four rectangle and four square objects that appeared sponge like. The rectangles were coloured green, yellow, orange and red while the square cubes were three shades of blue, with two on the side of light blue and the third and fourth being a dark aqua blue.

Sileas moved his hand to suggest the guests to dive into their food – of sorts as it was – and they did – with Robert hesitating a moment to gather in context of how to proceed.   He looked over at Tawna and she eagerly pursued the green rectangle in her right hand, with a slight nibble at the dark bluish cube after taking four or five chunks from the green one.   Her ferocity was out of character for her fine, complete, and reserved nature.

With Gordon and Sileas each choosing a rectangle and cube Robert decided to join in. He took the green rectangle as Tawna had and bit off a fair portion. As it fell into his mouth his palate reacted to an amazing and full presence of taste. It was as if a fresh salad – with combined freshness and crispness – had arrived all at once.   The sensation was manifest delight.

He nibbled and then chunked off the dark blue cube and immediately recognized it as fast, fresh cold and satisfying pure water that was as clean and satisfying as he could imagine. He thought back to a trip at age 12 to Greenwood in British Columbia where the water was said to be as pure and clean – and tasteful – as any in the physical world.   "Amazing" he thought.

He worked through the other rectangles, saving the light blue cubes until the end, given the example of the others. The largest cube he had worked through was the red one that he reasoned most closely resembled a meal on Earth. The last bite tasted like seafood with a moist full taste whereas the initial sections seemed more like beef, then chicken.

The last two cubes were tastes of rich deserts, both creamy and soothing and as if each bite should be slowly enjoyed to ceremoniously honor the explosion of flavour.   As with his style of eating the last portion of dark blue cube finished the meal, cleaning the palate and throat.

As the meal concluded Sileas took on the role of tour guide again, leading his guests through several of the lower floors and eventually to the beach where the group walked for what must have been two or more miles before returning to the massive terraced villa a few hours later.

During the walk Robert had felt strangely morose, not really depressed or melancholy, just quiet as he walked slightly ahead of the others. Sileas and Tawna had talked quietly between themselves while Gordon walked astride them, saying nothing. As Robert could make out, Sileas and Tawna had talked about souls they were mutually familiar with.

Robert searched his soul memory for why he was feeling so solitary. Wasn't this journey to the light realm the time for learning on his ultimate path of knowing?

It occurred to him that Sileas and Tawna had information about him that they weren't sharing. While he didn't think that the two harboured any ill will, it troubled him all the same. The reason he concluded, was that he felt like a junior again, still less informed than others and again being an outsider looking in.

He was also puzzled at himself for not having thought more of Anna during his visit to the high realm. For a moment he considered that perhaps he hadn't loved her as he had thought. After all, they had only known each other a brief time – and both were seeking something more to enrich their seemingly incomplete existences.

Anna had said she had started to want to be with someone, and so, perhaps she had jumped prematurely at the first available soul-mate she came across.

As the thoughts twisted and gnawed at his mind, somewhere inside he knew this line of reasoning to be untrue. A rush of emotion swept over him and he looked up at the horizon. There, to his surprise was a bright dark reddish globe of a sun poised as mid to late afternoon, and a hot, arid wind blew across his face and took his hair back. He breathed in deep at the alien, strange landscape and sky he came to find himself in, in that moment. A moment where there is realization of an event that marks a transition in a person, in a soul, and that a point of departure had been reached.

Robert's soul body tingled and gave off the sensation of spiritual goose bumps, the innate hidden and sub-conscious realization that a truth has just occurred and been registered by the conscious mind.

He surely did love Anna.

He thought of her kind touches, her loving ways, her deep beauty and long dark hair, her perfect face and soft skin. His eyes watered so that a tear formed and ran down his cheek. He missed his soul companion suddenly, with full completeness, and he knew it was time to go back to her.

As the thought matured to resolve, Robert felt his left hand scooped up by a rushing Tawna and she pulled him hard enough that he was compelled to trot forward a few strides. Tawna turned to him so that she took both hands while facing him and said "come, Sileas has asked that we stay for a time and we have rooms on the second level".

Robert was startled and somewhat taken off guard. Tawna had been quite reserved and polite since their arrival and initial meeting in the light realm, and this was the first that he had seen emotion – and a burst of emotion at that. Then he thought, what does "staying for a time" mean?

Regardless, the table appeared to have been set so to speak and it intrigued Robert's curiosity. As Sileas and Gordon arrived at the entrance way to the bottom floor of the terraced villa structure where Tawna and Robert already stood, Sileas said "I have rooms for you all friends on the second floor, shall we go see them"?

With collective nods the group exited what appeared to be a run of the mill elevator and as the doors closed, they seemed to immediately open again to a floor that seemed to be a lone, very lovely, suite.

A large curved viewing area presented with couches offering a grand panoramic vista and bordered eloquently with a long coffee table and end tables between the sitting areas. Into the distance was the long blue canvass heading to the distant unseen horizon owing to the mist that forms when seen edge on.

To the right of the sitting area was a modern-esc kitchen designed for large eatery events – buffered by a long sitting bar and multiple stools with backs for comfort. To its right was a glass double doorway leading out to a concrete walking lane placed upon the rocks to allow a narrow, but spectacular view of the beach stretching on into the distance. The walkway allowed for sitting to its right – as if the architect had carefully utilized them for optimal effect.

Sileas said "Ah, here friends are all that you need. And here to the left are the resting rooms for your relaxation". The group followed him toward a long hall, marbled and with doors partially open every so often. Robert followed the way down, seeing sparsely furnished rooms that had but a bed, night table and lamp. The only windows found high, rectangular and without a view unless one were to stand upon the beds.

A sense of tiredness came across Robert and as he looked at the bed in one room it seemed to call to him with a voice he could not protest, and so with a polite nod of acceptance, he surrendered to its flat inviting surface. He fell almost at once into a deep sleep. The words of the others drifted away.

After a time he awoke, flipped over and stared at the ceiling. His first thought was that perhaps he'd missed something important with the group. The next thought, was that perhaps he'd offended the others by taking to such a complete and immediate sleep. He checked his mind and decided that those thoughts were probably nonsense – as rest is what he had been offered and found.

He looked upward at the window above his bed and to his surprise he saw light that indicated that late afternoon – even dusk had arrived. The light was reddish and his instinct was that a sunset was taking place. He rose to his elbows on the bed as he thought about a change in environment in the light realm, and that pushed him to a sitting position, and then to his feet.

He headed out the room and into the hall that led to the large sitting area. He looked to the door to his right onto the long flat sitting and viewing area next to the rocks. He headed there and once outside, found a comfortable sitting area and put his back to it, his legs hanging over the side so that his feet found a comfortable platform that agreed with his overall sitting posture.

Warmth met his face and body in the reddish light of setting suns and he took a deep long breath. He felt a deep contentment throughout his body and it led to a growing sense of well-being, that grew to laughter and he let some of it out, and then a lot. He took a moment to reflect on what he was feeling and the answer came rushing over him – he was happy, happy with light that bathed him entirely and that was of love. Love, not the kind that evaluates and experiences and then emits for and to another; but rather, a kind that exists in entirety and that was as complete as Robert had ever experienced.

Robert felt that love as warmth upon his body and mind and he had no point of reference. His head bowed, and a smile was across his face, and he thought "Yes, this is the warmth of love, complete love".

After a few breaths he said in a volley of laughter "My God, my God" as if the words themselves would moderate the sensation he was feeling. He turned his face from side to side to evenly bask it in the immersive rays of warm light. Robert closed his eyes to assist his adjustment to this new experience, and he could feel the warmth of the sun pressing into his eye lids, forehead and face, arms, legs and deep within.

It was the most wonderful sensation he had ever had.

Robert heaved a great breath in and pressed it out quickly so that he could draw another, even deeper. As he did his back straightened and a calm peace swept over him. The peculiar sun seemed to hold all that he had sought since his arrival in the Subtle Domain. "Perhaps" he thought "of everything I have sought since the very, very beginning.

Robert again sensed the tingling that signalled to him that he was in possession of a truth, an aspect of existence that was at the point of verification. He thought of the stories that sat on the shelf in the cottage. He remembered about his life a young Maori tragically cut short in an ill considered cliff drive, and of his death as a poor boy lost under an unforgiving sun in an Indian desert. Those words weren't just words bound in a dusty old book now – they seemed like memories of earlier events in a single life, distant, but still poignant.

The words read and deeds done from the books now felt like stepping stones along a long path and eventual destination point, which was where he now sat; all necessary steps to bring him to his current destination along to what appeared to him to be the time line of his existence. The experience was tremendous and he knew instinctively that a time of significance was upon him. He sat alone sweeping it in until the door to the suite opened and Tawna walked out and joined him.

Her hair was damp with the look of having just left the shower and not enough attention having been paid to drying it with a towel. Tawna was dressed in a one piece garment that was cotton like and that had an elastic of sorts across the top to ensure a snug fit along the top of her chest while leaving her shoulders bare and flowing down to her upper thighs, leaving her legs bare as well.

She smiled at Robert and as she came close, her lovely lips curving upward at the sides – revealing again her perfect white teeth – the glow of her radiant and sun darkened skin and sandy colored hair and eyes, created a stunning aura of a human figure. The reddish glow of the distant orb perfectly suited the appearance of health and youthful womanhood – present in her skin and sandy hair and eyes. Robert was amazed at her beauty, and that as a figure of a woman, she was to him, perfect.

Tawna placed her hands just above her knees as she took up a seated position next to Robert.

"I have seen this only once before and I thank you."

Robert chuckled a little and said "No problem", not having a clue as to why Tawna should thank him for anything."

Perhaps, he thought, she was just appreciative to have another soul to share the event with. Robert knew that feeling well enough when he was alone on Earth; how a splendid scene of nature was proportionately diminished when there was no other to share it with, to discuss and remember the beauty of the moment, to share the sensations of the event.

The two souls sat together in silence for a time, each with the radiant red glow upon their face and a hot wind across their body that carried a very slight wisp of sand that gave more of a sense of a desert close to equator than of a tropical humid climate.

Eventually, Robert broke the silence. "Tawna, how long have you been here, what is your life story, or would it be better to say, soul story?"

The ever pleasant soul turned toward him so that the wind blew her now dried and somewhat tangled sandy hair across her beautiful face.

"I am somewhat of an anomaly Robert. My pattern of existence is very different than most others. I and those like me are called 'children of the light'. My soul was first born here in the light realm and all but a short series of incarnations have been spent here, amongst these souls."

"I did live on Earth for a short while, perhaps three lives, serving in the court of the Pharaohs of Egypt as a maiden to the high priests who worshiped Ra, the Sun God. The last was during the realm of Auknaten. During this time a strong connection existed empathically between the priesthood and the light realm. Those within the order and close to them could feel the presence of the afterlife and their religion aligned to it. They were able to draw knowledge directly from here to there and as a result the guilds were able to build great structures and excel in mathematics and astronomy."

"My kind's only purpose was in support of the Earthly soul's journey to the light realm and after a time our resonance allowed the priesthood to develop the direct empathic connection to the higher beings here. That made them very powerful of course and permitted them to transition the Pharaoh and themselves to the light realm."

"After a time, human jealousy, envy, and hatred took hold and the priesthood order was destroyed and with it, worship of the Sun God, that really only used the Sun as a symbol for the light realm. By the time of the 23rd century before the Christ visitation the connection to the light realm was severed and with it, my time on the physical plane."

After Tawna had playfully swayed her feet forward and back, and from side to side a few times, she rested her outstretched hands behind her and added "Our kind, children of the light, have always served in the higher light plane, helping those on the Earth or in the Subtle Domain to ascend to this plane and occasionally we witness ascension to the highest realm; the realm of the Masters where the physical world, the spiritual world, and the ego's pursuit of the material and its quest for knowledge no longer have any meaning or context."

Robert reflected back on Tawna's comment during the meal they had shared with Sileas of her seeing his crossing and of his "joining with a companion". He felt compelled to ask Tawna on this point. In reply, she said "The union of two souls is a sacred event and is completely different than just a physical union on the physical plane. Yes, the energy shared between you and the soul Anna registered – that is – was felt in the higher planes."

"I feel very shy about that" Robert said, his face blushing even in the sun's red glow about the two.

"Oh no, no, Tawna said "this wasn't like an unwanted viewing or observation, the luminosity of a joining as you experienced is a very powerful exchange that sends a ripple across the fabric of the Cosmos – of the very fabric of existence – and even more so in the light realm."

Tawna paused for several moments, and after looking downward as if to carefully select her words said "You see, nothing is more dynamic in existence than the joining of souls together. So the Masters have said – at the time of the beginning consciousness and the Universe were born, created, came to be, and in the end time, after the turning of the wheel, the cycle is complete, consciousness again becomes one. One in completeness, one in beauty in love and in light – and when you and the soul Anna came together – your joining was as this end time. You glowed with the luminosity of completeness."

Robert felt a tremor throughout his soul body as it registered another incredible truth. He gazed at the distant hot sun and coastal landscape in amazement – with a unique and powerful sense of coming of age that far eclipsed those that had led his evolution previously. This was the maturation of the very seat of his soul and being.

The realization now in full bloom was that the completeness of the spiritual essence is not the materiality of the physical plane or the ego's long march through successive failures and successes, nor through the gaining of knowledge and wisdom. Instead, it is in the bonding of one soul to another and in the love and affection, humility, kindness and empathy that can connect one soul to another.

It dawned on Robert in this moment that for the Universe the scale of the consciousness that is able to evolve to manifest kindness and empathy is beyond enormous as it ranges into infinity. Consciousness being given individuality to initiate the process of learning through experiment, growth through trial and error and liberated through free will and determinism – and limited only by the expression of that free will to explore and adventure.

Once complete that the symphony of multiple points of expression becomes bound together by love. In the end time, the symphony becomes a crescendo as the points of individuality, of souls, recombines into a collective of experiences that forms one sole body of knowledge.

The door to the second floor of the complex unexpectedly swung open and Sileas, draped in a bright red Tibetan Monk robe, presented and walked to the two sitting as they were. With his back turned to the hot red sun he outstretched a hand to Robert and said one word, "ready".

Robert gathered together the pieces of a thought he recognized as an intuitive cognition - and he knew that Sileas invitation was for one last grand journey. His only hesitation was to wonder where Gordon was and if he would join the adventure.

Robert rose and met Sileas hand with his own, as they met the seascape, building, red sun and Tawna disappeared.

He was back in the void again.

The Realm of the Masters

Robert sought to gain perspective. His normal inventory of senses produced nothing that registered input. What seemed like a few minutes past but the sensation of time seemed nonsensical. This, he thought, was a place where time has no meaning, no bearing, and no points of reference. Time suddenly became obvious as only a construct of the physical Universe to be companion of the other three dimensions of height, width and depth – retained in the Subtle Domain and even the light realm to allow context - but only a construct, fleeting and disappearing in this realm.

Robert reached his thoughts out to grasp onto his own points of reference. He projected into the void and scanned the opaque for a horizon. As he did he began to recognize some structure, deciding it was either real or just his own mind needing to find a definition of the space. He decided the latter and as he did, the sense of being above an immense flat plateau formed in his mind – set atop a mountain with an enormous mountain, vast at the base. The surrounding environment he reasoned was light blue-greyish tone and extending to and above distant ridges.

With the perception that the realm had some form, he then realized he did not. His soul body was not evident, which he thought was a reasonable explanation why he was not registering any information from the senses. He was pure spirit, thought only.

The realization gave no sense of distress or alarm, or fear; only a sense of contentment as his current location – if it could be called that – was the absolute antithesis of peace, calm and acceptance. No doubt existed here, no judgement, no desires, and no ambition.

As his mind searched his mental horizon Robert felt a presence approaching at a distance and as it did, he was engulfed in joy and love that completely overtook him. Robert knew that even a concept of respect for this entity had little meaning. He was in the presence of the same grace as the Christ, of the Buddha in liberation.

He was at the very source.

Robert's first sensation was of being youthful in the presence of spirit infinitely older and wiser, infinitely wider. The sensation gave way to the notion of a validation of being, his being. In turn, that sensation yielded to one of being entitled to be in the presence of a spirit so immense. The audience he was experiencing with this awe inspiring spirit was his entitlement, and the sensation he began feeling when sitting with Tawna, of being complete, was now fulfilled in entirety.

The entity of the Master did not speak to Robert in voice or thought; instead Robert felt his own mind and consciousness unfold revelations. He was welcomed to this experience because he had determined to reach truth about his existence. While Sileas had assisted his transition, the audience was intended for him.

Robert's readiness was confirmed by his experience joining with Anna and the unison that had connected their souls. His journey was now upon a different path. The student surely no more; he had finally crossed over to being the teacher. Robert intuitively sensed that he did not need to reflect on why or for whom he would teach – those moments of understanding would come in the experiences ahead. Those experiences ahead, were the greatest gifts of all now.

With the Master entity at his side the sensation of being over a great plateau expired and he saw himself in a darkness that felt like the depth of space he and Gordon had gone to in the end time of the Universe.

Instead of the fear and horror he had felt then as the light had gone out of the Universe, Robert now felt overwhelming glee as at first a few, then many, then millions and then many trillions, of speaks of light appeared and began to turn about a spiraling centre.

The appearance was of a galaxy turning in space, drawing its arms inward to the core. The light intense and radiating pure essential love – like the happiest moments experienced in a life time but to a massive exponent.

These, Robert knew, were the individual souls that were the sparks of the creation coming back together in the end time; having leapt into creation from the initial query of 'what am I', to the fulfillment of the expression 'I am' in the end time. The 'I am' constituted from many, many parts now come home from the multi-dimensional Universe and the realms of experience and knowledge of the physical and spiritual.

This time, this experience, this event as it unfolded was completeness in its entirety. Robert knew that this time stood side by side with all other times, and being not so much an end time – but the time when completeness should occur – like all the ticks of a clock face that are required by process - to complete the swing of the hands back to the moment when they first began to move.

Robert gazed in amazement for a long, long time, unable to look away. The spirit entity next to him seemed as transfixed in silence and wonder. This place and time was of spiritual equality. All were one.

Eventually Robert's eyes grew heavy and he lapsed into what was like a deep sleep. When he awoke, he was on the sleeping nook in the cottage by the sea.

One and One as One

Robert lay on his side, surveying the cottage interior, his emotions uncommonly flat for the experience he had just witnessed. He winked a few times and rubbed his hand across his eyes and the cheek not pressed against the pillow. Maybe had had just dreamt it all.

His mind reflected on the experiences he had since arriving at the cottage; his making of meals, his drinking port as he sat sitting gazing out at the chaotic storms on the Sea of Chasms and the multi-verse that appeared and unfolded in front of the fireplace hearth with its complex entanglement of cause and effect manifestations.

Then it occurred to him, Gordon, where was Gordon?

He rolled from a lying to a sitting position, looked out the small window above the sleeping nook toward the grassy slope leading toward the cliff edge, then stood. Had his teacher left him, after all the Master entity presence had left him with the conclusion that teacher was now his role to fulfill. Had his teacher ever been there at all?

Robert turned on his heels and headed for the door. Once outside he surveyed the front of the cabin and the cart path down to the road as it led in from the interior where he had initially come from, and away along the cliff edge where Gordon had arrived from.

He rushed to the back of the cabin to the garden area, and there, by the old tree stood Gordon. Robert heaved a deep sigh of relief; his experiences were as real as his mind told him they were. A flood of questions popped into his mind followed by the need to relay the full weight of the experiences since they had last been together, of the Master realm and spirit which had verified the earlier lessons Gordon had given him.

As the weight of those experiences overtook him he realized that he had witnessed the solely most amazing event since the point of creation itself. He was awe struck. Robert took a few side steps to present himself fully in front of Gordon, who stood emotionless, his grey eyes fixed forward as if in a trance.

His teachers standing position and demeanor led to calm in Robert so that he felt compelled to emulate the mood suggested. Robert stood about four feet away, fully facing Gordon. Both stood in silence. Robert looked deep into Gordon's light grey eyes that had always appeared to be of a different resonance than his own.

As he did his soul body transitioned and as it did he lifted each arm slightly above his waist and away to each side. For a moment he and Gordon's soul bodies were indistinguishable, both luminous and vibrant.

When the moment had passed Gordon was gone. Robert stood alone his body oscillating at a slightly higher frequency and his now light grey eyes fixed forward.

The sense of synchronicity and irony overtook him. He slowly came to understand, he and his teacher were one in the same, the same being separated only by time and living experiences in the physical and reflection and learning in the spiritual. The difference in time as perceived in the physical realm had given way, had yielded, in the spiritual realm where the need for its relative measure is not needed.

What did matter - the measure of their experiences - had now coalesced in the spiritual. The meeting point had been realized. Robert, who had felt the outsider living and when not-living, the novice and the learner, had really been the teacher all long; a great irony prevailed.

As the event transpired Robert thought of Sileas at the lecture amphitheatre saying 'transportation for three' rather than 'transportation for four' for he, Tawna, Sileas and Gordon. The journey was really only for three entities as one and one, were one.

His journey of discovery had now come to an end. He had seen his full transition to teacher and he knew his destiny led from this point forward.

It was time to leave the cottage and return to Anna, and that destiny.

Once More upon the Sea that is me

Anna swept the floor from the children's ward and into the hallway. As the meager dust particles left the floor and rose into the air they disappeared in puffs of little sparkles. The effort Anna was providing toward cleanliness was more to do with resolving tedium than any real hygienic purpose. The new arrival ward for children hadn't any customers recently requiring her care and comfort – which was Anna's speciality for those little souls needing to adjust to the transition from life to after life – without the caring provided by the role of their parents.

Anna's hair was shorter now, about shoulder length and drawn back by a band so that it was fitted snugly atop each ear as it swept to the nape of her neck. Her carefree and random thoughts were interrupted by footsteps down the hallway and she lifted her head upward expecting to see the mid-fifties former nurse whom she shared her duties with at the ward. Instead, she saw the impressive body of a man and then the face of Robert approaching her.

"Oh my God" she thundered, covering her mouth with her right hand at first, then with both hands. As the tears streamed at once from her eyes her hands moved to wipe them from her cheeks so that she could present a smiling face to the soul so missed and now returned to her. Her attempt partly succeeded, but her face continued to contort with emotion and her tears running freely.

Anna flung her arms around Robert's neck and drew him close and held him tightly. She raised her right arm up the middle of his back and then moved her left hand up to Robert's cheek and held it there, in part out of genuine need to touch him, but then, to register more closely the apparent change in her companion. She looked closely at Robert's skin and clothes, and could easily see the change in the luminosity of him, and then slid her hands down Robert's arms and held his hands in hers, looking directly into Robert's smiling light grey eyes and the impressive aura they cast outward.

Anna squeezed Robert's hands in hers tightly and then led him by one hand into the children's ward where they took up seats astride one another.

"Robert, what has happened to you, what has your journey taught you, did you find lessons, what did you do?" As the words tumbled out Anna recognized they were far from the mark given the luminosity and oscillation of the soul before her which indicated a profound change had occurred.

More questions began to formulate into a queue in Anna's mind and as she searched for the next few words to get out Robert took her hand softly in his own. "Anna, it is hard to describe to you all that has happened to me on the journey. It is far more than I had expected could happen and really has changed the soul that I am."

Anna knew deep down that Robert's words did not mean any loss of affection for her, and that the love emanating from the soul next to her was deeper and fuller than it had been when they had parted. "Well every journey leaves a traveler hungry and in need of rest to tell their tale" she said, "let's go home and talk."

The two rose and arm entangled in glowing arm turned out of the ward and down the hall.

Once at Anna's apartment the two had made a meal from a few simple things on hand – fresh bread, two types of cheese, a coil of pastrami and a rich red wine. A second bottle opened and the two took to the couch, glasses in hand.

Robert had recounted the journey as it had unfolded – the horse drawn cart ride to the sea and cliff edge, the cottage, the lessons given by Gordon, the visit to the dark end of the physical Universe, then on to the light realm and the lessons learned with Sileas and Tawna. Finally, of course, the soul changing experience of the realm of the Masters and the scene of the coming back together of the multitude of souls and their vast experiences.

"I don't quite understand Robert, how could Gordon be your teacher sent to guide you, but, well, really be you? It is so hard to understand, especially all, that, all that you are now, with this different energy about you?"

"My intuition, as far as it goes, lets me know that our experience, our lives, our time in the spiritual, can all exist side by side. I may in one life be Gordon, or be Robert, so that really, Robert was just a euphemism for Gordon, where he was knowledgeable and refined, and I, well, was a soul wandering in the dark mist of being unknowing, but in reality the same expression of a soul along different points of reference in its experience."

"The funny thing to me is that my Robert life was so consumed by doubt and self-need, that I never gave any sort of chance of opening my mind to a larger reality, and what now seems obvious, that our purpose is not to suffer tragedies, but to celebrate our own reality of being able to experience. And when that is known, that love, kindness and acceptance is the true reality. Really, if we are all one in the end of things, then, why would we need to be jealous, envious, hateful and hurtful of each other? Wouldn't that be like one cell in your eye harming another, so that neither can see, nor detect the light?"

"I am, who I am, and once I had lived and learned enough to travel the distance from student to teacher, the distance between Gordon and Robert had slipped from the ages to the moment. At the cottage, those moments became the present, and we, were no longer any different by any discernible amount of experience. The distance in time no longer had any meaning."

"I know this" Robert said "of knowledge, that it is a vehicle to the abolishment of ego. Knowledge being just knowing, knowing that a greater existence does exist – a journey that can only be travelled through determination to make it happen and the eventual desire to move forward from the material to the spiritual and beyond."

"It is through this willingness to continue to move on, to experience, that we as souls aid in the expression of possibilities – capable by consciousness collectively that allows for as many possibilities as is possible to be known."

After a time, Anna jumped into the long telling of the story "Then to return to life, to experience and have desires, that type of determinism is good, for all, for everyone and everything?"

"Yes Anna." Robert replied, sensing a rise in emotion in the lovely figure next to him in body and figure he had grown to believe was his spiritual twin.

"Oh Robert, I haven't known how to tell you this" Anna's head fell to her chest and then rose so that her eyes met his "but, having worked with children here, and wanting children. Oh my God, I want to return to life to teach children, to, to have children, to be a mother."

Anna let out an emotional breath. "But now you are on a journey to the higher planes, to a higher purpose, and no longer wanting to return to the living plane? Or, or, are you even able to now that you have changed energies?"

Robert moved slightly toward Anna and embraced her with such emotion that their two bodies once again began to share energy. He kissed her shoulder and her cheek, then briefly her lips.

"Anna, my purpose, whatever it becomes along this path, is with you. If that means a return to life then that is what we shall do. I feel inside that fate, the synchronicity and symmetry of the Universe will keep us together, somehow."

Anna's head fell forward and a stream of tears poured down her cheeks. Her own journey from her previous life and far too young death, her time in the Subtle Domain had taken a decisive turn; her path forward now being decided and with the splendid gift of 'being' shared with another.

"But Robert, I am not even sure how to go back to life. I mean, to be honest, I haven't explored any of that; maybe I should have – spoken to someone about it?" Anna's sentence ended with a hint of embarrassment as if she'd forgotten to buy bus fare for a trip.

Robert smiled widely and said "Well I know where we can get some advice." Anna looked into his eyes inquisitively and both said at the same time "...the gentleman's Club!"

Surely Adam and Andrew would have some advice on the topic.

With Robert's words being enough said, the two rose and went into the bedroom, undressed and fell into a long deep sleep, their two soul bodies pressed together and meshed at the legs and arms. As they slept energy silently swam freely across their body boundaries, like a trillion tiny bees busily at work, and just as if each body were really one.

When they awoke the two decided to go out for breakfast and coffee which Robert realized he had been without for so long, and settled for scrambled eggs and latte, with Robert having three.

Later in the day they walked on the beach in the full sun along the stretch where they had looked out over the sparkling waves the first night then had met. The time was spent very care free, both souls content that they had made a plan together – even though a return to life represented great unknowns.

Both knew they could spend as much time as they wanted or needed in the Subtle Domain, yet, the desire Anna had to care for and nurture was particularly strong and Robert could feel it in her. It was more than conviction or even determination, it was compulsion.

After three days spent in the same leisurely way, they decided it was time to visit the gentleman's club and afterward, to return to the Grand Buffet as they had that first day together.

Robert recognized the stairs he, Adam and Thom had bounded up on his first visit. He bolted up as the three had, leaving Anna scrambling to catch up as he held the door to the building open for her.

Once up the stairs and into the club the two found the place buzzing with activity on what was apparently a very busy afternoon which was in contrast to their last visit. Robert swung his head from left to right scanning the crowd for familiar faces.

He took a few steps to the right and toward the bar to the table that he and Anna had last sat at and sure enough there was portly Andrew's back with his head turned toward a standing and pointing Adam, who was obviously making a point of some import. The others at the table seemed to be indifferent and were engaged in chatter of some sort.

As he and Anna drew their way through the crowded assembly of souls, dodging a chair here and a pool cue drawn like an arrow there Adam caught site of them and his jaw and pointed finger dropped. He raised his hands, open palmed at his waist and drew them back in a welcoming 'for heaven sake' sort of motion.

The sudden dropping of the point and gestures by Adam caught Andrew off guard and he turned his heavy neck to the left so that he could catch a glimpse of what Adam was looking at, resting his left elbow on the chair back. By the time the two arrived at the table Adam was on his feet and turned to embrace first Anna, who Robert had paused to let take the lead, and then Robert, shaking his hand vigorously like a merchant just having made a grand sale.

"Robert my boy" Adam thundered "Why my God man you look superb. What has happened to you good fellow? You look, like a man who has transitioned a great, great distance." Adam drew back slightly, holding Robert by the forearm and looking intensely into Robert's eyes, and at his soul body.

Andrew was doing the same, and smiling widely "Did the sea air prove to be that beneficial, you look radiant?"

Robert was only able to mutter the single word "...well..." before Adam cut in and said "I've seen this once before some ages ago, when a fellow visited the light realm."

"Oh but surely" Adam sputtered out before Robert's gesture of his hand for Anna to sit down cut him off, and the polite necessity of the task became evident to the better manners of the two souls standing. As Anna, then Robert took to chairs they nodded in politeness to the others sitting at the table, including Thom, whose hand Robert stood slightly back up to shake before settling into his chair.

"Yes Adam, I did journey to the light realm and, beyond; beyond to the realm of the Masters."

As the words spilled out the table assembly, and even nearby souls fell silent. One soul at the end of the adjacent table muttered "bullshit" however, as they looked at Robert, proof of sorts was in the personage. Robert was clearly oscillating at a different frequency than all others, the nature of which gave off an aura unto itself of a soul in a clearly different range of experience. The energy being emitted spoke of a knowledge and wisdom at a different, greater level. His cool, grey eyes revealed that considerable experiences had come to be for this soul.

"The matter of the fact is, my friends, that these domains of light are the rightful property of us all, and in time we all will be bound back together, rejoined in the high light realm of the Masters. This is all of our future, our determination over the eons of countless lives and the experiences they permit."

Adam pulled hard on the gin and tonic in his left hand as he pointed in an agreeing way with the words Robert had just spoken. "Ah, yes you lot, like I have always said, determinism is the answer, and, the vehicle by which all these sub-structures exist. We determine, currently, to be here and in time we determine to grow and to progress, even right up to the light realm and that of the Masters. Here is the proof. I was right all along!"

Robert noted Anna ordering a drink from the barkeep who had approached the table and guessed he was in for another round of gin and tonics so prevalent at this table and guests, as he turned to Adam and said "Yes Adam through determination we steer our path and through knowledge we shed ego, vanity, even the need to be right in opinions we bring to discussions in order to reach the destinations of our purpose."

Adam blushed slightly at his boastful assertions.

"Interesting, interesting" Andrew said "Tell me young Robert, was my cottage in good order. Was all at the ready for you?" As Andrew completed his sentence - which was trivial to the enormity of the discussion soon to follow - Adam glumly muttered "I was still right" before deciding to leave it alone.

Robert thought for a moment and it occurred to him for the first time that the books on the shelf in the cottage were specific to his journey, his past and future lives and he wondered if Andrew had them placed there, and if so, how.

"Yes Andrew, all was in good order and the simplistic, lovely cottage was as you said that I would find what I needed. I do wonder how those very curious little books on the shelf came to be."

Andrew looked perplexed replying "Books, I don't recall any. You know, this Subtle Domain of ours and the physical Universe have many synchronicities that just pop up, when you are ready to look for them."

Robert thought deeply for a moment, shutting out the chatter around him as he did. He considered that there are guide posts along the journey of discovery, conveniently placed for sentient conscious beings to discover, once eyes are wide open to see beyond the veil of bias, ego and what appears real from moment to moment in life or after life.

The books, Robert decided, were between him and the fabric of the Universe and the field of energy that underlies it and from which consciousness arises and reports back its myriad of experiences. He was prepared through an open mind desiring truths to have the Universe unveil the majesty of synchronicity – and the books were just that – timely arriving for his perusal as sign posts along the route to his destiny.

Sitting with the eager assembly, Robert again recounted his story of the events, amazing as they were, since their last meeting. The debate that followed ranged from whether or not the souls truly had free will to the need for a petition of those in the Subtle Domain to cause the high Master spirits to enrich all souls with such experiences. Perhaps even a preparatory school that would lead souls through the stages of enlightenment and determinism - so the reasoning went.

Robert nodded politely to each opinion and counter opinion that was offered and debated, and answered the many questions about experiences at the cottage, with Sileas and in the end time of the rejoining. After a time he grew silent as debates raged and he took Anna's hand. As he did Anna leaned forward and said "Well a discussion like this must make you all very hungry, I suggest we all head for the Grand Buffet?"

The clamour of debate subsided and heads nodded in approval of the proposition, some more animated with gin than others, and slowly the group took to their feet as they finished their dearly departed drinks.

As Robert rose he thought to himself that debates about free will and petitions for this and that would eventually give way to each soul's desire for a different path, to determine one's own evolution and with it each expression of consciousness fulfilling its potential to explore all possibilities available.

Once at the landing before the street the assembly began the instantaneous change of attire for dinner, and Anna once again obligingly provided Robert his fine white dinner jacket and slacks by a simple touch on the shoulder, and her intent. It pleased him and he felt comfortable and very much at ease, even a little proud to have Anna on his arm and his breadth of experiences under his belt. He knew that he had become a celebrity of sorts and that he shouldn't ponder that to long lest it implant an egotistical notion or two.

The group rolled up the great promenade and into the grand facade of the massive structure. Robert and Anna selected their dinners; with Anna's plate colored mostly green with fresh vegetables while Robert preferred a large feast of fresh shrimp and scallops and a cocktails sauce and a few large crab legs for good measure. His greenery limited to a few lightly cooked asparagus spears.

Once the group had settled into their seats on the deck overlooking the beach and ocean glistening once again with sparkling moon light, the chatter of discussions great and small subsided as plates were eagerly cleared of their culinary treasures. The fine wine washing down the tastes supplied by the amply laden - plates as the eager bunch of souls tested and experienced all that they had set out before themselves.

With plates mostly empty Adam turned to Robert and Anna and said "So my dear friends, what is next for you? Will you use mental constructs to create a lovely home for yourselves here in the Subtle Domain, or, will you both live in Anna's quaint apartment in the town centre area?

The two hesitated for a moment and Anna eventually spoke saying "We've decided to go back to life."

Mouths stopped chewing and a fork was inadvertently dropped by its handler making a clanking sound as it hit the empty platter below. A collective word sprang out from the stunned group. "Why?"

Anna positioned herself more upright, her bare shoulders lovely as she curled her hair on the left side of her head neatly behind the left ear, exposing more of her radiant beautiful face. "I want to be with children, to tend to them" and after a moment she added "I want to parent them, I want to be a mother so very much."

Andrew's face smiled widely and he said "To once again sale upon the sea that is me."

"Yes" Robert jutted in "Exactly like that. Like the ripples of waves on an ocean, each wave life like a cresting wave, seemingly its own entity but really part of a much larger whole, the whole that we are all a part of. We seek to sail on that sea again, an adventure to another distant shore yet to be discovered."

Anna added "But we don't really know what to do, how, well, to make it happen."

Andrew smiled again "Oh you'll find what you need."

Adam cut in "You'll have to plan it of course. You'll have to consult the council for advice on the circumstances of your previous and coming lives."

Andrew pulled at his chin as if debating his own procrastination on taking to another life. "It's quite a risk you know, the council can advise, but in reality it's all one great toss of the coin."

"Well then, a coin toss it is" Robert said as he cupped Anna's far shoulder with his arm and hand, drawing her closer.

"If you are very certain on this" Adam said "then I can advise the council."

"We are" the two said, and Adam replied "Alright then, I am sorry to see the two of you go, but, meet me at the Hall of Souls on the morrow and we'll see you on your way."

After the meal was completed goodbyes were said Anna and Robert returned home and got into bed straight away. For a time they remained silent, Robert lying on his back and Anna on her left side her back to Robert. Each silently pursuing their own thoughts and fears, like any new couple who intend on much together but know that in doing so they are risking their lives as they have known it to date.

Eventually Robert leaned up on one arm and gently pulled Anna so that her shoulders squared and she was on her back. He kissed her and the two found a long and deep love making.

As they fell to sleep they knew their destinies were decided and interwoven together and their fears surrendered to their shared intent.

The Matter, of Matter

In the mid-afternoon Anna and Robert rendezvoused with Adam in front of the Hall of Souls, a large square building of immense size and no distinguishing architectural features. Just a large building with few windows and what appeared to be a polished granite exterior.

Once inside the two walked behind Adam who maintained a business like brisk walk down the finely polished marble floor. Neither knew what to expect and they felt a little like being led to the principal's office in school.

The building had the smells and feel of a large bureaucratic place where matters are officiously tended to through the careful measure and application of rules and processes. At the far end of the long hallway Adam turned and opened an etched glass panelled door and held it open for his companion souls.

Once inside Adam motioned them forward to a desk where an officious looking woman, her hair bunched up into a bun with a pin holding it in place, pushed an old style intercom and said merely "they are here sir, your two o'clock."

"Alright, send them in please" was the dry reply.

As Anna and Robert turned to go through a door the woman had kindly opened for them, Adam abruptly took each into a strangely close embrace and said "This us up to you now, it's your matter to tend to and as far as I go. Good luck, I wish you both the very best of luck and I know we'll meet again. Well, anyway, you know where to find me. Break a leg."

With that he turned and quickly left the office. Robert watched him go and suddenly felt melancholy. He recalled how lost he was when Adam had appeared at Thom's life recall tent, and how with Adam's arrival his journey in the afterlife had really begun.

Upon entry into the adjoining office space the two found themselves standing in front of a long table and five souls sitting and watching their approach, pens in hand and paper in from of them.

"Ah yes" the soul, a man, in the middle of the table said, Mr. Robert and Miss Anna. Let' see here, ah yes."

Robert and Anna looked at each other, dumfounded and not knowing what to expect.

"Yes, Miss Anna, we have reviewed your lives to date and see you have a strong intent to care for children as you have done here in the Subtle Domain. We see that you have had several incarnations where this intent has not matured fully."

The soul to the man's left, a woman, rubbed her thumb and forefinger down the length of her pen "You do realize that motherhood in the physical will bind you to other souls, who will incarnate through you? The two of you may or may not be together in the life to come, but surely as a mother and possibly a father, you will be bonded to other souls" the woman said in a stern, challenging way.

"I'm counting on it" Anna said confidently.

"Well then, that's all fine, lets' get you to the embark station." As the man spoke the other souls closed their open files and smiled politely at the two.

Robert and Anna were caught off guard and Robert struggled to spit out a few words. "What of me, do you not want to discuss my lives, I have had several really, I mean, I have read about them."

"No, no, Mr. Robert you are in good order. It's all just a matter of becoming matter again. Now, let's get you both to the embark station."

"What, now?" Robert said. Anna took his hand to show solidarity with the question.

"Yes, yes, now, we've got you all set" the man said.

The other souls left the room and outer office and the man led Robert and Anna out and down the hall a little further.

Robert and Anna were startled but silent, holding hands tightly as they walked. In their minds they felt some time would pass before they journeyed back to life. What would happen to Anna's apartment, wouldn't they have a good-bye party with the souls they knew on this side, perhaps a sending off meal at the Grand Buffet?

Yet inwardly they also recognized that the full consequence of their decision to return to life was upon them and that it required being met with resolve. What was a little longer in the Subtle Domain to do for them, they had resolved together to take this step, and the steps were being taken now. That was it, the matter of the matter at hand and they silently followed, wanting to accept rather than bargain.

The man whirled to his right and opened the door to one large very bright, white room with nothing other than two gurney styled tables in it, covered with white linen and a woman standing between the two clad in a brilliantly white dress. The man shook first Anna, then Robert's hand and said simply "good luck" before leaving the room without even so much as an introduction to the woman or any indication of what was to follow.

The woman said nothing outwardly to the two, communicating empathically for them to lie face up on the gurneys, which they did. Her message was very soft and soothing while answering a question that had formed in Anna's mind, which was whether the journey could be made together.

The empathic answer came back "You may start the journey together but upon arrival into the physical you must be separate, no two souls enter the same body."

Robert and Anna lay flat and they worked to calm their minds. Robert looked over at Anna and as she returned his gaze they smiled, reaching out to touch fingers and palms together one last time. Robert let his emotions go flat, and in his mind he thought this is really it.

The woman took a few steps so that she stood at the end of the gurneys looking down at the two subjects head's below. She reached out and cupped Anna's ears and stood motionless for a few long seconds. She then rubbed Robert's forehead and brow before cupping his ears an equal length of time. Her manner was meditative and gentle.

When done she simply tapped each on the forehead simultaneously with the index finger of each hand. The two souls disappeared from the room.

Robert felt himself circling as if slowly spinning. The motion left him feeling noxious. He could only see a greyish fog. Then he sensed feeling constricted and unable to move his hands or his feet. Panic set in and it grew swiftly to terror. Something had gone wrong he thought and as he did he tried to cry it out so that someone would hear him and come to help. He thought, my God, I can't breathe; I'm going back to when I died at the end of my Robert's life. I'M NOT SUPPOSED TO GO BACK TO THAT BODY, TO THAT LIFE"

He felt great pressure on and in his head and the alarm grew greater, he felt a squishing pain all around him and then a brilliant flood of light as he finally could flail his arms and legs. He cried out loudly as he gasped for air. One first, deep and fulfilling gulp of air!

He cried out again, louder, and he heard words...

"It's a boy."

Epilogue

A group of boys played an improvised game of soccer on as much grass as they could reasonably invade and take over at the State fair, with its rides, judging stations for this best pie or cake, or largest squash or pumpkin, and kiosks for games of chance filing most of the park.

The game play was interrupted as one boy kicked the ball far wide of the goal and into town's people just arriving for their Sunday afternoon, with lazy cloud's meandering in the sky above.

One boy, about nine, ran from the group of boys to retrieve the ball. As he did, young parents with their nine year old daughter, with long flowing black hair approached him.

As the two children's eyes met they stopped, transfixed with each other's gaze, their hands falling to their sides, standing motionless.

The strange behavior immediately caught the attention of the girl's parents. "Isabel dear, come now, let the boy get his ball and go back to his friends" the mother said.

The words went unheeded. The woman knelt down and clasped her daughter's hand in her hand. She looked at the emotionless expression in her daughter's face and then at the little boy who mirrored the demeanor. She looked deep into her daughter's transfixed eyes, then into the little boys eyes and then back into her daughters. Reflected in their pupils were seemingly millions of tiny specks of light, brilliant and specific and slowly turning, as if a galaxy in space.

Made in the USA
San Bernardino, CA
28 July 2018